A WELL-ARMED L[...]
A DISARMING LAD[...]

"One day you'll fall in love and wish to wed," Miss Bonnie Gordon predicted to the earl.

"You are wrong on two counts," he answered. "First, I am firmly persuaded that love is a myth foisted on humanity by poets and novelists. I have survived for six and thirty years without suffering the distressing symptoms they describe."

Having made love sound less a myth than a disease, the earl continued, "And if I *were* to experience such symptoms, I shouldn't dream of wedding the object of my . . . ah . . . abberation. I have encountered hundreds of beautiful women, and I daresay I'll encounter hundreds more. To restrict my attentions to one would be akin to . . . What is your favorite food, Miss Gordon?"

"Chocolate," she said, puzzled.

"But fond as you may be of it, you could scarcely live on it alone," he said. "My own is roast beef, but I certainly don't wish to have it at every meal."

Thus Bonnie, forewarned of the earl's attitudes and appetites, became suitably forearmed. . . .

(For a list of other Signet Regency Romances by Diana Campbell, please turn page . . .)

The
Earl's Invention

Diana Campbell

A SIGNET BOOK

NEW AMERICAN LIBRARY

NAL BOOKS ARE AVAILABLE AT QUANTITY DISCOUNTS WHEN USED
TO PROMOTE PRODUCTS OR SERVICES. FOR INFORMATION PLEASE
WRITE TO PREMIUM MARKETING DIVISION. NEW AMERICAN LIBRARY.
1633 BROADWAY. NEW YORK. NEW YORK 10019.

SIGNET, SIGNET CLASSIC, MENTOR, ONYX, PLUME, MERIDIAN AND NAL BOOKS
are published by New American Library,
1633 Broadway, New York, New York 10019

First Printing, October, 1986

1 2 3 4 5 6 7 8 9

PRINTED IN THE UNITED STATES OF AMERICA

1

*T*he wardrobe was empty, as were the desk and chest of drawers, and Bonnie frowned into her portmanteau. The bag had been full when she arrived in London; in fact, she had been compelled to tie it round with ropes in order to keep it closed. Now, however, it was scarcely half-filled, and she gazed about the room wondering what she could have forgotten. She had certainly packed all her dresses . . .

Her dresses; that was it, of course. She had brought six gowns to town, and during the ensuing five years, two had simply worn out. Then, last spring, the Powell boys had appropriated one of her remaining dresses from the laundry and ripped it into "banners," which were subsequently carried into battle by the Knights (Teddy and Samuel) and the Saracens (Lucas and Oliver). Bonnie supposed that, as the children's governess, she should have been pleased to discover they had learned enough about the Crusades to reenact the Battle of Acre; but in the event, she judged this dubious evidence of their educational attainment scant compensation for the loss of her best gown.

Reduced to only three dresses, Bonnie had expended the whole of her meager savings on a simple but handsome frock of apple-green jaconet, and that was the dress the boys had destroyed this afternoon. She glared at the crumpled heap of muslin on the bed and fervently hoped the ink was soaking through to the counterpane. She had been unable to determine which of the wretched Powell brood had poured a pool of black ink on the seat of her chair in the schoolroom; the boys had all howled with equal glee when she sat down and leapt immediately back to her feet. Any of them could have perpetrated the prank, and—more to the point—any of them was eminently capable of plotting and executing a similar trick in future. Which was why she did not intend to spend another night, another *hour*, under Theodore Powell's roof.

Bonnie turned the dress over, gingerly touched the great black spot on the back of the skirt, and found it still wet. If she put the gown in her portmanteau, the ink might well spread to the rest of her clothes, and what would be the use? The damage was almost surely irreparable, unlikely to be disguised by cleaning or dyeing or clever patching. Furthermore, she doubted that life with Aunt Grace would require an extensive wardrobe.

Aunt Grace. From the moment she'd fled the schoolroom, Bonnie's thoughts had been clouded with rage, and she now experienced a belated jolt of reason. She could not be certain Aunt Grace would agree to take her in, she realized, sinking weakly onto the bed. Indeed, when it came to that, she was not even sure her father's elder sister was alive. They had exchanged brief letters every Christmas since Bonnie's removal to London, but this was the first week of May. Aunt Grace was nearly eighty and had complained of delicate health for years; it was entirely possible that she had at last succumbed to one of her numerous vague maladies.

But she would have been notified of her aunt's death, Bonnie decided. If—as she had been given to understand— she was Aunt Grace's principal heir, she would have heard from a solicitor; barring that, she would have received some sort of communication from the housekeeper. So the odds were excellent that Aunt Grace was alive and would be perversely delighted to see her wayward niece. Aunt Grace had predicted that Bonnie would come to regret her employment most bitterly, and Aunt Grace loved nothing more than to be proved Right.

"Did I not tell you?" Bonnie could almost hear the shrill, grating voice. "Did I not say you should have come to Nantwich in the first place? Particularly inasmuch as it was your dear mother's dying wish." Since Aunt Grace had never approved of Mama and had hardly spoken to her sister-in-law throughout the thirty-odd years of their acquaintance, Bonnie could only collect that her constant posthumous references to "your dear mother" were a peculiar form of canonization.

Which would not have been altogether inappropriate, Bonnie reflected, for Mama was the saintliest person she had ever known. She had kept her final illness a secret as long as she could, brightly attributing her increasing debility to "silly little flutters" in her heart. It was only when she grew too weak to leave her bed that she revealed the terrible prognosis Dr. Harding had pronounced months before: her heart was hopelessly diseased, and she had but a very short time to live.

"You are not to cry," Mama said sternly as Bonnie emitted an involuntary gasp of grief. "Certainly not on my account; I shall be joining your father in a better place. And you needn't tease yourself about your own future, for I have arranged for you to live with Grace."

She gestured toward an envelope on the bedside table, and Bonnie repressed another gasp when she observed how pale her hands were, how thin her fingers had become.

"As you know," Mama continued, "Grace and I do not . . . do not get on. But you mustn't tease yourself on that head either because she is *exceedingly* fond of you."

If that was the case, Bonnie thought grimly, Aunt Grace had hidden her fondness prodigious well. Insofar as she could recall, she had never detected the slightest flicker of warmth in the icy blue eyes, the tiniest trace of a smile on the small set mouth. Apparently her doubts were written on her face, for Mama assumed a brilliant smile of her own.

"And you will be with Grace only a brief while after all," she said cheerfully. "Every young man in Nantwich will soon be pounding on her door, and I daresay you'll be wed before a year has gone."

Bonnie did not suppose there could *be* many young men in a small town in southern Cheshire, far from any major city. Nor that Aunt Grace, a lifelong spinster, would much welcome whatever suitable *partis* there were "pounding on her door." But she could not shatter Mama's brave optimism, and she bobbed her head in agreement.

"My one regret is that I shall not live to see you settled." Mama's amber eyes clouded for the first time. "But you are not a child, are you? You are nineteen; nearly a woman grown. And I'm confident you'll be quite happy with Grace until such time as you marry."

"Yes, Mama," Bonnie choked. "Yes, I'm confident I shall."

Her words to the contrary, Bonnie did not believe, then or during the few remaining weeks of her mother's life, that she would be in the least happy with Aunt Grace. Worse yet, she entertained a nagging fear that circumstance had doomed her to follow in her aunt's footsteps. She could not but wonder if—half a century hence—she, too, would be an embittered spinster, lacking even the companionship of a niece to brighten her old age.

Had Bonnie clung to any vague hope that residence with Aunt Grace might be bearable after all, such hope would have been dispelled when the formidable Miss Gordon arrived in Stafford the day after Mama's death. Having spent blessedly little time with Aunt Grace in recent years, Bonnie had forgotten her habit of complaining—loudly and endlessly—of every inconvenience—real or imagined—that intruded on her life. After describing at length the current lamentable state of her health, Aunt Grace began to grumble about her journey from Nantwich, the recital of her grievances requiring nearly as much time as the three-hour trip itself. By nightfall, she had voiced her negative opinions on a whole host of additional topics, ranging in importance from the color of the dining-room draperies to the conduct of the government; and in the morning, she delivered a long, furious indictment of the mattress on which she had been forced to sleep. Though she managed to hold her tongue during the funeral, she hastened to point out—as soon as it was over—that the rector had "mumbled" throughout the service and twice lost his place in the prayer book.

At some juncture, between complaints, Aunt Grace had declared that they would repair to Nantwich as soon as possible; and on the evening of the funeral, she instructed Bonnie to put her affairs in order the following day. Bonnie—her stomach churning with panic by now—cast desperately about for some means by which to persuade her aunt that this endeavor would take considerable time, but nothing credible came to mind. Aunt Grace was well aware, as Bonnie was, that she and Mama had all but exhausted Papa's minuscule estate; their solicitor would need virtually every remaining pound to pay their outstanding bills. Since Papa's death, his widow and daughter had occupied a leased, furnished house, and Bonnie estimated that their personal effects could be packed up in under half a day. Hard as she thought on it, she could conjure up only one other small task which had to be performed: that of advising the landlord of her intention to vacate the house. She realized she could readily dispatch him a letter to this effect, but she was so eager to escape Aunt Grace that she elected to visit his office in person.

In an effort to prolong her respite as much as she could, Bonnie fairly crawled toward the leasing office, and as she did so, she glimpsed a slender ray of hope: perhaps the landlord would refuse to terminate the lease. Well, not the landlord, she amended; Theodore Powell would take no personal interest in the rental of one insignificant property. But maybe his agent would fly into the boughs and threaten her with legal proceedings if she did not continue to pay the rent until the lease had expired. How she *could* pay the rent, she had no notion; but since a term in Newgate seemed distinctly preferable to life with Aunt Grace, she rushed past the last few streets and through the door of the leasing office.

Bonnie's perverse hope began to dim the instant she identified herself to the man behind the desk.

"Miss Gordon!" He sprang to his feet, solicitously guided her to the chair in front of the desk, then stood beside her, sadly shaking his head. "I was most dreadfully sorry to hear of your mother's death. I do trust there is some relative to ease the pain of your loss and provide you a comfortable home."

"Mama did arrange for me to live with my aunt in Nantwich," Bonnie murmured. "But as the lease on the house has not yet expired—"

"Oh, my poor Miss Gordon." He patted her awkwardly on one shoulder. "I should hate to think you've been troubling yourself about the lease in the midst of your great sorrow. The contract was with your mother, and it ceased upon her death. You are quite free of any legal obligation, entirely free to vacate the premises and go to Nantwich."

"I see," Bonnie muttered. "Well, thank you anyway. I realize the situation is beyond your control."

Divorced from the context of her dismal thoughts, her final remark was an utter non sequitur, and, not surprisingly, the agent frowned in puzzlement. Bonnie gave him a bleak smile, rose, and started to trudge back toward the door.

"Miss Gordon?"

The voice which caught her up was not that of the agent, and when Bonnie spun around, she beheld a second man emerging from a doorway at the rear of the main office.

"Forgive me," he said, striding across the room, "but I could not avoid overhearing your conversation with Maynard. I am Theodore Powell."

He reached her side as he finished speaking, and Bonnie strove to mask her astonishment. Mr. Powell was reputed to be the wealthiest man in Staffordshire, one of the wealthiest in England; and inasmuch as he had amassed his whole enormous fortune himself, she had assumed him well into middle age. But the man who swept her a bow was not much above forty, she judged, and had he not been altogether too plump, she fancied he would be quite handsome. As it was, his heavy jowls sagged over the top of his neckcloth, and the buttons of his elegant waistcoat threatened to pop at any moment.

"I collect you're the daughter of the late Reverend Mr. Gordon?" he said. Bonnie nodded. "And that you've no great wish to remove to Nantwich with your aunt?"

"I . . . ah . . ." She could not confess her dislike of Aunt Grace to a perfect stranger, and as she attempted to formulate an innocuous response, Mr. Powell's fleshy cheeks creased in a smile.

"I quite understand, Miss Gordon," he said soothingly. "A pretty young woman such as yourself is naturally looking to make a good marriage, and there can't be many young bucks in Nantwich, can there?"

Though this was not Bonnie's primary objection to Nantwich, neither was Mr. Powell entirely wrong, and she flushed and dropped her eyes.

"Fortunately," he continued in the same soothing voice, "I am in a position to tender a proposition which could be of benefit to both of us."

A proposition! It was commonly known that Theodore Powell was a man of dubious background, far from a "gentleman," but Bonnie could scarcely conceive that he would offer a *carte blanche* to a respectable girl he had encountered only five minutes before. She opened her mouth, but before she could deliver the stinging rebuke he so richly deserved, Mr. Powell went on.

"Yes, I am in desperate need of a governess to educate my two daughters. Maria, who is nine, and Anne; Anne is seven. As you're the daughter of a clergyman, an educated woman yourself, I daresay you're amply qualified to fill such a post."

"I . . . I . . ." Further words eluded her because, in truth, she had no notion what she planned to say. She believed she *was* qualified to be a governess—Papa had supervised her education and often praised her quick mind—but she had never considered the prospect of employment in any capacity.

"I should provide your room and board, of course," Mr. Powell said, "and pay the prevailing salary. And you'd soon have suitors in droves, I'll warrant," he added with another smile. "I fancy you'd meet dozens of suitable young men in London."

"London?" Bonnie echoed sharply. She had been quite certain Mr. Powell resided in Stafford; indeed, she vaguely remembered Papa pointing out his house.

"Did I fail to mention that?" Mr. Powell said rhetorically. "Since the end of the war, my business interests have expanded to the Continent, and a month since, I relocated in the capital. In fact, that is why I require a governess: Mrs. Baker did not wish to reside in the city. At any rate, I traveled back to Stafford yesterday to attend to a few final details, but I shall be returning to town tomorrow. And I believe *you* would quite enjoy living in London, Miss Gordon. I've a large home in Portman Square . . ."

His voice trailed provocatively off, and Bonnie wondered if he was somehow reading her mind. If he perceived that of all the blandishments he might have offered, this was the one most likely to gain her acquiescence. She had never been to London, and she longed to see it, longed to stroll through the parks and visit the shops and attend the theaters. And, yes, she longed to meet the dozens, the *thousands* of suitable young men who must surely throng the streets of the city.

"Have we a bargain then?" Mr. Powell asked briskly. "If so, I should like you to accompany me back to town tomorrow. Unless you have some compelling need to stay on in Stafford a day or two."

Tomorrow? Bonnie thought wildly. Her head was whirling with the shock of Mr. Powell's proposal, but in truth, she had no compelling need to stay. To the contrary, if she remained in Stafford, Aunt Grace would undoubtedly feel obliged to stay on as well in order to chaperon her niece. And Bonnie calculated that Aunt Grace would be quite sufficiently overset without the injection of additional complications.

In the latter regard, Bonnie was not disappointed.

"You are going to *London*?" Aunt Grace screeched after Bonnie had announced her precipitate decision. "To serve as governess to that *horrible* man?"

"I found Mr. Powell exceedingly pleasant," Bonnie protested.

"Humph," Aunt Grace snorted. "His sort are invariably pleasant when it serves their ends to be so." She heaved a tremulous sigh. "I can scarcely bear to contemplate what your dear mother would say to such a plan."

Bonnie had deliberated this very factor as she raced home from Mr. Powell's office and had concluded that—beyond all else—Mama would have wanted her to be happy. And she was persuaded she would be far happier in London with Mr. Powell and his family than in Nantwich with her odious aunt. But she could hardly express this opinion to Aunt Grace, and she bit her lip and said nothing.

"However, your dear mother did not see fit to appoint me your legal guardian." Aunt Grace punctuated this disclosure with a fearsome scowl. "Consequently, I cannot prevent the rash, foolish course you have elected to follow. I can but warn you that you will soon come to regret most bitterly that you did not heed your dear mother's wishes."

In the event, Bonnie reflected, glancing round the room again, Aunt Grace had erred only in respect to the "soon." And not even entirely on that head, she admitted, for though she had not immediately regretted her decision, she had been disillusioned almost at once.

As Mr. Powell had indicated, his home was a grand brick structure in Portman Square, but the bedchamber to which Bonnie was assigned proved a good deal smaller than her room in Stafford. She supposed she should be grateful not to be banished to the attic with the rest of the staff, and she tried not to mind that the bedchamber was so crammed with furniture that it was prodigious difficult to walk about. As she grew familiar with the house, she discovered that every room, whatever its size, was similarly crowded; and she shortly concluded that Mr. and Mrs. Powell were so excessively wealthy that they were hard pressed to find ways to spend their fortune.

Mrs. Powell's wardrobe certainly tended to confirm this theory, for during the entire first year of their acquaintance, Bonnie did not observe her in the same garment twice. Unfortunately, despite her plethora of clothes, Mrs. Powell never looked truly handsome. She was not an attractive woman to begin with—as lean as her husband was fat, with light brown hair, pale brown eyes, and a sallow face that seemed to run all together—and as if these deficiencies were not enough, she was always hideously overdressed. When she went out in the afternoon, she wore an evening gown suitable for dinner; to dinner, she wore a ball dress. On the rare occasions Bonnie had seen her rigged out for an actual ball, Mrs. Powell had been wearing a gown so elaborate, jewelry so ostentatious, that she might well have been mistaken for a cyprian holding court in her opera box.

In view of her execrable taste, it was scarcely surprising that Mrs. Powell had failed to achieve her fondest ambition: that of being granted entry into the London *ton*. Bonnie could tell when the Season or Little Season was under way, for during these months, Mrs. Powell was from home the better part of each day. Bonnie had collected from the remarks of the servants that her employer spent the absent hours driving up one street and down the next, doggedly presenting her calling card to the butler of every lord, lady, and honorable in her path. Insofar as Bonnie knew, Mrs. Powell had never been received by any of these exalted personages, and none of them had ever returned her calls.

When the *ton* quit London, Mrs. Powell—undaunted—began to plot her campaign for the next Season; and from time to time, Bonnie would feel a stab of pity for the wretched woman. But her heart would harden again the instant she entered the schoolroom because she firmly believed that maternal neglect lay at the root of her endless problems with the children.

The children. Bonnie instinctively shuddered, then cast another baleful glare at her ruined dress. She had encountered no difficulties in the early months of her employment, when—as

Mr. Powell had stated—her only pupils were his two daughters. In addition to their mother's homeliness, Maria and Anne had inherited Mrs. Powell's rather obtuse mind, and neither could be described as an apt student. But the girls were malleable and, for the most part, well-behaved—generally content to sit quietly at the table they shared and at least pretend an interest in the day's instruction.

Six or eight months had passed, placidly if not really pleasantly, before Bonnie learned of the grave—and, she suspected, deliberate—oversight Mr. Powell had committed when he engaged her services. She was well aware by then, of course, that Maria and Anne were but the eldest of the Powells' six children and had four little brothers—aged five, four, three, and two. In fact, she felt sure that all the neighbors for miles around were aware of the Powell boys because it was a rare day indeed when an irate homeowner or servant did not drag one of them to the front door and report some dastardly depredation. In the course of Bonnie's brief employment, two nannies had fled in terror, and the current nursemaid betrayed every indication of following in their wake.

Thus it was that Bonnie heard with alarm—nay, *horror*—Mr. Powell's casual pronouncement that as each boy reached the age of six, he would be joining his sisters in the schoolroom. Nor did she derive significant comfort from Mr. Powell's addendum that his sons would remain in her charge only until they could be sent away to school. That would be several years per boy at the least, she reckoned, and probably far more, for she strongly doubted that any boarding school in England would tolerate Mr. Powell's unruly offspring above a day or two.

But she could not decline the responsibility, not without resigning her post, and she figuratively squared her shoulders and resolved to make the best of the situation. A governess worthy of the name could control even the most obstreperous six-year-old, she reasoned; and during the week prior to the scheduled arrival of Teddy—the eldest boy—in the schoolroom, she composed and rehearsed a firm little speech on the

subject of gentlemanly conduct. Teddy listened to her address
with rapt attention and, upon its conclusion, loosed a mouse
from a box beneath his desk, sending his sisters and Bonnie
herself shrieking into the corridor.

The mouse was but the first specimen in a vast zoological
array. Over the course of the ensuing years—or so Bonnie
was persuaded—the Powell boys enlivened the schoolroom
with every species of rodent native to Britain and a number of
the indigenous reptiles, amphibians, and insects as well. When
inclement weather inhibited their search for loathsome crea-
tures, they were inclined to turn their hands to devilish feats
of engineering. For example, on the rainy day of Lucas'
debut in the schoolroom, he and Teddy nailed shut the drawer
of Bonnie's desk, and she broke all her fingernails before she
glimpsed the metal heads in the wood. This trick so delighted
its perpetrators that the following year, when Oliver came to
join his brothers, the three boys nailed the schoolroom door
closed. Having recently decided that the boys might cease
their pranks if she ignored them, Bonnie refused to acknowledge their pounding until it was too late; and she and the girls
were trapped inside the schoolroom for upwards of two hours.

However, most of the boys' escapades were not so compli-
cated. They often tied strings between adjacent pieces of
furniture, and twice Bonnie had been sufficiently incautious
to trip over one of these obstacles. No, she amended, she
had *tripped* on innumerable occasions; twice she had actually
fallen. A favorite variation on this theme was to tie the items
on Bonnie's desk together—cleverly hiding the string, of
course—so that when she picked up the text of the topic
under discussion, all her books, papers, pencils, et cetera,
tumbled to the floor. She had long since lost track of the
number and variety of unsavory articles that had dropped on
her head when she opened the schoolroom door; crashed into
her back when she dared to turn it; been planted on, in, or
under her desk.

All of which might have been bearable, she sometimes
thought, if her life outside the schoolroom had offered any

compensation for her trials within. But it did not, for her
roseate dreams of London had failed most abysmally to mate-
rialize. She had seen enough of the city to own that it boasted
a myriad of charms and entertainments, but her duties left her
too little time, too little energy, to enjoy them. And—the
primary obstacle—she had far too little money to finance the
shopping excursions and theater outings she'd planned. She
did not know the "prevailing" wages of a governess, for she
was not acquainted with any other women in her profession.
She only knew that the tiny salary Mr. Powell provided
barely covered her expenditures for underclothing and the
occasional book or box of candy. Her "new" dress—the one
which now lay in ruins on the counterpane—had cost every
farthing she had saved in nearly four years of employment,
and in the year since its purchase, she had accumulated but
five pounds more.

The strains of a piano wafted up from the music room
below Bonnie's bedchamber, and she could not repress a wry
smile at this reminder of the last and greatest of her disap-
pointments. Endowed with the bitter wisdom of hindsight,
she wondered how she could possibly have believed Mr.
Powell's assurance that she would have "suitors in droves"
once she came to London. How she herself could have entertained visions of "thousands" of young men thronging the
streets, all wildly eager to court a greenheaded governess
from Stafford. The truth was that after four years and ten
months in the Powell household, she had met but one prospective *parti,* and him only six months since, when Mrs.
Powell had engaged Mr. Percy Crawford to instruct the girls
in music.

There was no denying that Mr. Crawford was "suitable":
Bonnie estimated him to be about thirty years of age, and he
had once mentioned that his father was a clergyman as well.
Nor was there much doubt that he was, in fact, eager to
initiate a courtship. They had first met at Mrs. Powell's
insistence to discuss the practice sessions Bonnie was to
conduct between the girls' weekly lessons, and Mr. Crawford

had subsequently seized upon this excuse to have Bonnie summoned to the music room nearly every week. Here— randomly, maddeningly striking the keys of the piano all the while—he managed to extend what should have been a five-minute conversation to half an hour or more. Mr. Crawford's discourse was normally as pointless as his idle plunking on the piano, but on the occasion of their last encounter, he had broadly hinted that Bonnie might wish to accompany him to Vauxhall Gardens some evening.

Bonnie had affected not to comprehend his invitation because she did not find Mr. Crawford in the least attractive. From her childhood, when Mama and Papa had told her tales of bold knights and handsome princes, Bonnie had carried a mental portrait of the quintessential man—tall and lean, with coal-black hair and eyes of sapphire blue—and she was hard put to imagine a human male who resembled this image less than Mr. Crawford. She had long since recognized, of course, that the man of her dreams—like the London of her dreams— probably did not exist; and she was prepared to overlook one or two deficiencies. She might have forgiven Mr. Crawford his diminutive stature or his stooped shoulders, his dun-colored hair or his small gray eyes; but she couldn't accept them all in combination.

Which was a rather high-handed attitude, Bonnie conceded, for she was no longer the "pretty young woman" Mr. Powell had professed to admire in Stafford. Her hair was still an arresting shade of pale red (though it hadn't been properly cut in months), and she did have Mama's lovely brown-gold eyes. But she had lost almost a stone since her arrival in the city, and by the end of an exhausting day in the schoolroom, she feared she looked positively gaunt. She would study her reflection with dismay, noting how very sharp her cheekbones seemed, how hollow her cheeks, how pointed her chin. She was only four-and-twenty, but when she was in a particularly pessimistic frame of mind, she would fancy she appeared nearly as old as Mrs. Powell.

The mantel clock struck half past three, and Bonnie started.

The girls' lesson ended at four, and if she was to leave, she must escape the house before then, before Mr. Crawford could desire a servant to call her to the music room. And there was no "if" about it, she chided herself. However painful the prospect of slinking back to Aunt Grace, it was an inevitable fact of nature that her aunt could not survive much longer. The Powell boys, on the other hand, would still be alive, thriving, and no doubt wreaking havoc in the schoolroom a dozen years hence, by which time Bonnie would have grown so old and haggard that even Mr. Crawford would no longer wish to court her.

There remained only to inform Mr. Powell of her decision, and Bonnie had concluded as she packed that a personal conversation might well lead to an argument about her failure to grant him proper notice. She had consequently left a sheet of stationery, an envelope, and a pencil on the desk; and she now rose from the bed and traversed the few steps to the writing table. She perched on the chair in front of the desk, nervously aware of the minutes ticking away on the mantel clock, and abandoned her effort when it chimed a quarter till four. What was she to say? That his beloved sons were such bestial monsters that she couldn't bear another day of their torment? No, Mr. Powell would simply have to infer from her empty bedchamber that she had left his employ forever.

Bonnie jumped up from the chair and returned to the bed, closed her portmanteau and set it on the floor. She had previously laid her threadbare pelisse and battered French bonnet on the counterpane, and she hastily donned them, hung the chain of her reticule over one arm, and picked up her bag. It was so light that she frowned around the room again, but with the exception of the ink-stained dress and the items on the desk, it was, indeed, empty. She crept to the door, cracked it open, and—hearing the reassuring trill of scales from the music room—stole along the corridor, down the stairs, and out the front door.

Eager to distance herself from the house as speedily as she could, Bonnie hurried down Orchard Street toward Oxford, which, at any rate, she judged the best place to hail a hackney coach. It was an unusually warm day for early spring, and by the time she reached the intersection, she was perspiring most uncomfortably. She set her bag down, removed her cloak and draped it over her arm, then retrieved her portmanteau and began to search the approaching traffic for an empty hackney.

It was a busy time of day in Oxford Street, the time when many of Bonnie's betters repaired to Hyde Park for an afternoon drive, and she soon grew quite entranced by the passing parade of barouches and curricles and phaetons and the elegant passengers they bore. The experience was rather akin to pressing one's nose to a shop window, she reflected—admiring merchandise one couldn't possibly afford—and she was so very intrigued that she momentarily failed to register the identity of an oncoming landau. When she did, her knees weakened with dread, for there was no mistaking Mr. Powell's distinctive carriage. He normally did not return from his office in the City till half past four, half an hour before dinner, but Bonnie lacked the leisure to wonder why his schedule had been disrupted. She would not confront him at this late juncture, she thought frantically, and as she gazed desperately about for some avenue of escape, she glimpsed a hackney coach on the opposite side of the street.

One vehicle now lay between her and Mr. Powell's landau, but it was still some yards away, and Bonnie dashed in front of it and halted in the middle of the road. The hackney was also at a considerable distance, but it was proceeding toward her at a rapid pace, as was the curricle just ahead of it. However, Bonnie calculated that she could outrace the latter carriage, and she jerked up her portmanteau, rested it against her hip, and darted forward.

She remembered her pelisse only when it was too late, only when it slipped off her arm and tangled round her pounding feet. She began to stumble, and she instinctively dropped her bag, but it was, again, too late; she was hopelessly off-balance. She heard the shout of the curricle driver, the protesting squeal of his horses as he sought to rein them in, but she could only lurch ahead, closer and closer to the flying hooves and clattering metal wheels. Until, at last, she collided with a hard obstacle and everything went black.

2

"Come now, try to look at me. That's right; I want to see your eyes."

Bonnie had had this experience before: that of being aware, within a dream, that she was dreaming. Specifically, she was dreaming of her eighth birthday, when—against Papa's express instructions—she had climbed the oak tree in the rear garden of the rectory and fallen almost ten feet to the ground. Her first memory following the fall had been of Dr. Harding prying her eyes open one at a time, peering into them, asking her to look at him. Though, as so often occurred in dreams, Dr. Harding's appearance was wrong. His eyes were warm and kind and brown, and the eyes staring intently into hers were a frosty gray.

"She does not seem to have been concussed." The physician's words to Papa were precisely those Bonnie recollected, but his dream-voice was as distorted as his dream-eyes: a high-pitched voice entirely unlike Dr. Harding's pleasant baritone.

"And you're certain she has no broken bones?"

Papa didn't sound like Papa either, Bonnie reflected. In fact, Papa sounded rather like Dr. Harding *should* sound; dreams were so peculiar.

"I said I am certain none of her *major* bones is broken,"

Dr. Harding snapped. "When she begins to move about, she may well discover a small fracture or a cracked rib. Indeed, I shall own myself astonished if she does not. I should not expect a slight young woman to crash full tilt into a moving carriage without suffering *some* ill effect."

The dream was altogether ceasing to make sense now, Bonnie thought groggily. Which was just as well because she did not care to relive the well-deserved paddling she had received the day *after* her eighth birthday. Papa and Dr. Harding continued to talk for a time, their words a mere buzz in her ears, and at length, she drifted into dreamless oblivion.

Bonnie opened her eyes and lay still a moment, frowning in puzzlement. As nearly as she could gauge from the shadows in her bedchamber, it was early evening, and she never slept in the afternoon. Well, she amended, she did occasionally nap on a Sunday, after church and midday dinner, but she was quite certain this was Monday. Which meant that if she had, in fact, fallen asleep and dozed till six or seven o'clock, she had missed dinner; and she wondered why no servant had been sent to wake her. Thin as she was, she could ill afford to skip a meal, and she judged it best to go to the kitchen at once, before Mrs. Parr—the enormous cook—could wolf down all the leftovers herself. She sat quickly up and gasped as an unexpected bolt of pain shot through her right shoulder.

"Ah, you are awake."

It was a male voice, and even as Bonnie bristled with fury at the notion that Mr. Powell had invaded the sanctity of her bedchamber, she began to remember the events of the day. Someone had poured ink in her chair, she recalled, and she had packed her portmanteau and left the house in Portman Square. And then . . .

A dim figure materialized from the shadows, bent and lighted the lamp on the bedside table, and when he straightened, Bonnie gazed up at him. And then she had been struck by a carriage, she recollected. And apparently she had died and ascended to Mama's "better place," for the man who stood beside the bed looked exactly like the one she had envisioned. No, not exactly, she corrected: this man's nose was a trifle longer than that of the man she'd pictured, and his black hair was threaded here and there with gray. But the tall, spare frame was the same, and the dark, lean face; and his eyes truly were the color of sapphires.

She continued to stare at him until he perched on the edge of the bed, at which point she decided that he probably wasn't an angel after all. She was under the impression that the "better place" was inhabited by incorporeal spirits, and the mattress definitely gave under the weight of her companion. Furthermore, upon consideration, she strongly doubted that an angel would be clad in snugly fitted white pantaloons, a white waistcoat edged with crimson, and a splendid tailcoat of azure Bath.

"Where . . . where am I?" she stammered.

"Let us address first things first," he said soothingly. "Do you remember that you were involved in an accident?"

"Yes." Bonnie nodded. "Yes, I was run down by a carriage."

"Umm." He grinned, and Bonnie observed that he had beautiful teeth. "It would be somewhat more accurate to say that you ran the carriage down. Be that as it may, I brought you to my home—which is in Grosvenor Street at the intersection with Duke—and summoned my physician to attend you. Selwin is a rather chilly fellow, but I've always found him competent, and he could detect no serious injury."

It hadn't been a dream then, Bonnie realized; she had overheard a portion of Dr. Selwin's conversation with . . . with . . . "Who are you?" she blurted out.

"The Earl of Sedgewick." In lieu of a bow, he inclined his head. "I was driving the curricle you had the misfortune to encounter. At any rate, Selwin did indicate there might be injuries he could *not* detect, and we should explore that possibility without delay. Move about and advise me if you feel any pain."

Bonnie obediently flapped her arms and stretched her legs and twisted her torso, gasping again from time to time as her muscles shrieked in agonized protest. "I feel pain everywhere," she reported grimly.

"But not in any particular place?"

"Particularly in my shoulder." She gingerly touched the spot.

"Yes, that was the point of your impact with the carriage, and Selwin said you'd sustained an excessively nasty bruise. And that you'd be generally stiff and sore for a day or two. But I count it an excellent sign that you've no excessive pain in any other location. I believe we can safely conclude that you emerged from the accident virtually unscathed."

That was easy for him to say, Bonnie thought grouchily. He was not the one who ached in every limb and organ of his body.

"What is your name, by the by?" Lord Sedgewick asked.

"Bonnie," she muttered. "Bonnie Gordon."

"Bonnie." He knit his brows, and Bonnie noticed that—unlike his hair—they were untouched with gray. "Surely that isn't your legal name."

"No, my legal name is Elizabeth."

"Elizabeth." His frown deepened. "Would it be rude of me to inquire how 'Elizabeth' came to be shortened to 'Bonnie'?"

"It was my grandfather's doing. He came down from Scotland as a young man, but he never lost his accent. And when he first saw me—or so the story goes—he said, 'My, what a bonnie little lass.' I've been called Bonnie ever since."

"I trust someone commended his sharp eye? You *are* a bonnie lass, if not so little any longer." The earl's own blue eyes swept her face, then suddenly narrowed, and he tilted his head as if to obtain a better perspective. "What an odd coincidence," he murmured. "You look astonishingly like my sisters."

"Then I can only collect that your sisters do not look in the least like you," Bonnie snapped. She regretted her sharpness, but his scrutiny was rendering her prodigious uncomfortable.

"In point of fact, they do not," he said mildly. "My sisters keenly resemble our late mother, and I'm told that I myself am the very image of our father. But let us return to you. Since I assume you are not in the habit of jousting with carriages, I am compelled to wonder why you were in such a monstrous hurry."

"I was . . . was escaping," Bonnie said.

"Ah." He flashed another grin, and his eyes began to twinkle. "Escaping from a man, I'll warrant."

"Five men actually," Bonnie said. She perceived no reason to mention Mr. Crawford. "Mr. Theodore Powell, my employer—whose carriage was bearing down on me from the opposite direction—and his four sons. The eldest of whom is ten," she added hastily as Lord Sedgewick's mouth dropped open with shock.

"You were their governess then," he said with unmistakable relief. "The boys' governess, I mean." Bonnie nodded. "But am I to understand that Mr. Powell was *pursuing* you in his carriage?"

"No, no; he was not even aware I was gone. I left without notice, you see . . ."

There was nothing for it but to relate the entire story, and this Bonnie proceeded to do—starting from the day the mouse had been loosed in the schoolroom and ending with the moment she had charged into Lord Sedgewick's curricle. The earl began to chuckle before she was half-through, and by the time she finished her tale, he was roaring with laughter.

"Oh, I say." He pulled a handkerchief from one pocket of his coat and mopped his streaming eyes. "My mother often declared that I was the wickedest child in Britain, but I fear I should have lost that distinction at once had the Powell boys been my contemporaries."

"It is not amusing," Bonnie said sternly. But his merriment was infectious, and she was hard put to stifle a giggle of her own.

"And where precisely were you going?" Despite her admonition, Lord Sedgewick was still chuckling a bit.

"I intended to engage a hackney to drive me to the Swan with Two Necks. From there, I planned to take a public coach to my aunt's home in Cheshire."

"I see." The earl had overcome his mirth at last, and he shoved his handkerchief back in his pocket. "Then I daresay your aunt will be most alarmed when you do not appear. We must write and advise her of the delay—"

"No," Bonnie interposed. "Aunt Grace wasn't expecting me, and I doubt she'd be much alarmed in any case. We never did get on, and we've scarcely communicated during the past five years."

"I . . . see," Lord Sedgewick repeated, this time stringing the words out. His eyes searched her face again. "In short, Miss Gordon—or so I infer—you are presently accountable to no one."

Bonnie rather liked his phraseology: "accountable to no one" sounded far kinder than "alone in the world." "That is correct," she confirmed aloud.

"Well, well, well."

His tone suggested that she had revealed a startling piece of information, but before Bonnie could puzzle his reaction out, he rose from the bed.

"Are you hungry?" he asked. "Never mind. You must eat even if you aren't hungry; you're altogether too thin. I shall send Nell up to help you change for dinner."

Evidently, Bonnie thought irritably, he had decided that—having narrowly failed to kill her—he was now free to order her about as he pleased. She started to protest that she didn't want to change for dinner, but when she glanced down, she discovered her dress quite ruined: black with dirt from top to bottom and featuring a great rent on one side of the skirt. Nor had the earl afforded her an opportunity to object, she saw, looking up again; he had left the room and closed the door behind him.

Bonnie sighed and eased herself out of the bed. Lord

Sedgewick's reference to a change of clothing had led her to assume that her portmanteau had been rescued from the street and brought to his house, and after peering about a moment, she spied her bag—considerably the worse for its recent travail—situated between the door and a tall mahogany wardrobe. She hobbled across the room, distantly noting the Aubusson carpet underfoot, retrieved the bag, carried it back to the bed, and laid it on the counterpane. Since she had packed her two remaining gowns near the bottom of the portmanteau, she was compelled to remove her nightclothes and undergarments in order to reach the ancient white muslin dress beneath. She withdrew it from the bag, shook out the wrinkles, draped it over the footboard of the canopied bedstead, then gazed uneasily at the rest of her things.

She did not know the exact hour, but she surmised from the dim light poking between the draperies that it was well into the evening. By the time she and Lord Sedgewick had finished their meal, it was likely to be half past nine or later—a most inconvenient hour to resume her interrupted journey. So though the earl had not specifically stated that she was to spend the night under his roof, Bonnie had to suppose this was his intention; and she belatedly wondered whether there was a *Lady* Sedgewick. If not, the situation was highly irregular to say the least—

A great pounding at the door ended Bonnie's speculation, and before she could instruct the party to enter, the door flew open. Bonnie initially fancied she was witnessing nothing short of a miracle, nothing less than a living mountain; but the mountain soon proved to be a massive woman clad in a voluminous black dress. How she got about at all, Bonnie could not conceive—she was far from young, her hair entirely white—but she fairly bounced over the threshold and strode briskly across the carpet.

"I'm Nell," she announced gratuitously, reaching Bonnie's side. "As his lordship is holding dinner, there'll be no time for a bath, so I brought some water for the basin."

She indicated the pitcher in her hand, marched to the far

wall of the bedchamber, emptied the pitcher into the basin atop the rosewood washstand, marched back to the bed. All in under twenty seconds, Bonnie calculated, marveling anew at her speed.

"Is that what you think to wear?" Nell demanded, frowning at the muslin dress. "There's a spot on the sleeve. A red spot."

"Yes, I . . ." But how did one explain that one had been caught between opposing forces in a furious red-currant-tart fight? "I know," Bonnie concluded lamely.

"I'll tend to it while you wash up," Nell said. "Hurry now, for I'll be back by the time you're done."

Bonnie had little doubt of this, and as soon as the door had closed in Nell's wake, she stripped off her clothes and limped as quickly as she could toward the washstand. A satinwood dressing table stood just beside it, a mirror above, and Bonnie paused a moment to study her reflection. Except for a smear of dirt on her right cheekbone, her face bore no mark of the accident, but she sucked in her breath when her eyes fell to her right shoulder. She had sustained a nasty bruise indeed—a ragged purple-black circle fully four inches in diameter—and she was almost grateful that the high neck of her old-fashioned dress would hide it.

Nell was as good as her word: Bonnie had scarcely completed her washing and donned a fresh set of underclothing when the door crashed open again. The elderly servant was a trifle deficient in courtesy, Bonnie felt, but clearly an accomplished ladies' maid, for the currant stain was gone. Nell assisted her into the dress, and as she began expertly fastening the hooks and eyes at the back, Bonnie glimpsed a perfect means of ascertaining her host's marital status.

"Are you Lady Sedgewick's abigail, Nell?" she inquired with studied casualness.

"*Was*, miss," Nell responded sorrowfully. "Yes, I was her ladyship's abigail until the dear woman died."

"How . . ."

Bonnie had started to say "splendid," and though she

succeeded in biting back the word, the thought lingered. She was inexplicably pleased to learn that the earl was not presently married, but the fact that he was widowed somehow rendered the situation less compromising. Or was that specious reasoning? Widower or no, he was a remarkably handsome man, not much above five-and-thirty, she judged—

"How what, miss?" Nell once more shattered her reverie.

"How . . . how tragic," Bonnie murmured.

"That it was." Nell heaved a tremulous sigh. "She was a saint, was Lady Sedgewick, and she's sorely missed. But there, I've finished." She patted Bonnie's back in confirmation. "I don't have time for your hair; Alice will be needing me in the kitchen. And I'm afraid I couldn't do much with it anyway."

Her keen black eyes traveled from the unruly red curls on Bonnie's forehead to the stray tendrils snaking toward her shoulders, and she drew another sigh. "Comb it yourself as best you can. But do hurry because his lordship is waiting in the dining room."

On this decidedly uncharitable note, Nell sailed out of the bedchamber, and Bonnie snatched her comb and brush from the counterpane and rushed back to the dressing table. Since her hair had grown so long, she hadn't been able to do much with it either, and ten full minutes of effort produced no visible improvement. But what did it matter? It didn't signify a whit whether Lord Sedgewick approved her coiffure or not. With a sigh Nell might well have envied, she dropped her ineffectual instruments on the dressing table and—her muscles beginning to throb again—trudged across the room, out the door, and into the corridor.

Bonnie had neglected to inquire whether Lord Sedgewick had children, but the two bedchambers she passed en route to the staircase suggested that he did not. Or—if he did—that the children had not accompanied him to town, for the bedchambers were furnished much like hers, and she saw no toys or other personal effects. In fact, she reflected, stopping to peer briefly into the rooms on the first story, the entire house looked rather sterile; and she surmised that the earl—like most of the *ton*—spent but a few months of the year in London. It seemed a pity that the fine Adam furniture in the saloon and the two smaller parlors was so little used, and she entertained the same impression she had that afternoon in Oxford Street: that of observing a world she could never be a part of.

Bonnie had also failed to ask the location of the dining room, and when she reached the ground floor, she arbitrarily approached the door on the left side of the vestibule. She realized at once that she had erred, but she lingered on the threshold of the library, her eyes enviously raking the floor-to-ceiling shelves. Shelves laden with books, she noted; this room, at least, was used. She remembered, with a stab of dismay, that she had left her own books in the schoolroom in Portman Square. Not many books; over the years, she had "lent" much of her collection to the Powell children, and few of the volumes had been returned. But now she possessed no books at all, and she was sorely inclined to forgo dinner and devote the evening to an investigation of the treasure spread before her. However, she supposed Lord Sedgewick would soon desire Nell to hunt her down, and she turned reluctantly away and traversed the foyer to the archway on the opposite side.

As Nell had stated, the earl was awaiting her, already seated at the head of the table, and he did not rise when Bonnie entered the room. Instead, a male servant—the butler, she presumed—stepped forward to assist her into the chair at Lord Sedgewick's right. He then proceeded to the mahogany sideboard and returned to the table with two steaming bowls of soup.

The earl began immediately to eat, and—following his lead—Bonnie discovered herself hungrier than she'd fancied. Indeed, she amended, she was ravenous, and the mulligatawny was superb, but she could not quell a vague sense of disappointment. His arrogance notwithstanding, she had found Lord Sedgewick quite charming, a thoroughly amusing companion; and his unexpected reserve was most disconcerting. She looked up from her bowl, wondering if she had somehow offended him, and perceived—to her further discomfiture—that he was watching her. Not merely glancing in her direction from time to time, as would be normal in the circumstances. No, he was *studying* her, his sapphire eyes once more narrowed in speculation; and at length, Bonnie grew so nervous that she was hard put to finish her soup.

"The . . . the food is excellent," she stammered at last. Five full minutes had elapsed since the butler had removed the soup bowls and delivered the entrées, and she could bear the silence no longer.

"Umm?" The earl shook his head, as though physically dislodging a spell. "Ah, yes, the food. Yes, Alice has been in the family since I was a boy. In fact, my city staff is a family in itself. Alice is Nell's sister . . . I trust Nell's services were satisfactory, by the by?"

"Oh, yes," Bonnie assured him. She elected not to add that Nell's services would be somewhat more satisfactory if she did not burst unbidden into the bedchambers of his lordship's guests.

"I'm delighted to hear it. At any rate, Alice is a widow, and Kimball"—he nodded toward the butler—"is her son. I bring only the three of them from Dorset when I come up to London. A small staff by any standard, but sufficient for a bachelor who spends little time at home."

"Yes," Bonnie murmured, "I was deeply sorry to learn of your loss. Did your wife die recently, Lord Sedgewick?"

The earl was seized by a fit of frenzied coughing—apparently he had choked on a morsel of lamb—and Bonnie regarded him with concern, belatedly regretting that she had introduced such a painful subject. Lord Sedgewick groped for his wineglass and, after two or three great swallows, succeeded in clearing the obstruction from his throat.

"My wife?" he sputtered. "However did you conceive the notion that I'd been married?"

"Nell told me she was Lady Sedgewick's abigail—"

"Nell was my *mother's* abigail," he interjected. "Mama died five years ago, and there's been no Lady Sedgewick since. Nor will be, not in my lifetime. No, Miss Gordon, I've never been wed and never intend to be."

"What a foolish thing to say!" she chided. "One day you'll fall over head and ears in love and change your mind in an instant."

"That I shall not," he said smugly, "for you are wrong on two counts. In the first place, I am firmly persuaded that love is a myth foisted on humanity by generations of poets and novelists. If it is not a myth, how is it I've survived for six-and-thirty years without suffering a single one of the distressing symptoms they describe?"

He made it sound less a myth than a disease. Nor did Bonnie have a ready answer to his question, which was obviously rhetorical in any case.

"And if I *were* to experience such symptoms," the earl continued, "I shouldn't dream of wedding the object of my . . . ah . . . aberration. I have encountered hundreds of beautiful women, and I daresay I'll encounter hundreds more before I'm done. To restrict my attentions to only one would be akin to . . . What is your favorite food, Miss Gordon?"

"Chocolate," she said. "Though I fail to see what possible connection—"

"Chocolate." He nodded. "But fond as you may be of chocolate, you could scarcely live on it alone, could you? And if you could, if you tried, you would soon grow most dreadfully tired of it, would you not? My own favorite food is roast beef, but I certainly don't wish to have it at every meal."

Apparently Lord Sedgewick viewed the female sex as a banquet laid out for his exclusive delectation, and Bonnie could not but wonder her place on the table. He had already remarked her thinness, and as she was somewhat taller than the average and had pale red hair, she fancied he might well perceive her as a carrot. But she would not dignify his odious analogy by deigning to discuss it any further.

"You have quite made your point," she said stiffly. "However, I should think a titled peer might judge himself compelled to give some consideration to the matter of an heir."

"How very intriguing that you should mention that, Miss Gordon."

His eyes narrowed again, and he sat back in his chair and laced his fingers over his ribs. Intriguing or convenient? Bonnie now wondered. She had an odd but distinct impression that she had blundered into a trap.

"The fact is I have an heir," the earl said.

Bonnie could only collect that he was referring to an illegitimate child, but before she could convey her disapproval of this indelicate turn in the conversation, Lord Sedgewick went on.

"My nephew, Francis. The son of my eldest sister, Judith, and her husband, Sir Robert Hellier. And I have given the matter a great deal of consideration in the weeks just past because I am excessively distressed by several recent developments."

"Distressed by Francis, you mean," Bonnie said.

"Not so much by Francis." He shook his head, and the gray strands woven through his hair gleamed silver in the flickering light of the chandelier. "Francis has been involved in his share of scrapes, but young men will sow their wild oats."

"As will older ones," Bonnie said coolly.

"I must concede that point to you, Miss Gordon." He flashed his winsome grin. "But if we may return to Francis, he's not really a bad sort. A bit skitter-brained in my opinion, but a tolerably good lad nonetheless. The problem lies with his parents."

Bonnie understood the problem all too well: Papa hadn't much cared for Aunt Grace either. "You and your sister do not get on," she rejoined aloud.

"It is not a question of 'getting on.' " He shook his head again. "Although, to say the truth, there was never any great love lost between Judith and myself. No, the problem is that Judith and Robert seem determined to exhaust my fortune long before it can pass to Francis.''

"But how?" Bonnie peered around the room, half-expecting to find Sir Robert and Lady Hellier lifting the silver from the sideboard.

"Nothing so overt as theft." The earl might have been reading her mind. "But equally effective for all its subtlety. Judith and Robert and I patronize many of the same merchants, and I am given to understand that Robert has always been prodigious slow to pay his bills. Be that as it may, he did—until the past few months—eventually meet his obligations. Lately, however, he has left a number of major debts to languish so long that his creditors discreetly brought the situation to my attention. Indeed, I was advised only this morning that Robert still owed Hatchett for the phaeton he purchased nearly six months since." Lord Sedgewick scowled at the memory. "My payment of that bill was the fourth I have made in Robert's behalf, and I shudder to contemplate what additional debts I shall be obliged to settle in future."

"Obliged?" Bonnie echoed. "Surely you aren't legally responsible for your brother-in-law's debts."

"No," the earl agreed, "but I hold myself *morally* responsible. Were it not for his connection to me, Robert would have been denied credit years ago. As it is, the merchants are well aware that Francis is my heir, and I fancy they assume I am quite prepared to contribute to his parents' support."

"And Robert and Judith are confident of their position as well," Bonnie said, beginning to comprehend the magnitude of his dilemma. "Or so I presume, for they must know you do not intend to marry."

"Oh, they more than merely *know;* they have taken great pains to ensure that I remain unwed. If I stand up twice with the same woman at a given assembly, I shortly spy my dear sister whispering in her ear. No doubt warning her of my scandalous reputation and rakeshame habits." He sketched a sardonic smile. "I suppose I should be grateful to Judith for defending my bachelorhood so assiduously, but in the circumstances, I bitterly resent her interference.''

"I daresay they would mend their ways if you threatened to cut Francis from your will," Bonnie mused. "But you can't do that, can you? Not when an estate is entailed."

"An interesting observation, Miss Gordon."

"Interesting" jangled in her ear much the way "intriguing" had, and she entertained the same peculiar notion of entrapment. A notion reinforced when Lord Sedgewick sat forward and propped his elbows on the linen tablecloth.

"In point of fact," he said, "the bulk of my estate is *not* entailed. Our family seat in Dorset is, of course, and a small seaside home in Hampshire, but that is essentially all. By far the larger portion of my fortune derives from the legacy of my maternal grandfather. I might add that Judith also received a handsome bequest from Grandpapa, but she and Robert have squandered every farthing. Whereas—if you will pardon my immodesty in saying so—I invested my inheritance very carefully, and it has nearly quadrupled over the years.''

It was fortunate the earl did not feel compelled to apologize for all his immodesties, Bonnie thought wryly, or he would have time for little else. "So you *could* modify your will," she commented aloud. "Except—or so I collect—that you've no other relative but Francis to designate as your principal heir.''

"No, I have not," he acknowledged, "but I suddenly discover myself with a golden opportunity to invent such a relative. You, Miss Gordon. I've had it in mind for some hours now to pass you off as my niece."

He had sprung the trap at last, and for a moment, Bonnie could only gape at him, her jaw sagging with shock. "One cannot simply *invent* a niece," she protested when she finally found her tongue. "Well, an infant niece perhaps," she amended, "but I am four-and-twenty years of age."

"Which is perfect as it happens," Lord Sedgewick said,

"because Cornelia wed Thomas Carlisle *five*-and-twenty years ago."

"Cornelia?" Bonnie's brain was whirling with confusion, and she wondered if she might have been concussed after all. "Thomas Carlisle?"

"You must recollect my remark that you look astonishingly like my *sisters*," the earl said by way of reply. "Indeed, it was that observation which prompted me to consider an imposture. Cornelia is the younger of my sisters—younger than Judith, that is, but nine years my own senior."

Far from dissipating Bonnie's confusion, his explanation served to bewilder her even further. "And you have it in your mind to persuade Cornelia to pretend she has a daughter? A daughter she has chosen to hide for nearly a quarter of a century?"

"Fortunately, no such persuasion will be necessary. Or unfortunately, perhaps I should have said, because I was immensely fond of Cornelia." His sapphire eyes briefly clouded, grew distant, then returned to Bonnie. "Be that as it may, you should quite appreciate her story, Miss Gordon, for Cornelia's head was stuffed with the same sort of romantic nonsense you yourself subscribe to."

Bonnie opened her mouth to object, but Lord Sedgewick waved her to silence.

"Cornelia conceived a great *tendre* for Thomas Carlisle," he continued, "and one would be hard put to imagine a more unsuitable *parti*. He tenanted one of our farms at Sedgewood, which meant, of course, that Papa counted him barely a notch above the servants. As if that were not sufficiently horrifying, Tom's father was a criminal; he'd been hanged some years earlier for a murder he'd committed during a taproom brawl. Tom himself was a bang-up fellow, or so I thought with all the wisdom of my eleven years. But whatever his character, he was no proper match for the daughter of an earl; and I suspect that had Papa ignored the situation, Cornelia would soon have recognized her folly. However, Papa forbade her

any further association with Tom, and I daresay I needn't tell
you what happened next.''

"They eloped," Bonnie said, and the earl inclined his
head. "And *did* she come to recognize her folly?" Bonnie
hoped not, for she did rather like the story. "Have she and
Tom been happy, I mean?"

"That I can't say because we've heard nothing from them
since the night they fled to Scotland. I wasn't privy to Papa's
final conversation with Cornelia; he gave us only the gist of
it. However, I surmise he informed her that if she defied his
wishes in respect to Tom, he would disown her—financially
and personally as well. And if that is the case, I additionally
surmise that Tom and Cornelia's pride has not permitted them
to attempt to effect a reconciliation. At any rate, Cornelia left
a note stating their intention to emigrate to Barbados, and that
is the last I know of them.''

"I see," Bonnie murmured.

"Is that a mere figure of speech," he demanded, "or do
you *really* see? It's entirely plausible that Cornelia might
have a twenty-four-year-old daughter neither Judith nor I has
ever heard of. Entirely possible that—in her daughter's
interest—Cornelia might swallow her pride at last and send
the girl to England to make a good marriage. The story would
be credible even did you not chance to resemble my sisters,
and the fact that you do renders it the more so.''

Lord Sedgewick punctuated his commentary with a bite of
lamb, then—evidently finding it cold—pushed his plate away
and signaled for dessert. This proved to be chocolate blancmange, which was one of Bonnie's favorites, but her brain
was spinning so dizzily by now that she had altogether lost
her appetite.

"I do see that the story would be credible," she conceded
at length. "That Judith would probably believe I was your
mutual niece. What I do not see, however, is how you can
expect me—me or any other young woman—to play such a
role for the indefinite future—''

"But I expect nothing of the kind," he interposed. "You

would be required to pose as Bonnie Carlisle only a few weeks, only until the end of the Season, let us say. Whatever her deficiencies, Judith is far from stupid, and she would perceive in an instant that Francis could no longer be assured of inheriting my whole estate. Though I should not leave it entirely to her to draw the proper inference; I should naturally drop the occasional remark about a possible redistribution of my wealth.'' His grin was one of considerable relish.

''And then?'' Bonnie pressed. ''After the Season?''

''After the Season, Bonnie Carlisle would discover herself wretchedly homesick and return to Barbados. She would never be seen again, but the damage would be done. Judith and Robert would fairly tremble at the prospect of provoking me; they'd fear that the slightest annoyance might lead me to bequeath my personal fortune to my dear niece. I doubt Robert would risk saddling me with the bill for a new neck-cloth, much less another phaeton.''

He glowered again, grinned again, finished his pudding, shoved the bowl aside.

''When Bonnie Carlisle returned to Barbados,'' he went on, ''Bonnie Gordon would join her aunt in Cheshire. Some weeks later than originally planned, but her aunt would never be the wiser, would she? That is the second factor which so conveniently simplifies our project: the circumstance that you've no relatives of your own to tease themselves about your absence.''

Our project, Bonnie noted; he spoke as though she had already consented to abet his scheme. Nor was he far from wrong, for she could perceive no reason to decline. If nothing else, he had offered her a brief respite—six or eight blessed weeks before she would be compelled to confront Aunt Grace. Who, as the earl had pointed out, would never learn of her escapade. She reached for her spoon, thinking to toy with her blancmange while she reviewed his proposal, and observed that Nell's deft removal of the currant stain had revealed a hole in her sleeve.

''I fear you've overlooked one difficulty,'' she said. ''Cornelia would not send her daughter to England without an adequate wardrobe, and mine is far from that. The dress I was wearing this afternoon was ruined in the accident, and I've only two others—''

"But that presents no difficulty whatever!" Lord Sedgewick interrupted brightly. "As it happens, Judith and her family are on holiday in France. They won't reach town till late next week, and if we visit the mantua-maker tomorrow, you'll be suitably rigged out well before then. Indeed, I am confident Mrs. Pruitt will have you ready to attend Lady Lambeth's assembly next Tuesday."

Lady Lambeth. An assembly. She was no longer peering wistfully through the shop window, Bonnie reflected; the door had cracked open, and she had been invited inside. There did remain one complication, one she had somehow forgotten as she pondered the earl's proposition. She had worried, not two hours since, about the impropriety of spending a single unchaperoned night beneath his roof, and if she agreed to portray his niece, her stay would extend to upwards of a month. To say nothing of the wardrobe he had so airily promised to provide: her acceptance of such a gift would rightly be judged compromising in the extreme.

But judged by whom? a tiny voice within her whispered. Aunt Grace would never know of her scandalous conduct, the Powells would never know, and Bonnie was acquainted with no one else in London. Only she and Lord Sedgewick would know the truth of their situation, and the truth was that it was nothing more than a business arrangement.

"Have we a bargain then?"

The earl's words were precisely those Mr. Powell had employed so many years before, and Bonnie experienced a little jolt of apprehension. Surely, she thought, Fate would not be so unkind as to propel her into a second post as disastrous as the first. No, she *could* not be tricked again, for what could conceivably go amiss?

"Yes, Lord Sedgewick," she murmured aloud. "Yes, I fancy we do."

"Excellent." He patted his lips with his napkin and tossed the napkin on the table. "As I've an appointment tomorrow afternoon, I should like to go to Mrs. Pruitt's in the morning. We shall leave at half past nine if that is agreeable to you."

"Yes, Lord Sedgewick."

"Excellent," he said again, rising from his chair. "I also have an engagement this evening, so I must beg to be excused. Finish your pudding like a good girl. You are, as I mentioned, rather too thin, and I shouldn't wish the world to think I am starving my poor niece. Feel free to request another bowl if you're still hungry."

"Yes, Lord Sedgewick."

He strode to the archway, then turned back round. "Since you *are* to be my niece, you must henceforth call me Uncle David. Practice that while you eat your pudding, lest you err when we meet Mrs. Pruitt."

"Yes, L . . . Yes, Uncle David."

He walked on into the vestibule, and Bonnie stared in his wake, unable to quell an impression that she was dreaming after all.

3

"Miss Bonnie?" As was her wont, Nell opened the bedchamber door without knocking and bounded over the threshold. "Ah, I'm happy to see you're awake, for his lordship wishes to leave at half past nine precisely. He desired me to serve your breakfast here."

She nodded toward the silver tray in her hands, then strode across the room, and Bonnie gritted her teeth at the agonizing prospect of rising from the bed. Had she entertained any lingering notion that she was dreaming, it would have been most rudely dispelled some ten minutes earlier, when she'd awakened and incautiously sprung to a sitting position. She had expected, per Dr. Selwin's prediction, to be somewhat "stiff and sore"; but in the event, she felt as though she had spent the entire night on the rack. She had thus far succeeded in lowering both feet to the carpet, but how she was actually to stand and walk, she could not conceive.

"Come now," Nell said. She had deposited the tray on top of the dressing table and was waving the linen napkin rather like a battle flag. "I daresay you're a trifle achy this morning, but you'll feel better if you move about. And *much* better when you've had your breakfast."

Bonnie strongly doubted that anything short of death would ease her discomfort, but it was clear Nell would brook no argument. Indeed, Bonnie judged it quite likely that the enormous abigail would forcibly bear her to the dressing table if she declined to go unaided, and she gritted her teeth again and drew herself gingerly up. To her unutterable relief, the pain did moderate a bit as she hobbled across the room—the white-hot bolts in her muscles and joints shrinking to mere nails—and she was able to sink into the chair with only a muffled groan.

"There, did I not tell you?" Nell beamed and laid the napkin on her lap. "And look at the splendid breakfast I brought. His lordship instructed me to give you a whole pot of chocolate; he said you particularly favored chocolate. But he left the rest to me, so I added a little of everything else as well."

Nell's idea of "a little" would readily feed a small village, Bonnie observed: a veritable mountain of scrambled eggs, six rashers of bacon, two kidneys, a great bowl of porridge, and three muffins. "Thank you," she murmured, "but I can't possibly eat so much. Though I'm certain the food is excellent," she added quickly as the abigail's black eyes flickered with suspicion. "As was my dinner last evening. I hope you will tell your sister how greatly I appreciate her cooking. In case Lord Sedgewick neglected to relay my compliments."

"Uncle David," Nell corrected. "He said I was to remind you should you make a mistake. Remind you that you must call him Uncle David."

Bonnie had heretofore failed to consider the servants' role in her and the earl's charade, but she now realized that he would have been compelled to advise the staff what they were at. To *confirm* what they were at, she amended: Kimball had been present throughout their conversation and had surely provided his mother and aunt a full report.

"You know of our . . . our project then," she said gratuitously, breaking and buttering a muffin. "What is your opinion? Do you approve?"

"It's not my place to form an opinion," Nell said primly. "But if I was forced to venture one"—the black eyes twinkled in the mirror—"I'd have to say I favor any scheme that looks in the way of giving Miss Judith a proper setdown. She was a wicked child, and she's grown into a wicked woman. Not to mention the scoundrel she wed. I wouldn't pay you tuppence for the both of them."

"And Lord . . . Uncle David?" Bonnie seized the opening Nell had provided. "He told me yesterday that his mother believed him the wickedest child in Britain."

"He did create more than his share of mischief as a boy," Nell conceded. "But it was harmless for the most part, and even when it wasn't, he never _planned_ to do harm. That was the difference between him and Miss Judith; there's not a malicious bone in Mr. David's body. Which is why I lend no credence to them as says he's a rake."

Bonnie choked on her muffin, and Nell clapped her resoundingly on the back.

"No," the abigail continued, "it's my feeling that a rake takes his pleasures without regard to the other party, and that isn't Mr. David's way. He's broken more than a few hearts in his day, of course, but I fancy he can't be blamed for that. The ladies of his acquaintance know very well he has no thought of wedding, and them that _aren't_ ladies—"

"I . . . I perceive your point," Bonnie interposed hastily. She had not intended to invite a full recounting of the earl's personal life, and it was rendering her cheeks prodigious warm. "And I'm delighted to learn we shall have your cooperation during the course of our . . . ah . . . endeavor."

"That you will, miss." Nell eagerly bobbed her head. "In fact, I was the one to suggest we call you 'Miss Bonnie.' The staff, I mean. I told Mr. David we'd address you so if you were Miss Cornelia's _real_ daughter, and he agreed. And I assure you that I, for one, will treat you like a member of the family in every other regard as well."

Bonnie wryly suspected that this treatment would be a decidedly mixed blessing.

"You finish your breakfast," Nell commanded as if in confirmation, "and I'll fetch you up a bath. You'll feel much better indeed after a nice hot bath. And while you're bathing, I'll unpack your bag and put your things away."

She scurried across the room and through the door without awaiting a response, and Bonnie gulped down what food she could, cut the remainder into tiny pieces, and artfully distributed the pieces round her plate.

The curricle came to a smooth halt, and Bonnie heaved a ragged sigh of relief. She had been excessively alarmed to discover that she was to ride in the very vehicle which had run her down, particularly when she saw how monstrous far the seat was from the ground; and she had kept her eyes firmly closed for the better part of their drive from Grosvenor Street to Leicester Square. Having survived the journey, she could now own that David was an excellent driver and his team of matched black geldings extremely well-behaved. Indeed, she realized, if such were not the case, she probably would not be alive to render judgment.

David clambered nimbly down from the seat, strode around the carriage, and assisted Bonnie to the footpath. It was the first time they had stood side by side, and she noted that he was taller than she'd fancied. Considerably taller; were she not wearing a hat, she doubted the top of her head would extend much above his chin. He smiled down at her, and though his expression was appropriately avuncular, Bonnie experienced an odd little tremor in her midsection. Which wouldn't do at all, she sternly counseled herself. Whether the earl was a rake or not—and that remained to be seen—she must take care to regard him as nothing more than her "Uncle David," and she determinedly dropped her eyes.

"I trust you were not jostled about too dreadfully?" he said.

Bonnie tentatively moved her arms and legs and marveled anew at how little they protested. Nell had been right on this head as well: the hot water of the bath had proved remarkably soothing. She was still a trifle stiff, of course, but the agonizing stabs of pain had faded to dull twinges, and she was able to walk without a limp.

"Not dreadfully at all," she murmured.

"Then let us place you in Mrs. Pruitt's capable hands."

David nodded her ahead of him, and as they approached the door of the shop, Bonnie caught a glimpse of their reflection in the display window. She was hard put to quell a laugh, for she could scarcely conceive a more ill-matched pair. The earl was immaculately clad in buff pantaloons, a coat of dark blue superfine, and a pale blue waistcoat—his ensemble crowned by a high, glossy beaver hat. In shocking contrast, Bonnie wore the ancient black bombazine dress she had inherited from Mama and—clashing hideously with the gown—her canary-colored French bonnet. Well, the bonnet *had* been yellow before the accident, she amended; now it was liberally adorned with streaks and splotches of dirt. Added to which, the front of the brim had been dented so deeply that it nearly touched her forehead; and the ostrich feathers, mortally wounded, dangled limply from the crown. She swallowed another giggle and wondered what Mrs. Pruitt would make of his elegant lordship's pathetic niece.

David opened the shop door and ushered her inside, and as the tinkle of the bell died away, Bonnie gazed around the interior of the mantua-maker's establishment. She had just begun to register the chandeliers sparkling overhead, the delicate gilt chairs and pier tables against the walls, the tall cheval mirrors, when a woman emerged from the rear of the shop and hurried across the Brussels carpet. She was well under five feet in height, Bonnie judged, and as she was wearing a brown dress the precise shade of her hair. she resembled nothing so much as a sparrow.

"Ah, it is you, Lord Sedgewick!" Though she had nearly reached them, her brown eyes were squinted to the merest slits—a circumstance from which Bonnie inferred that she was prodigious shortsighted. "What a fortunate coincidence! I was in the very process of composing a note to advise you that Miss Godwin's order is ready for the final fitting." Her eyes shifted to Bonnie. "And I'm confident you will be quite pleased, Miss . . ."

Her voice trailed off, her mouth snapped closed, and she fumbled for the spectacles which hung from a ribbon round her neck. "Oh, dear," she moaned, peering at Bonnie through her glasses. "Oh, dear."

"Pray do not tease yourself about it, Mrs. Pruitt." His soothing words to the contrary, the earl's lean face had turned noticeably pink. "I am sure my niece well understands that a man in my position will gift his female . . . er . . . friends with the occasional new gown."

Occasional? Bonnie felt her own eyes narrow. She had naively assumed that David knew Mrs. Pruitt only by reputation; now she would have wagered her last groat that he was one of the mantua-maker's premier clients.

"Your niece, you say." Mrs. Pruitt's tone was one of manifest relief at having so narrowly avoided a shocking faux pas. "Yes, she does bear a keen likeness to your sister. Although"—her brown brows knit in a frown—"I was not aware that Lady Hellier had a daughter."

"Nor does she." David shook his head. "Permit me to present Miss Carlisle, Mrs. Pruitt. Bonnie is the daughter of my other sister, who lives in Barbados."

"I see." The seamstress granted Bonnie a distracted nod of acknowledgment before returning her attention to David. "Then perhaps it would not be too . . . ah . . . indiscreet of me to mention a rather troublesome matter, Lord Sedgewick. I naturally declined to bring it up when you were here with Miss Godwin, but since Miss Carlisle is a close relative . . ." She coughed. "The fact is Lady Hellier's account is considerably in arrears, and I was in hopes you might be so good as to remind her."

"Poor Judith." The earl emitted a most persuasive sigh, but Bonnie detected an unmistakable hardening of his jaws. "I fear she's grown excessively forgetful now she's reached her middle years. Be that as it may, she is presently in France, so I shall pay the bill in her stead, Mrs. Pruitt."

"How *very* good of you." The mantua-maker clasped her hands in gratitude and—the "troublesome matter" so happily resolved—looked back at Bonnie. "Then let us discuss what it is we're to do for Miss Carlisle." Her birdlike eyes darted from the dented brim of Bonnie's hat to the toes of her worn satin slippers and widened with shock. "Oh, dear," she clucked.

"Yes, as I fancy you can see for yourself, my dear niece will require a complete new wardrobe." David patted his "dear niece" fondly on the shoulder. "My sister recognized that styles in the Indies tend to be rather outdated and judged it best for Bonnie to be rigged out here in England. As she provided a considerable sum for that purpose, we need stint on nothing, Mrs. Pruitt."

The seamstress had never unclasped her hands, and she now rubbed them together with undisguised glee. Bonnie supposed she should be pleased that their charade had passed its initial test so well, but in the event, she judged it most alarming that the earl could lie with such glib facility.

"And I shall also buy Bonnie a gown or two." David patted her shoulder again. "I've been quite generous with Francis over the years, and I am of the firm opinion that I should do no less for my niece than I have for my nephew." He hesitated and bit his lip, as if he had said too much. "Though I do hope you won't repeat my words to Judith, Mrs. Pruitt," he added conspiratorially. "I should hate her to obtain the impression that Bonnie could in any way *supplant* Francis in my affections."

This, of course, positively guaranteed that the mantua-maker *would* repeat his words the very instant Lady Hellier next stepped through her door, and Bonnie cast him a suspicious glance from the corner of her eye. But the earl's demeanor was one of abject and perfect dismay that his ill-chosen remarks might inadvertently wound his beloved sister.

"I shouldn't *dream* of betraying your confidence," Mrs. Pruitt assured him. "And I quite agree that your generosity should extend equally to your niece."

Particularly inasmuch, Bonnie thought dryly, as Lord Sedgewick's nephew was not a candidate for the seamstress' services.

"Sit down"—Mrs. Pruitt gestured toward the nearest pair of gilt chairs—"and I shall fetch my stylebooks."

As David seated Bonnie in one of the indicated chairs, the mantua-maker raced into the rear of the shop; and shortly after the earl had occupied the other chair, Mrs. Pruitt came scurrying back, panting with the burden of the several great volumes she bore. She set the books on the carpet at David's feet, plucked a third chair from the adjacent grouping, placed it just beside David's, and sat down.

"In view of Miss Carlisle's coloring," she said breathlessly, snatching the top volume from the floor, "I believe we should do her predominantly in greens and yellows. Do you not concur, Lord Sedgewick?"

"Yes, I fancy those shades would be the most becoming."

"Excellent. Then, since she is a bit tall, permit me to recommend"—Mrs. Pruitt leafed through the book—"this type of walking dress. We can vary the trimmings, as is done here and here." She indicated the pages immediately before and after. "My point is that the shoulders and sleeves of the spencer should be rather narrow."

As it happened, yellow and green were Bonnie's favorite colors, and she was dismally aware that her knowledge of fashion was nearly as outdated as if she *had* lived in the Indies for four-and-twenty years. But David and Mrs. Pruitt were discussing her as though she were a piece of furniture to be re-covered—evidently counting it quite as gratuitous to solicit her opinion as to ask the sofa or chair what upholstery it preferred. Nor was there any way she could unobtrusively detect what they were at: a pier table lay between her chair and David's, and the stylebook, lying across his and Mrs. Pruitt's knees, was a good three feet distant. Close as she wriggled to the edge of her chair, much as she craned her neck, she couldn't make out the drawings; she could only listen to their enthusiastic commentary.

It was by dint of this commentary that Bonnie learned she was to have six walking dresses and two morning dresses, in various hues of yellow and green, and half a dozen ball gowns. In the interest of variety, one of the latter would be gold and one a periwinkle blue. Blue was so very far from green that Bonnie started to venture a protest, but even as she parted her lips, Mrs. Pruitt explained that her brother had recently received a bolt of elegant periwinkle satin. During the course of the ensuing conversation, Bonnie further learned that Mrs. Pruitt's brother was a linendraper, that his shop was conveniently located just next door, and that—"as usual"—he and Mrs. Pruitt would select the best fabrics for Bonnie's clothes. "Best" meaning "most expensive," Bonnie wryly translated.

But the earl offered no objection to this procedure, and Bonnie had long since perceived the futility of posing any objection of her own. David did, however, caution Mrs. Pruitt not to cut his niece's ball dresses "too low."

"I shouldn't wish them to be unfashionable, of course," he elaborated, "but if there is any question in your mind, I should prefer you to err on the side of modesty. Frankly, Mrs. Pruitt, the situation is somewhat awkward. Though Bonnie is four-and-twenty years of age, she will be introduced into society for the first time—"

"I quite understand, Lord Sedgewick," the mantua-maker interposed. "And I assure you I shall alter my designs to your *complete* satisfaction. There remains only to measure Miss Carlisle, and if she will accompany me to one of the fitting rooms . . ."

Mrs. Pruitt closed the ball-gown stylebook, returned it to the floor, rose, and—for the first time in above two hours, Bonnie calculated—looked directly at her.

"I'm sorry to put you to such trouble," Bonnie snapped. "Had I thought to have Uncle David measure me at home, I shouldn't have needed to come at all."

"What a merry sense of humor she has!" Mrs. Pruitt tittered in appreciation. "She's much like you in that regard, Lord Sedgewick. But come, Miss Carlisle; it will only take a minute."

In fact, some fifteen minutes elapsed while Bonnie removed her dress, subjected every conceivable portion of her anatomy to the mantua-maker's measuring tape, and donned her gown again. Mrs. Pruitt left her to accomplish the latter task alone, and by the time Bonnie returned to the main room of the shop, the seamstress had filled two full pages in her order book and was eagerly calculating her profit.

"There!" She looked up with a brilliant smile; evidently the total exceeded her most optimistic estimate. "As you requested, Lord Sedgwick, I shall have Miss Carlisle's clothes finished next Tuesday. *If* you bring her for an initial fitting on Thursday," she added sternly, "and a final fitting Saturday. On Thursday I shall give you swatches of the materials we are using so you can procure the requisite accessories."

Bonnie was not in the least surprised to hear that Mrs. Pruitt's brother—in addition to the fabrics he carried—also maintained a vast inventory of headdresses, gloves, shoes, et cetera; and would, "as usual," welcome his lordship's patronage.

"Then, of course, Miss Carlisle *must* have her hair styled," the mantua-maker continued.

"Of course," David agreed.

"I personally feel that Monsieur Michel is the most accomplished *coiffeur* in the city," Mrs. Pruitt said. "As you no doubt recall, Lord Sedgwick, he is the one who styles Miss Godwin's hair." Bonnie clenched her hands. "At any rate, since I collect that your niece is to make her first appearance at Lady Lambeth's assembly, I shall arrange for Monsieur Michel to call at your house next Tuesday afternoon."

"That is very kind of you, Mrs. Pruitt."

The earl sounded curiously uncomfortable, and he abruptly snaked his fingers round Bonnie's elbow and began to tug her toward the door of the shop.

"Speaking of Miss Godwin . . ." The seamstress' voice caught them up before they had traversed half the room. "I do trust you will soon bring her in for her final fitting, Lord Sedgewick. With the Season just ahead, I am monstrous busy, and I can ill afford to have partially finished orders cluttering up my workrooms."

"Yes," David mumbled. "Yes, I shall bring Miss Godwin shortly. Good day then, Mrs. Pruitt."

He ushered Bonnie on across the Brussels carpet and out the door, assisted her into the curricle, took the driver's place, and clucked the black geldings to a start. Bonnie thought—nay, *prayed*—his cheeks had colored again, and she gazed stonily at the passing buildings and people and vehicles on her side of the carriage.

"Umm." They were well along Piccadilly before the earl cleared his throat. "As Mrs. Pruitt pointed out, this is a busy time of year for those merchants who specialize in women's fashion, and we must consequently be certain to return for your fitting Thursday. Nor should we want Mr. Mercer to sell his best hats and gloves before we visit his establishment."

Bonnie inferred from this discourse that Mr. Mercer was Mrs. Pruitt's enterprising brother, in which case she could not but own that he was aptly named. "I daresay I shall have to go for my fittings," she snapped aloud. "However, I perceive no reason to burden you with my presence at Mr. Mercer's. You can simply take my hat"—she furiously indicated her bonnet—"and one of my gloves and a shoe, and make the selections yourself. Having chosen all my dresses and ball gowns, you shouldn't find it in the least difficult to pick out a few headdresses and the odd pair of slippers."

"You disapprove the garments I ordered?"

David's tone seemed one of genuine astonishment, and when Bonnie forced herself to look at him, she found his brow furrowed in confusion. But he had proved himself a splendid actor, she reminded herself, and she once more ground her fingernails into her palms.

"I was granted no opportunity to approve or disapprove either one," she responded warmly. "I could not even *see* Mrs. Pruitt's drawings from where I sat. I could only leave it to the two of you to decide that I was to have one of this and two of that, all in shades of yellow and green except for the periwinkle blue Mr. Mercer is apparently eager to sell . . . ." She ran out of breath and lapsed into silence.

"But that is the way we have always done it," David protested. "Mrs. Pruitt and I, that is. She has impeccable taste, and none of my friends has ever tendered the slightest objection—"

"I am not one of your *friends*," Bonnie hissed. "Not one of your *chères amies*, to describe the connection somewhat more accurately. Though I fancy I shall quite fit the mold before you and Mrs. Pruitt have done with me, shall I not? I suspect the clothes you ordered for me are remarkably similar to those awaiting Miss Godwin's final fitting, and as I'm to have my hair styled by her *coiffeur* . . ." She stopped and swallowed an inexplicable, infuriating lump in her throat. "You did not even trouble yourself to ask whether I wished to change my hair."

"Women!" David shook his head and cast his eyes upward, as though seeking divine assistance in the midst of his many trials. "I shall never puzzle out why it is women think as they do." He transferred his sapphire eyes to Bonnie. "You're a very bonnie lass indeed—or could be if you rid yourself of all that excess hair. I assumed you'd be delighted when I consented to engage the finest *coiffeur* in London to attend you; I assure you it would have cost me dearly. However, if you really want to go about as you are, with your hair spilling over your eyebrows and tumbling round your shoulders . . ." His voice trailed provocatively off.

Bonnie was sorely inclined to retort that this was *precisely* what she wanted, but she recollected the proverbial danger of cutting off one's nose to spite one's face. "No," she said with as much dignity as she could muster. "No, I am willing to have my hair restyled. I should merely have liked to be *consulted*."

"Then I am sorry if I offended you. As I indicated, I am accustomed to having my way with women."

In other circumstances, Bonnie would have found his double entendre highly amusing; as it was, his phraseology served to rekindle her wrath. "And as I hope *I* indicated," she said frostily, "you will have to modify your custom. I elected to pose no objection at Mrs. Pruitt's because I didn't wish to jeopardize our project. But be warned that I shall not be so reticent in future. You may ultimately bring me to look like one of your . . . your playthings, but I shan't permit you to order me about as you do them. I trust we are clear on that head?

"Oh, *abundantly* clear."

His voice was quite as frigid as hers had been, and when he said nothing more, Bonnie redirected her gaze to the passing scenery.

"Hell and the devil!" the earl muttered at length.

Bonnie initially fancied his expletive to be a delayed reaction to their quarrel, but when she glanced out the front of the curricle, she saw that David's house lay just ahead and that a small landau stood before it. She could only presume that Lady Hellier had returned prematurely from France, and her stomach knotted with panic. It was one thing to fool Mrs. Pruitt, who knew nothing of the earl's family history, but Bonnie recognized that she was wretchedly unprepared to deceive her alleged Aunt Judith.

"Is it . . . is it . . ." She looked fearfully at David and attempted to moisten her lips, which had gone altogether dry.

"It is *Kate*," he growled through gritted teeth. "Good God."

Since his lordship had mentioned no relative named Kate, Bonnie surmised that the visitor must be Miss Godwin, and she was at a loss to conceive why the earl should find her call so oversetting. Nor did she have a chance to inquire, for even as David reined the geldings to a halt, a young woman descended from the landau and hurried toward them. An exceedingly handsome young woman, Bonnie noted as she reached the curricle—her great blue eyes and blond curls artfully framed by the enormous leghorn hat she wore.

"This is most embarrassing, Kate," David said grimly, fairly jumping down from his seat. "As I explained last night—"

"That is what I wanted to speak to you about." There was a catch in her voice, and upon closer inspection, Bonnie observed that her small pink mouth was trembling. "I wanted

to tell you I would agree to see you only rarely. Only when
you could get away without your niece's knowledge . . .''
She peered up at Bonnie for the first time, and her eyes
narrowed. *"This* is your niece?'' she demanded.

"Ah . . . yes.''

David seized her elbow, clearly thinking to lead her out of
Bonnie's hearing, but she jerked it from his grasp.

"You told me she was a child,'' she said accusingly.

"I *told* you no such thing.'' The earl's face had turned
quite scarlet, and Bonnie felt the prickle of an odious suspicion. "You may have *inferred* that Bonnie was a child—''

"Well, you made certain I would, didn't you?'' The catch
in Kate's voice had given way to a tremor of rage. "Saying it
wouldn't do at all for a young girl to discover you had a
liaison with an actress. And I daresay she's no younger than
I am. Miss . . . Miss . . .''

"Miss Carlisle,'' Bonnie supplied. "And you are. . . ?''

"Miss Elwell. Katherine Elwell. Though my friends call
me Kate—''

"Yes, yes,'' David interjected hastily. "And now the two
of you have met, I fear I really must ask you to go, Kate.''

"Oh, no, David. No, please. I'm not angry; I didn't mean
to sound angry. I fancy it was all a misunderstanding—''

"Yes, I fancy it was,'' Bonnie interrupted pleasantly. "And
if *Uncle David* will be so good as to help me down, I shall
leave you to resolve your differences in private.''

She took keen delight in the look he cast her—a roughly
equal blend of vexation and entreaty—but he could hardly
decline to assist her out of the carriage. With a polite nod at
Miss Elwell, Bonnie strode toward the house, gleefully envisioning the grave difficulties David would encounter as he
tried to extricate himself from the bumblebath he had created.
Her sole regret was that she would be unable to hear the
forthcoming conversation, but she could certainly *watch* it;
and when she was safely out of sight in the vestibule, she
raced up the stairs to the second floor, pounded down the hall

to her bedchamber, dashed to the window, and tweaked the draperies carefully apart.

David and Miss Elwell occupied approximately the same positions they had when Bonnie exited the scene, but the latter's face was now buried in her gloved hands, and her shoulders were prettily heaving. Inasmuch as Miss Elwell was an actress, Bonnie did not attach undue importance to her sobs; but evidently David did, for he was shuffling his hessians in an apparent agony of discomfort and vainly attempting to stuff a handkerchief behind Miss Elwell's fingers. At length, he succeeded in this endeavor, and after dabbing at her eyes for a time, Miss Elwell began to talk, her voice eventually growing so loud that Bonnie could almost hear her after all. The earl, for his part, had never ceased to shuffle his feet, but his movements now assumed a pattern: he was slowly, inexorably herding Miss Elwell toward her landau. Though the vehicle was situated only a few yards distant, their tortuous passage required some ten or fifteen minutes; but at last, David handed Miss Elwell into the carriage, closed the door behind her, and signaled the coachman to start. The earl bounded across the footpath before the wheels of the landau had even begun to turn, and Bonnie dropped the curtains and speedily retreated to the dressing table. The front door slammed as she was untying her bonnet ribbons, and—to her utter lack of surprise—there was soon a tap on the door of her bedchamber.

"Come in," she snapped.

"Bonnie."

To her renewed delight, David's appearance had degenerated to a sad travesty of its former splendor: rivulets of perspiration trickled from beneath the band of his beaver hat, and his shirt-points and neckcloth had wilted to a single shapeless mass of fabric round his jaws. He belatedly removed the hat, stepped over the threshold, and shut the door.

"Bonnie," he repeated. He was unmistakably panting. "Pray permit me to apologize for Kate's unfortunate intrusion. I assure you I do not normally invite my . . . ah . . . friends to call at the house."

"Oh, I am sure you do not," she said sardonically. "I quite believe that Miss Elwell's visit was altogether *un*invited."

"I'm so relieved you understand." He had obviously failed to register her tone. "As you no doubt collected, I saw Kate last evening after dinner and advised her of my wish to terminate our . . . er . . . friendship—"

"Oh, I collected much more than that." Bonnie flung her hat on the dressing table and leapt to her feet. "You told Miss Elwell that your niece had unexpectedly arrived from the Indies and would be residing with you for the indefinite future. You cleverly implied that this niece was an innocent young girl who would be prodigious shocked to discover that you were . . . were disporting yourself with an actress. I must admit to some puzzlement as to why you elected to rely on insinuation; you've demonstrated yourself a remarkably accomplished liar. Be that as it may—"

"Bonnie, Bonnie." David had recovered his normal aplomb: he rested his broad shoulders against the door and flashed his winsome grin. "You must also have collected that Kate and I have been at daggers drawn for some time. We did not get on at all when I was in town last autumn, and since then—"

"Since then, you have made the acquaintance of Miss Godwin," Bonnie hissed. She was distantly gratified when his lordship flushed. "And I represented the perfect excuse for you to sever your relationship with Miss Elwell so as to devote your full attention to Miss Godwin. I should merely like to ask whether you had that objective in mind from the start or conceived it after I consented to pose as your niece."

"I . . ." He stared down at his boots a moment, then raised his sapphire eyes and tendered another dazzling smile. "I saw no harm in killing two birds with one stone," he responded airily.

Which did not, of course, answer her question, and Bonnie once more clenched her hands. "There is a great deal of harm in it," she said icily, "and I want us to be clear on that head as well. You cannot retract your statements to Miss Elwell, but you are not to use me so in future. Your personal life doesn't signify a whit to me, but I will not serve as an instrument to extract you from one dalliance so you will be free to pursue another. Now, if I recollect aright, you have an appointment this afternoon, and you really must tidy up a bit before you go.''

"Yes." He stood away from the door, opened it, then turned back round and cleared his throat. "As I thought on it, I was compelled to own that your complaints were justified. Your complaints concerning my conduct at Mrs. Pruitt's, that is. If you prefer, I shall order out the barouche for you on Thursday, and you may complete your shopping without my interference.''

If this was a peace offering, it seemed woefully inadequate, but Bonnie bobbed her head. "Yes, I should prefer that," she said.

"Very well. You did correctly recall that I've an appointment this afternoon, but tonight we shall begin reviewing the facts you must know if you're to persuade Judith of your identity.''

"Tonight?" Bonnie echoed. "I should have supposed you'd be waiting upon Miss Godwin tonight." The earl colored again, and she nodded in comprehension. "No, Miss Godwin is your *appointment*, is she not? I do hope you will remember to take her to Mrs. Pruitt's for her final fitting. As you are aware, Mrs. Pruitt is most anxious to clear her workrooms.''

She whirled around, winced as the bedchamber door slammed closed, then turned back and gazed at the spot where David had stood. Though he had declined to confess it, she was convinced he had intended from the outset to use his "young" niece to rid himself of Miss Elwell; and she could not but wonder if there were other dimensions to their charade which she had yet to discover.

4

*T*he barouche jerked to a halt, and Bonnie wriggled to the edge of her seat and peered apprehensively round the box. But they had not yet reached their destination, she saw; six or eight other carriages lay between their vehicle and the brilliantly lighted entrance of Viscountess Lambeth's house. She sank back against the squab and—as she had throughout the drive from Grosvenor Street to Berkeley Square—nervously toyed with her ivory fan.

"Quickly now," David said. "What sort of dog did Cornelia receive on her tenth birthday and what did she name it?"

"It was a poodle," Bonnie replied with a tired sigh. "A white female poodle, and though Cornelia named her Marie Antoinette, she always called her Annie. Annie conceived a great *tendre* for your male spaniel, and between them, they eventually produced six litters of puppies. And I shall try," she concluded peevishly, "to work Annie's promiscuous history into my conversation with Lady Lambeth."

"Now Bonnie." David clicked his tongue reprovingly against his teeth. "I realize you've grown somewhat weary of our lessons, but we agreed at the outset that the smallest fact might ultimately prove important."

Somewhat weary was an understatement of monumental

proportions, Bonnie thought dryly as the carriage lurched
ahead a bit. For the past seven nights, the earl had devoted every
moment of their dinner conversation—and two or three hours
in the library after dinner—to her "lessons," and she fancied
she knew far more about the Merrill family than she ever had
about the Gordons. She had initially been puzzled by David's
apparent neglect of Miss Godwin, but she soon conjectured
that his new *amie* was otherwise occupied in the evenings.
Miss Godwin was probably an actress as well, she surmised,
or perhaps an opera dancer. Whatever the case, David evidently spent his afternoons with her, for he raced off in his
curricle at precisely two o'clock each day.

Which was not to say that he had left Bonnie's afternoons
unoccupied. No, his clever lordship had purchased several
books about the Indies and ordered her to study them while
he was from home. Unfortunately, the books dwelled upon
the tedious details of producing sugar—the paramount industry in Barbados and its neighboring islands—and described
very little of the residents' daily lives. Barbados was excessively warm, Bonnie had learned, and abounded in all manner of exotic vegetation; and as she and David had determined
to state that Thomas Carlisle was a successful planter, she
could safely claim to have grown up on a sprawling estate.
Should she be pressed for details beyond these, she would
have to manufacture them, and she could only hope she
would not encounter anyone familiar with her alleged home.

However, Bonnie reflected irritably, she would be required
to fabricate no details at all about the early life of Lady
Cornelia Merrill. David had begun his tutelage by drawing a
plan of Sedgewood, the family seat in Dorset, and Bonnie
was confident she could by now make her way from room to
room with her eyes closed. The furniture would certainly
pose no obstacle because David had insisted she memorize
the location of every piece, from the pedestal in the entry hall
to the bow-fronted commode at the western end of the second-
floor corridor. Upon opening her eyes, she would be able to
greet the servants of Cornelia's day by name—starting with

the senior Kimball, Alice's late husband, who had served as butler before his demise; and ending with Josh, the youngest of the footboys. The latter, it was widely rumored, was the son of David's father's younger brother, the Honorable Albert Merrill, now deceased, and Rose, the handsomest of the chambermaids. Rose herself, it was generally believed, had been sired by a Gypsy tinker . . .

After Bonnie was thoroughly acquainted with Sedgewood and—or so she was persuaded—knew the lineage and biography of every person associated with the Merrill household since approximately the Conquest, David turned his attention to "various anecdotes Cornelia might have related over the years." Bonnie shortly decided that even if Cornelia had related one "anecdote" per day for the whole four-and-twenty years of her daughter's life, she would scarcely have scratched the surface of her brother's prodigious memory. Bonnie did not mind being told that Lady Amanda Rawlins had been Cornelia's dearest childhood friend; such information, she owned, was probably essential. But did she really need to know that Lady Cornelia and Lady Amanda had crept into the dairy one summer day in 1785, upset half a dozen pails of milk, and been sent to bed without dinner as a consequence? Or that, several years later, they had been mortified to appear at their first London assembly in *identical dresses*?

From the beginning, David's interminable narrative set Bonnie to squirming in her chair, but several evenings elapsed before she admitted that her frustration resulted as much from disappointment as from boredom. When she had agreed that seemingly insignificant facts might prove important, she had entertained a hope that any discussion of Cornelia's youth must inevitably lead to a revelation of the earl's own character. They had shared the same parents, the same upbringing; how could David explain Cornelia without explaining himself? He would soon disclose—if inadvertently—when and why he had determined not to wed, how he had come to view women in such a dismal light . . .

But he had not. If their conversation had occupied an uninterrupted expanse of time, they would have talked above a day, yet Bonnie knew little more of him than she had at the start. No, that was not entirely true, she amended. She knew, in excruciating detail, much of what he had *done* in his six-and-thirty years, but he had provided not the slightest clue of what he'd *felt*. She sometimes suspected that he wrapped his wit around him like a cloak, using his winsome smile and clever tongue to hide his emotions. At other times—when, for example, he had driven her to the point of tears because she could not remember the color of the draperies in Cornelia's bedchamber—she was quite sure he *had* no emotions. She would stiffen her spine, clench her hands, remind herself that he was nothing more than a calculating rake; and then he would disarm her by solicitously inquiring if she were tired or if she wished a cup of chocolate or a glass of brandy. And she would wonder whether his kindness was sincere or merely another means of bending her to his will.

The carriage moved again, then halted in a pool of light, and Bonnie started and glanced fearfully up. But the light was only that of the streetlamp overhead, and when she essayed a sheepish smile at David, who occupied the rear-facing seat, she saw that his sapphire eyes were resting upon her.

"You must not be nervous," he said gently. "You've learned your lessons so well that I daresay you might almost fool Cornelia herself. And as I mentioned earlier, you are looking excessively handsome. Even handsomer than I had expected."

He had, in fact, stated this opinion at considerable length when they met in the vestibule, and—as had occurred then—his undisguised appraisal brought a flood of warmth to Bonnie's cheeks. She dropped her own eyes, but in the dim glow of the streetlight, the primrose flounce around the bottom of her skirt looked as white as her satin shoes. Not that it signified, for she well recollected the reflection she had studied before she descended to the foyer. And, false modesty apart, she could not have said whether she looked handsome or not because the image in the mirror had seemed that of an utter stranger.

Her gown had presented no surprise, of course, for she had obediently returned to Leicester Square for her scheduled fittings. During the course of these, she had been compelled to own, albeit grudgingly, that Mrs. Pruitt and her brother had chosen the perfect fabrics for her wardrobe—bold medleys far exceeding Bonnie's limited imagination. She was sure she would never have ordered the dress she wore tonight, but the moment she glimpsed the slip of deep yellow satin, the covering frock of lemon-colored net, the primrose lace trim, she was equally sure the dress would not be half so stunning were it made in any other way.

At any rate, Bonnie had been familiar with her gown long before Nell withdrew it from the wardrobe, and she had selected her headdress herself. She had, it was true, been armed with Mrs. Pruitt's swatches—and fortified with a generous dose of the mantua-maker's advice—when she ventured into Mr. Mercer's establishment; but once there, she had chosen the garland of primrose satin flowers quite unaided. So the only theoretically shocking modification to her appearance should have been that rendered by Monsieur Michel, who had come that afternoon to apply his scissors and numerous other mysterious implements to Bonnie's unruly hair. But the *coiffeur* had departed hours since, leaving her ample time to grow accustomed to the short, soft curls which framed her face and ended at the nape of her neck.

Therefore, Bonnie had concluded as she examined the alien reflection in the glass, she must be reacting to the sudden combination of all these factors. Her gown alone had not seemed strange, nor her headdress, nor even her new coiffure; but put together, they created quite a different person. Added to which, the earl and Nell had relentlessly pinched at her to eat just a little more of this or take another small portion of that, and her face had grown noticeably fuller as a result. Not that this was anything to lament, Bonnie assured herself. To the contrary, her feasting had served to moderate

her gaunt, haggard countenance to one of . . . Well, she
preferred to term her visage "arrestingly lean," and she
fancied that in this respect she had come to look rather like
the earl. A circumstance which would undoubtedly lend credence to their charade.

But however advantageous her plumper face might be, it
was another change, and Bonnie's fingers stole to her right
shoulder. She had initially hoped her bruise would heal before Lady Lambeth's ball, but she now regarded it as the last
tenuous proof of her identity. She entertained an irrational
fear that when the faint yellowish circle disappeared, Bonnie
Gordon would vanish as well, and the stranger in the mirror
would truly become Bonnie Carlisle.

"Although . . ." David cleared his throat. "Although your
dress is somewhat less . . . er . . . modest than I had
anticipated."

Bonnie had expected him to bring this up, but she bristled
with annoyance nonetheless. Mrs. Pruitt had originally cut
the ball gowns to his lordship's specifications, but on the
occasion of Bonnie's first fitting, she and the seamstress had
agreed that the high necks the earl had suggested quite destroyed the lines of the garments. Mrs. Pruitt had consequently altered the bodices in accordance with the current
dictates of fashion, and Bonnie could not suppose they were
nearly as revealing as those of the gowns David commissioned for his myriad "friends." She angrily raised her eyes,
intending to voice this rebuttal aloud, but she perceived that
his expression was one of puzzlement rather than disapproval.
He viewed her as she viewed herself, Bonnie realized—saw
her as a stranger—and she felt another prickle of fear.

The barouche crept ahead again, and even as Bonnie blinked
against a sudden blaze of light, the carriage stopped, and a
liveried footman bounded forward, opened the door, and
extended a hand to assist her out. Her nagging fear turned at
once to total panic, and she cast a look of frantic entreaty at
the seat across. But the earl was climbing out the opposite
side of the carriage, and Bonnie took the proffered hand and

stumbled down the step to the footpath. She swayed a bit when the footman released her, but before she could inform David that she was entirely too ill to attend a ball, he seized her elbow and began to usher her up the shallow stairs to Lady Lambeth's door.

Another footman escorted them from the entry hall to the first story and along the corridor to the second-floor staircase, which was clogged by a lengthy line of guests awaiting admission to her ladyship's ballroom. Bonnie was much relieved by this latest delay; with any luck, she thought optimistically, she would collapse and die on the stairs before she was required to speak to anyone. But she did not, and far too soon the butler was announcing them to the assembled multitude. At the sound of her name—"Miss Elizabeth Carlisle" —Bonnie fancied she would collapse after all; but the earl, as if he had sensed just such a possibility, tightened his grip on her arm and tugged her toward the receiving line.

"Carlisle?" Lady Lambeth echoed.

Actually, Bonnie now observed, the receiving line consisted solely of their hostess: a very plump, prodigious homely woman well into her middle years. Though David was bowing gallantly over her hand, the viscountess' gray eyes were fastened on Bonnie, and her brows had met in a frown.

"Yes, Lady Lambeth, pray permit me to present my niece. Miss Elizabeth Carlisle, who is familiarly known as Bonnie."

The earl nudged his "niece," none too gently, and she managed to bob her head in greeting. "Lady Lambeth," she murmured.

"Carlisle!" her ladyship repeated, the gray eyes widening in startled comprehension. "Yes, that is the man Cornelia married, is it not? That . . . that—"

"I daresay you will be delighted to learn," David interposed smoothly, "that Thomas has been immensely successful in Barbados. I infer from Bonnie's description that his principal plantation puts Sedgewood quite to shame, and it, of course, is but one of his many enterprises. But we should not be surprised, should we, Lady Lambeth? We have long been aware that those with the courage and foresight to emigrate to the colonies often accumulate vast fortunes.''

''Vast . . . fortunes.'' The viscountess moistened her lips, then kindly patted Bonnie's shoulder. ''My son is circulating among the company, but I shall be *certain* you meet him before the evening is over, Miss Carlisle.''

It seemed, Bonnie reflected wryly, that a ''vast fortune'' could atone even for the sin of dubious breeding.

''David may or may not have mentioned that his late mother and I were close friends. Your grandmother, Miss Carlisle.'' Evidently the subject of breeding was on Lady Lambeth's mind as well. ''As a result of our friendship, I had the good fortune to be well acquainted with Cornelia in her girlhood, and I was enormously fond of her. For many years, as I recollect, she had the most *adorable* dog. Did she chance to mention it to you, dear?''

''A-Annie,'' Bonnie stammered as the earl succumbed to a sudden fit of coughing. ''Her poodle, Annie.''

''Annie; that was it. Yes, Cornelia was always mad for dogs, and I should guess you have *hundreds* of them on your estate in the Indies. Fortunately, my son also loves dogs, so you and Hugh will have a great deal in common. I shall definitely be sure you meet him, Miss Carlisle. My son, Viscount Lambeth,'' she added, lest there be any lingering confusion as to his identity.

''It is very good of you to extend such a warm welcome to my niece,'' David said.

Perhaps she knew him better than she'd fancied, Bonnie thought distantly. To the untutored ear—and apparently Lady Lambeth's were among these, for her plump face was wreathed in a happy smile—the earl's tone would sound as pleasant as his words, but Bonnie detected an unmistakable sharpness round the edges.

"However, we must take no more of your time. Others are waiting to greet you." David inclined his head toward the entry, and the gray threads in his hair turned to purest silver in the soft light of the chandeliers. "We shall consequently beg to be excused." He executed another courtly bow, seized Bonnie's elbow again, and jerked her unceremoniously into the ballroom.

"Lambeth!" he hissed when they were safely beyond her ladyship's hearing. "His mother has been attempting to marry him off for years, and her failure can come as no surprise to anyone who knows him. He is quite the dullest fellow I have ever met and as knocker-faced as she is."

"Umm," Bonnie grunted noncommittally.

"As knocker-faced as she and the same sort of insufferable hypocrite. Lady Lambeth and Mama were very far from being close friends, and I doubt she encountered Cornelia more than half a dozen times. And she certainly could not have found Annie *adorable*. Indeed, she would not remember the dog at all were it not for the circumstance that Annie bit her ankle during the course of a ball at Sedgewood. The poor creature was not herself at the time, being in an advanced state of pregnancy—"

"David!"

Bonnie had never before seen him so mifty, and she could not conceive why Lady Lambeth's innocuous "hypocrisy" should prompt such a venomous outburst. Whatever its genesis, his tirade was beginning to border on the shocking, and she glanced apprehensively about, fearing to discover a horrified eavesdropper nearby. But most of the guests were on the dance floor, stepping through a quadrille, and Bonnie experienced a sudden rush of excitement.

This was the London she had dreamed of, and, from a distance at least, the scene fulfilled her expectations. From her perspective at the perimeter of the floor, the women were colorful clouds of muslin and net, silk and satin—clouds lent definition by the ostrich plumes gracefully swaying above their heads and the glitter of jewels in their ears and round

their necks. Nor was the glitter altogether confined to the
female gender: the men attired in military uniform fairly
sparkled with the medals arrayed upon their chests.

However, the majority of the men were clad in traditional
evening garb, and they looked . . . Well, if David was any
indication, they looked rather better than they did in their
everyday clothes. Bonnie peered at the earl from the corner of
her eye and reminded herself that Papa had always preached—
publicly and privately—that appearances were unimportant.
But without Papa to guide her thoughts into suitably lofty
channels, she had been unable to refrain from remarking that
David's breeches and stockings and wasp-waisted coat rendered him excessively handsome indeed. Made him appear
even taller and leaner than he was and revealed muscular,
shapely calves—

The quadrille ended, and Bonnie hastily redirected her
attention to the center of the room. The orchestra retuned
their instruments a moment, then launched into a waltz, and
the assembled company began to whirl around the floor.

"But let us talk no more of Lady Lambeth," David said.
Bonnie judged this a monstrous good idea. "I now realize
that I neglected to inquire whether you know how to dance."

On this head, if on no other, Bonnie was compelled to own
a debt to her former employer. She had not, in fact, known
how to dance when she left Stafford; but several years after
her arrival in London, Mrs. Powell—as part of her inexorable
campaign to school Maria and Anne in the social graces—had
engaged a Viennese dancing master. Apparently fearing that
the physical contact requisite to his instruction might drive
Herr Mueller to tender an indecent advance to her innocent
daughters (which seemed prodigious unlikely in view of the
circumstance that he was fully seventy years of age), Mrs. Powell
desired Bonnie to supervise the girls' lessons. However, Herr
Mueller, who spoke very limited English, clearly failed to
understand Mrs. Powell's explanation of Bonnie's role, for he
at once took to addressing her as "Fräulein Powell" and
directed his tutelage more to her than to her "little schwesters."

After an interval of vain argument, Bonnie determined to capitalize on his confusion; and over the ensuing months, she had mastered the quadrille, the waltz, the boulanger, the quick step, and a whole host of other dances, which, she suspected, were so esoteric as to be unknown to any but Herr Mueller and his fellow professionals.

"Yes, I know how to dance," she responded aloud.

"Then I daresay no one will look askance if I stand up with my niece."

David had never released her elbow, and he now guided her onto the floor and spun her smoothly into the rhythm of the waltz. He was an excellent dancer, Bonnie judged—nearly as accomplished as Herr Mueller himself—and she was at a loss to comprehend why she found it so difficult to follow his lead. Probably, she surmised at length, it was because the earl was far taller than Herr Mueller, whose bald scalp had barely reached Bonnie's nose. His lordship, on the other hand, fairly towered over her, and the disparity in their heights created the illusion that he was terribly . . . terribly *close*. Indeed, he seemed so very close that Bonnie could scarcely breathe, and the insufficiency of oxygen set her heart to pounding most painfully against her ribs. She was confident she could recover if David moderated his movements a bit, but he was vastly stronger than Herr Mueller as well—his arm like a steel vise around her waist—and she could only struggle to match his steps as he whirled her dizzily about the floor.

The set ended at last, and Bonnie gazed guiltily up at the earl, thinking to apologize for her clumsiness. But he was regarding her with the same odd expression of puzzlement he had worn in the carriage, and in the superior light of Lady Lambeth's ballroom, his sapphire eyes seemed peculiarly dark—closer to violet than blue. Somehow Bonnie found this scrutiny even more discomfiting than his customary bold appraisal and, altogether losing her tongue, she accompanied him silently off the floor.

"Lord Sedgewick!"

The female voice, which emanated from behind them, sounded quite as breathless as Bonnie felt; and when David dropped her arm, she turned curiously around.

"Lord Sedgewick!" the woman repeated, reaching his side. "I saw you when you arrived, but as I was dancing at the time, I had no opportunity to greet you. If I may say so now, you are looking exceedingly well."

"Thank you, Lady Pamela," David rejoined politely. "You are also looking very well."

Bonnie fancied he would have conveyed a similarly courteous sentiment had Lady Pamela been as "knocker-faced" as Lady Lambeth. However, at first glance, the former did appear a very handsome woman—considerably shorter than the average and extremely slight, with luxuriant golden-brown hair and large, thickly lashed green eyes. Only when one took a second, harder look did one perceive that Lady Pamela was no longer in the flush of youth: there was a tiny sunburst of lines round either eye and small telltale grooves at the corners of her mouth. She was far nearer thirty than twenty, Bonnie estimated, and a third and still more careful inspection suggested that Lady Pamela took advantage of her diminutive stature to create the impression that she was years younger than she was. The simple white muslin gown she wore would quite have suited a girl of eighteen, and Bonnie suspected Lady Pamela had chosen the dress with precisely that effect in mind.

"As I indicated, I was dancing when you arrived . . ."

Her ladyship's voice was a ruse as well, Bonnie conjectured. She had no doubt trained herself to speak in this breathless, uncertain, girlish fashion, rehearsing for endless hours in the privacy of her bedchamber . . .

". . . and when the quadrille was over, you stood up with . . . with . . ." Lady Pamela transferred her great green eyes pointedly to Bonnie.

"With my *niece*," David supplied, somewhat more heartily than Bonnie deemed necessary. "My niece, Miss Carlisle. This, Bonnie, is Lady Pamela Everett."

"Lady Pamela," Bonnie dutifully muttered.

"Miss Carlisle." Her ladyship flashed a brief, cool smile, and Bonnie was pleased to note that her front teeth were a trifle uneven. "Your niece. How lovely. Although"—her brows formed a pretty frown—"I do not believe I was aware you *had* a niece, Lord Sedgewick."

"Nor was I until dear Bonnie appeared upon my doorstep." David threw his arm enthusiastically round her shoulders, and Bonnie managed a tight smile of her own. "Appeared—was it a week ago yesterday, Bonnie?" She obediently bobbed her head. "Bonnie is the daughter of my sister Cornelia, who lives in Barbados. Perhaps your parents have mentioned, Lady Pamela, that Cornelia's marriage caused a most lamentable rift in our family. A rift—I am happy to say—that Bonnie is well in the way of healing."

"How lovely," her ladyship cooed again. "And how delightful that Miss Carlisle so unexpectedly graced you with her company."

Was the breathless little voice embroidered with sarcasm, Bonnie wondered, or was she hearing echoes of her own overwrought imagination? Whatever the case, David offered no response to Lady Pamela's final comments; and in the ensuing silence, the tuning of the orchestra grated most unpleasantly on Bonnie's ears. To her relief, the musicians soon seemed satisfied with their screechings and struck up a sprightly tune.

"The ride-a-mile!" Lady Pamela clapped her hands with joy. "As you know, Lord Sedgewick, it is my favorite dance, and I shall be bitterly disappointed if you do not ask me to stand up."

"I should certainly do so were it not for Bonnie," the earl said regretfully. His arm was still loosely draped around her shoulders, and he now pulled her closer and beamed fondly down at her. "However, since my niece is a stranger to London, I feel I should grant her my undivided attention—"

"Lord Sedgewick? Miss Carlisle!" Lady Lambeth sounded even more breathless than Lady Pamela, and she was fairly

sprinting toward them, dragging an as yet unidentifiable figure in her wake. "Forgive me if I intrude," she wheezed,
screeching to a stop, "but I did promise to introduce Miss
Carlisle to my son. And here he is, Miss Carlisle—my son
Hugh, Viscount Lambeth."

The viscount did bear an unfortunate resemblance to his
mother, Bonnie observed as Lady Lambeth prodded him
forward for her inspection. But he reminded her of someone
else as well, and after a moment of discreet study, she
realized that his lank brown hair and small gray eyes were
astonishingly like Mr. Crawford's. It seemed enormously, if
perversely, amusing that she should have at last gained entry
to the *ton* only to be confronted by this ghost of her former
parti; and she was hard put to stifle a rather hysterical giggle.

"I am sure Lord Sedgewick will not object if you stand up
with his niece, Hugh."

Lady Lambeth's tone was one of such authority that Bonnie doubted God himself would dare to pose an objection,
and with a stiff bow, David removed his arm from her
shoulders. Lady Pamela promptly grasped said arm in one of
her tiny hands and tugged the earl happily toward the floor,
leaving Bonnie and Viscount Lambeth to follow well behind
them.

"Mama advises me that you are excessively fond of dogs,"
the viscount said, awkwardly shuffling his feet as he strove to
find the beat of the orchestra.

In point of fact, Bonnie had never owned a dog, knew
virtually nothing about them; and she was at a loss to conceive what she would say if he demanded she enumerate the
many canine varieties which presumably inhabited her magnificent home in the Indies. In the event, however, she was not
required to utter a single word, for Lord Lambeth immediately launched into a description of the imaginative breeding
program he had applied to his own hunting dogs. His explanation of the details skirted the bounds of propriety more than
once, but Bonnie was so grateful to be spared the necessity of

conversation that she willed herself to appear fascinated rather than shocked.

The end of the viscount's discourse fortunately coincided with the end of the second set they danced—a waltz during the course of which Lord Lambeth revealed himself considerably *less* accomplished than Herr Mueller. Indeed, his numerous missteps had set Bonnie to limping again, but she was granted no respite because Sir James Clayton was waiting to stand up with her. (Or Clay*more* maybe; his flowery introduction was half-drowned by the inevitable retuning of the orchestra.) Whatever his surname, Sir James's interest was in horses, and at the conclusion of his lecture, Bonnie was persuaded she could make her fortune in one short day at Newmarket if only she had a farthing to wager.

Following their boulanger, Sir James presented Bonnie to one of his relatives, the Honorable Clement Aldrich. (She believed Mr. Aldrich was Sir James's cousin, but, again, the cacophonous squealing of the orchestra rendered the exact connection uncertain.) At any rate, Mr. Aldrich was evidently a radical reformer of some sort, for he punctuated both their dances with pithy quotes from *The Black Dwarf*, *The Republican*, and several other revoluntionary journals.

Despite, or perhaps because of, Mr. Aldrich's unorthodox political views, he was the last partner Bonnie entirely remembered; the young men who subsequently escorted her to the floor seemed to run more or less together. She could not recollect whether Lord Ravenshaw or Sir Lionel Varden expressed a particular affinity for the opera, and though she thought it was Captain Darnell who had recently served in India, she was compelled to own that it might be Major Niven. Eventually she insisted she could dance no more— which was far from being a lie inasmuch as her feet were throbbing and her ankles visibly swollen—and hobbled to a chair in the remotest corner of the room. Perhaps, if she sat very quietly, she would merge into the wallpaper, no one would notice her, and she would not have to move till the earl was ready to leave . . .

As it happened, Bonnie was not required to move, but
neither did she go unnoticed. To the contrary, a gaggle of
admirers soon clustered round her chair and began to vie for
the privilege of satisfying Miss Carlisle's every whim. Lord
Lambeth was the first to act, but even as he raced toward the
refreshment parlor to obtain a plate of oysters, Sir James
sniffed his opinion that oysters were out of season.

"Not much out of season," he conceded with another
sniff, "but questionable nonetheless. I consequently eschew
oysters at this time of year and eat cheese instead. Permit me
to fetch you some cheese, Miss Carlisle."

Sir James galloped off in Viscount Lambeth's wake, and
before he had disappeared, Captain Darnell volunteered to
search for a glass of champagne. His tone suggested that this
project was a perilous military mission, and he executed it
accordingly: threading his way across the dance floor as
though it were strewn with unexploded shells and the dancers
were enemy troops. However, his noble effort ultimately
proved gratuitous, for while he was gone, one of the many
circulating footmen passed by a few feet away; and Sir Lionel
bounded forward, plucked a glass from his tray, and triumphantly presented it to Bonnie.

Thus it was that Bonnie shortly found herself with a plate
of oysters, a plate of cheese, and two glasses of wine; and as
she attempted to juggle this bounty without spilling anything,
her companions embarked upon a lively verbal sparring match.
Their debate, if spirited, was polite enough until Mr. Aldrich
pronounced his opinion that the money squandered on horses
used for sport was a typical example of the decadent excesses
of the unjust society in which they lived. Sir James retorted
that Clement always had been a "muttonheaded sapskull,"
and Bonnie believed they might well have come to cuffs had
Lord Ravenshaw not stepped hastily between them.

Unfortunately, his lordship's intervention served to remind
Mr. Aldrich of another decadent excess, and he sternly advised Lord Ravenshaw that after the reformers had accomplished their objectives, opera would no longer be reserved for

the "privileged few." Indeed, Mr. Aldrich added darkly, it
was entirely possible that Lord Ravenshaw would be unable
to procure a seat at the King's Theatre. It soon appeared *they*
might come to blows, and Bonnie cast desperately about for
some harmless topic toward which to redirect to the conversation.

"I trust you will pardon my intrusion?"

Bonnie started, and the multitudinous plates and glasses
skittered alarmingly across her knees. Her imagination had
definitely outstripped her senses now, she decided, for she
would have sworn before any magistrate in the land that
David's polite words were once more tinged with sharpness.
Which was absurd, of course, because he had absolutely no
reason to be vexed.

She glanced cautiously up, but he was standing with his
back to the nearest chandelier, and the shadows reduced his
eyes to dark, unreadable pools in his face. In fact, she could
not even clearly see his face, and she chose to believe she
was also imagining his grim, unsmiling countenance.

"D . . . Uncle David!" she said brightly. "Permit me to
present my . . . my friends—"

"I am well acquainted with your *friends*," the earl interposed. "Good evening, Ravenshaw. Clayton. Varden . . ."
He continued to recite their names—sounding much as Teddy
Powell had when Bonnie instructed him to identify the Tudor
monarchs—until he had addressed the full circle. "Now, if I
may repeat myself, I trust you will pardon my intrusion. It is
long after midnight, and I should like to take Bonnie home."

Bonnie's newfound friends greeted this announcement with
suitable gallantry. Was it really so late? How swiftly time
fled in the immeasurably enjoyable company of one so charming as Miss Carlisle. Perhaps they would see her at Almack's
tomorrow evening or, barring that, at General Whitfield's ball
on Friday. And there was a whole host of assemblies next
week . . .

They were still chattering in this vein when David stepped
forward, snatched the plates and glasses from Bonnie's lap,
and belatedly looked about for a place to put them. There

was no such place, of course; Bonnie had long since ascertained that the nearest table was many yards distant. But the earl—evidently undeterred by the possibility of breakage—crashed the crystal pieces on the floor, yanked Bonnie up from her chair, and began to propel her out of the ballroom.

He *was* vexed, Bonnie admitted at last, and her feet started to throb again as she strove to match his long strides. Though she would not have believed it possible, he quickened his pace when they reached the stairs, and she tripped twice as they hurtled downward. Indeed, she fancied she would have fallen had his lean fingers not been snaked around her elbow; as it was, he jerked her upright and dragged her relentlessly ahead. He released her only when they were on the footpath, fairly flinging her arm away as he curtly desired one of Lady Lambeth's servants to summon his carriage.

"It . . . it was a lovely ball, was it not?" she ventured, discreetly massaging her elbow.

"Umm," he growled.

Bonnie interpreted this to mean that he had *not* thought it a lovely ball, but since another half-dozen of her ladyship's servants hovered just behind them, she elected not to pursue the subject. Instead they stood in silence until—at endless length, it seemed—the barouche rolled to a stop in the street. David stalked forward and climbed into the carriage, leaving Bonnie to the mercy of the footmen; and when she was safely seated, the barouche clattered to a start. They trotted round Berkeley Square, and as they turned into Davies Street, Bonnie could bear the silence no longer.

"Why are you in such a flame?" she demanded. The earl said nothing. "Don't deny you're vexed with me; it's prodigious clear you are." He did not deny it; he said nothing. "I can only collect I said something wrong, and you'd do well to tell me what it was lest I repeat the mistake in future."

"I have no conceivable means of knowing whether you said something wrong or not," he snapped. "Surely you recall that I was not privy to your numerous conversations. I fervently pray you did *not* commit any fatal verbal error, for if you did, it will be heard in every corner of London by dawn. Inasmuch as you stood up with every eligible buck in the city tonight. That was, of course, before you retired from the floor and began to conduct your own private assembly.''

"I was very far from wanting to conduct a private assembly," Bonnie protested. "In fact, I sat down to rest—"

"Ah, yes, forgive me," David interjected, his voice now dripping with sarcasm. "Yes, now you mention it, I do recall that you were frantically attempting to drive your suitors off when I arrived on the scene."

"What is your point?" Bonnie was growing excessively vexed herself. "Did your *niece* disgrace you by attracting undue attention?" The earl gazed stonily out of the carriage. "If so, I should like to remind you that you drew attention to me in the first place."

"I?" He spun his head back toward her.

"Yes, it was you who told Lady Lambeth my father possessed a vast fortune."

"I did not do so to draw attention to you," David said coolly. "To the contrary, I felt such a fabrication necessary to *dispel* unfavorable attention. To moderate the inevitable prejudice against Cornelia's daughter. You must understand that her marriage was the greatest scandal of its time, and those of Lady Lambeth's generation have not forgotten it."

"I do understand," Bonnie said. She did not wish—had never wished—to quarrel with him, and she tendered a conciliatory smile. "What you must understand is that your ploy succeeded all too well. Lady Lambeth obviously spread the news of my wealth, and I daresay most young men would rather court a rich girl than a poor one."

"Well, there is to be no more *courting*," he hissed. "Permit me to refresh your memory as to the nature of our project. When I engaged you to portray my niece, my objective was to frighten Judith and Robert into some semblance of responsible behavior. I did not undertake to give you a come-out."

Bonnie clutched her hands with fury, quite abandoning any

notion of a truce. "No, you did not," she agreed frostily. "But perhaps—like you yourself, milord—I saw no harm in killing two birds with a single stone."

She turned away and sightlessly watched the passing houses as she awaited his response. But the only further sounds were those of the carriage and the horses and Kimball's tuneless whistle floating down from the box above them.

5

"Miss Bonnie?" A hand gently shook her shoulder. "Come now; you really must get up."

It couldn't possibly be time to get up, Bonnie thought groggily as the shaking grew stronger. But the hand, like an annoying insect, would not leave her shoulder, and she raised her own hand and attempted to bat it away.

"Miss Bonnie!" The shaking became so very vigorous that she fancied she could hear the rattle of her teeth. "It is already noon, and you can't lie abed all day."

Noon? Bonnie's eyes flew open, and Nell released her shoulder and peered sternly down at her.

"Noon?" Bonnie croaked aloud, struggling upright in the bed.

She could not remember the last time she had slept so late. Indeed, upon reflection, she did not believe she had *ever* before slept till midday. Papa—reminding his wife and daughter that sloth was one of the seven deadly sins—had always insisted that breakfast be served at seven o'clock precisely, and Mama had continued this tradition in the years following his death. Nor had Bonnie been permitted any "sloth" in the Powell household, where her duties had compelled her to rise at half past six. Except on Sundays, when she could loll in bed till half past seven before dressing for her mandatory

appearance at St. George's, Hanover Square. (Mrs. Powell
was persuaded—mistakenly, it proved—that she might attract
the favorable attention of the *ton* if she, her family, and the
senior members of her staff faithfully attended services at
the premier church in London.)

"Yes, noon," Nell said, her black eyes softening. "And I
well understand you may still be tired. I expect it was very late
when you and Mr. David returned from the assembly."

It had been very late, Bonnie now recalled; the long-case
clock in the vestibule had been striking half past two as she and
the earl entered the house. As *she* entered the house, she
amended; his lordship had stormed through the door well
ahead of her and was already out of sight when she limped into
the entry hall. But late as it was, tired as she was, she had
been unable to fall immediately to sleep. She had, instead,
crawled beneath the bedclothes and lain awake an hour or
more, reviewing her and David's quarrel.

"Very late indeed, I'd guess," Nell added, "because I'm
told you were the hit of the ball."

"David told you *that*?"

Then he was no longer vexed, Bonnie reasoned, heaving a
tremulous sigh of relief. Not if he was boasting to the servants
of her social triumph—

"Oh, no, Mr. David didn't say a word about the assembly.
Didn't say a word about much of anything, in fact. He
seemed quite sunk in the mopes this morning, which isn't
like him at all. Ate hardly a bite of his breakfast and then
went tearing off to visit his tailor."

"I . . . I see." Bonnie's relief evaporated.

"No," Nell went on, "I heard about the ball from Lady
Roebuck's housekeeper, who got it from General Whitfield's
valet. Or maybe . . . ." She frowned. "Maybe Lady Roebuck's
housekeeper got it from Lord Blanchard's coachman, and *he*
got it from General Whitfield's valet. At any rate, one of
them—Lord Blanchard's coachman or General Whitfield's
valet— spoke *directly* to Lady Lambeth's butler, and he said
Miss Carlisle was undoubtedly the belle of the assembly."

"I see," Bonnie muttered again. She did not suppose the earl would be the least bit proud to learn that she had been unofficially declared "the belle of the assembly."

"Which is why I came to wake you," Nell concluded. "I fancy some of your *partis* will be calling this afternoon, and you must be ready when they arrive. I brought your breakfast"— she nodded toward the dressing table—"and while you're eating, I'll lay out your clothes."

Callers. Good God. Bonnie could scarcely bear to contemplate David's reaction if he returned from his tailor and found his saloon overflowing with her alleged suitors. However, she had long since recognized the futility of arguing with Nell, and she counted it best to eat and dress in accordance with the abigail's instructions. If any callers did appear, Kimball would be the one to present their cards, and Bonnie could simply decline to receive them.

She climbed out of bed and trudged to the dressing table, sat down, spread the napkin on her lap, and picked up the fork. But she had no appetite, and confident that even Nell's sharp eyes could not penetrate her back, she replaced the fork on the tray.

Evidently David was still angry, and during her fitful tossing and turning, Bonnie had been forced to admit that he had a point. He had been far too harsh with her, of course; he had no right to charge that she had sought to conduct a "private assembly" on the fringes of Lady Lambeth's ballroom. But she was compelled to own, in retrospect, that it might appear she had taken undue advantage of the situation. David had bought her clothes, paid for her stylish coiffure, created the myth of her fortune . . .

In short, she was the earl's invention, and perhaps he was entitled to fly into the boughs at the notion that she had deliberately used their project to gain a foothold in society. An erroneous notion, it was true, but one she had unfortunately reinforced with her waspish remark about killing two birds with one stone. She had *never* thought to convert their charade to a come-out for herself, and she wished for perhaps

the hundredth time that she could retrieve her impulsive
words.

But she could not; she had reached that dismal conclusion
at least a hundred times as well. She could not snatch her
comment back, so—grim though the prospect was—she perceived no alternative but to apologize to David. Not for her
actions: she remained convinced that she had in no way
invited the attentions she had received at the ball. But if she
confessed she had spoken rashly, he would surely concede
that he, too, had been unreasonable—

"Humph!"

As so often happened, Nell had stolen up behind her, and
Bonnie guiltily groped for her fork.

"I daresay you and Mr. David between you left enough of
your breakfasts to feed half the beggars in London. But come
along; we'll get you dressed."

Bonnie's jaw sagged with astonishment, for this was another
first. In Nell's personal lexicon of sins, "failure to eat"
ranked as the deadliest, and she normally lamented every
morsel of food left on Bonnie's plate. But—now judging it
best not to try the abigail's unexpected tolerance too far—
Bonnie leapt up, hurried to the mahogany chest beside the
wardrobe, stripped off her nightclothes, and donned her corset and drawers. Nell bounded to her side, carrying the
lime-green walking dress she had previously laid upon the
bed; and as Bonnie stepped into the gown, she detected the
clatter of a carriage in the street below.

"What did I tell you?" Nell said triumphantly, beginning
to fasten the hooks and eyes. "You've a guest already, and
it's not yet one o'clock."

Good God, Bonnie inwardly groaned; she had failed to
consider this complication. How was she to dismiss the caller
with Nell on the listen for her every word? She couldn't
instruct Kimball to report that she was still asleep, and she
certainly couldn't claim she was not yet dressed. So there was
nothing for it but to chat with her admirer a moment and then
affect the onslaught of a sudden mysterious indisposition.

And if she was quick about it, her *parti* would be gone long before David returned.

"There."

Nell finished her fastening at last, and Bonnie dashed to the dressing-table mirror to inspect her reflection. Fortunately, Monsieur Michel's coiffure required only a modicum of correction, and after patting a few wayward curls into place, she applied a dab of rouge to either cheek. She had just completed this endeavor when she heard the expected tap at her bedchamber door, and she watched in the glass as Nell threw the door open.

"Miss Bonnie?" As she had also expected, Kimball was bearing a small silver tray. "You have a caller." He proffered the tray, and Bonnie turned reluctantly around. "Lady Pamela Everett."

"Lady Pamela!" Nell grimaced with annoyance.

"Lady Pamela?" Bonnie echoed, expelling another sigh of relief. "I fear you misunderstood, Kimball. I'm sure she wishes to see David."

"She did inquire whether Mr. David was home." Kimball bobbed his head in agreement. "However, when I advised her he was not, she requested to speak to you."

"How peculiar," Bonnie murmured. She had obtained a distinct, if inexplicable, impression that her ladyship did not much welcome the sudden arrival of the earl's "niece."

"Perhaps she wants me to convey a message to David."

"Message indeed!" Nell emitted a snort of disdain. "Lady Pamela has been chasing after Mr. David above a year now, and I daresay she thinks to enlist you in her cause." She transferred her bright black eyes to Kimball. "Tell her Miss Bonnie is otherwise occupied—"

"No!" Bonnie interposed.

She was far from wishing to befriend Lady Pamela; to the contrary, she had instinctively disliked the woman from the moment of their introduction. But Nell's remarks had rendered her excessively curious, and she shook her own head.

"No," she repeated. "Please show Lady Pamela to the drawing room, Kimball, and advise her I'll be down shortly."

In the event, "shortly" extended to nearly fifteen minutes, during which interval Nell expounded her unflattering opinion of their visitor. At the crux of this opinion was the abigail's belief that her ladyship would have been wed long since did she not entertain such an exalted notion of her importance.

"Being as she's the daugher of a marquis, I mean," Nell elaborated with a sniff. "I fancy she expected to marry a duke. Or even a prince, if any of their royal highnesses had been readily available. But then, about a year ago, she must have woken up to the fact that she's not getting any younger. Must have decided to set her cap at the handsomest, richest earl she could find. Mr. David, to be precise. So she started trying to look like she was eighteen again . . ."

Nell was still grumbling in this vein when Bonnie judged that Lady Pamela—whatever her sins—had been permitted to cool her heels long enough; and with a nod at the crusty old servant, she left the bedchamber and descended the stairs to the first floor. She collected, as she approached the saloon, that Kimball had ordered tea for their guest: she could see a silver tray on the table in front of the Hepplewhite sofa. However, she further observed when she stopped in the drawing-room archway, Lady Pamela was not drinking the tea. Indeed, her ladyship was not even seated on the couch; she was slowly circling the room, pausing to study each individual item of furniture. At length, Bonnie surmised that Lady Pamela was planning the redecoration she would order when she won the hand of her rich, handsome earl; and though she could not have said why, her vague dislike swelled to intense animosity.

"You asked to see me, Lady Pamela?" she snapped, stepping on into the saloon.

"Ah, yes."

Her ladyship turned lazily toward the entry, and Bonnie noted that she was once more clad in a simple white muslin dress. But in the brilliant sunlight streaming through the open draperies, the lines in her face were deeper, harsher; and

Bonnie now estimated—with considerable satisfaction—that she was some years beyond thirty.

"Yes, I did request to see you, Miss . . . ah . . . Carlisle. Shall we sit down?"

Lady Pamela sank into the oval-back chair she had most recently been appraising and waved graciously toward the sofa. It was a clever attempt to seize the initiative, Bonnie conceded: an uninformed witness to the scene might well collect that Lady Pamela was the hostess and Bonnie the unwelcome intruder. An impression that would be reinforced if she took the designated place on the couch, and she consequently stood her ground in the archway and granted her ladyship a cool smile.

"I haven't the time to sit down," she said. "I was . . ." She elected to borrow from Nell. "I was otherwise occupied when you arrived. I consented to receive you because I assumed you wished me to relay a message to Uncle David."

"Uncle David." Lady Pamela chuckled, but the sound was utterly devoid of amusement. "Let us be candid with one another, Miss . . . Carlisle. I shall begin by frankly owning that I did not come to see Lord Sedgewick; I came specifically to speak with you. To speak *privately* with you. I inquired after Lord Sedgewick only to ascertain that he was from home."

She had been right about the voice, Bonnie thought absently: her ladyship was speaking firmly, crisply, with no trace of the breathless uncertainty she had employed the night before. Of more immediate import, however, Nell had been right about Lady Pamela's motives. She was obviously seeking to enlist the earl's niece in her campaign, and much as Bonnie misliked the woman, she didn't wish to be rude. It therefore seemed imperative to terminate the conversation before her ladyship could overtly solicit her assistance, and Bonnie groped for the polite—but unequivocal—words that would accomplish this objective.

"I fear you grant me too much credit," she said at last. "I'm quite incapable of influencing my uncle."

"You disappoint me." Lady Pamela shook her head. "I was honest with you, and I was in hopes you'd be equally honest with me. But apparently you've determined to play your part to the bitter end. Well, it will avail you nothing, Miss Whatever-Your-Name-May-Really-Be, because I know you are not Lord Sedgewick's niece."

How did she know? Bonnie wondered wildly. She had successfully deceived everyone else at the assembly; how had Lady Pamela, of all people, surmised the truth? She opened her mouth to ask, but it was so dry that the question died in her throat. And fortunately, as she moistened her lips, she realized that her ladyship's accusation might, in fact, be only a guess.

"Not Uncle David's niece?" Bonnie distantly commended herself for her indignant tone. "However did you conceive such an absurd notion?"

"Oh, come now." Lady Pamela issued another mirthless chuckle. "I am hardly a child."

"No, you are not," Bonnie pleasantly agreed.

A dull flush suffused her ladyship's cheeks, and Bonnie thought—nay, *prayed*—she was grinding her crooked teeth.

"My point being"—Lady Pamela's voice was now gratifyingly shrill—"that I am well aware of Lord Sedgewick's numerous *chères amies*. Indeed, his sister has warned me of his rakeshame ways at every possible opportunity. Since I am also well aware that it is in Lady Hellier's interest to prevent Lord Sedgewick's marriage, I shouldn't be in the least surprised to learn that she promoted this arrangement."

Arrangement? Bonnie knit her brows in puzzlement. For all the sense her ladyship was making, she might have lapsed into a foreign tongue. Not French; Bonnie was reasonably fluent in French. Greek maybe.

"I haven't the faintest notion what you're talking about," she rejoined aloud. "Evidently you're suggesting that I'm somehow in league with Aunt Judith, and the fact is I have not yet met her."

"Aunt Judith." Lady Pamela shook her head again. "You've

mastered your lines prodigious well; I'll give you that. However, I'm inclined to believe you do not know Lady Hellier, which renders the situation exceedingly surprising indeed. I can scarcely conceive that even Lord Sedgewick would ensconce a cyprian beneath his very roof. You must possess charms which are quite invisible to me."

"Cy-cyprian?" Bonnie stammered incredulously. "You think that I . . ."

But it was appallingly clear what Lady Pamela thought, and Bonnie was struck by a terrible suspicion. A suspicion so horrifying that her knees began to quiver, and she sagged against the doorjamb. Had David anticipated her ladyship's misapprehension when he contrived their charade? Had he plotted to kill *three* birds with a single stone?

"Be that as it may, you have created an excessively awkward situation." Lady Pamela seemed to be speaking from a vast distance. "I shouldn't like it to be said that I was compelled to pry a husband directly from the arms of his barque of frailty. I am prepared to make restitution, of course. Very generous restitution; state your price, and if it is remotely reasonable, I shall meet it."

"Are you . . ." Bonnie once more licked her lips. "Are you proposing—"

"I am proposing a far better bargain than you have with Lord Sedgewick," Lady Pamela interposed kindly. "He will tire of you in a few months—half a year at most—and cast you out. Whereas I am in a position to ensure your comfort for the indefinite future."

"No." Bonnie frantically shook her head. "You have altogether misconstrued—"

"I'm sure he's perfectly splendid in the bedchamber." Lady Pamela tendered a sympathetic smile. "But you cannot trade a lifetime of security for a week or two of passion."

"Half a year" had now shriveled to "a week or two," Bonnie noted, while "the indefinite future" had blossomed to "a lifetime of security." Had she watched such a scene upon the stage, she would have burst the seams of her dress with laughing; as it was, she could only lament that David wasn't present. Indeed, she lamented his absence most bitterly because she desperately wished to strangle him with her bare hands.

"You don't understand, Lady Pamela," she said as levelly as she could. "I am . . ." But she could hardly say she was the earl's invention, a figment of his vivid imagination, and she clenched her hands. "I am not a cyprian," she concluded lamely.

"No," her ladyship hissed, "it is *you* who do not understand. I intend to wed Lord Sedgewick, and I am accustomed to having my way. I have not permitted Lady Hellier to intimidate me, and I certainly won't be thwarted by a brazen little bird of paradise. I had hoped we could reach a civilized agreement, but since you have rejected that solution, I shall be forced to resort to other methods. Perhaps you are not aware that my father is the Marquis of Haverford."

"I was told your father is a marquis—"

"And my elder brother is the Earl of Walsingham." Lady Pamela flew heedlessly on.

"You are to be congratulated for your excellent choice of relatives," Bonnie said dryly. "However, I fail to perceive any connection between them and me."

"They have every connection to you." Her ladyship's green eyes were glittering with malice. "I believe I indicated that I am accustomed to having my way, and Papa and Richard are accustomed to seeing I do. Indeed, they go to considerable lengths to give me what I want. Such considerable lengths as occasionally to become . . . Shall we say *unpleasant?* Unpleasant for the obstacles to my happiness, I mean."

Bonnie was again reminded of a play, and at this juncture, she would have criticized the author for his amateurish lack of subtlety. Lady Pamela had not bothered to cloak her threat in even the thinnest of veils, and for a moment, Bonnie could only gape at her.

"Are you threatening me?" she asked gratuitously when, at last, she found her tongue.

"Interpret my words as you will." Her ladyship rose and brushed an invisible speck of lint from the skirt of her dress. "But do not profess to be surprised should something . . . something unfortunate occur. No, pray do remember that you were duly warned. And do not trouble yourself to ring for a servant to show me out. I have been here before."

She sailed across the Axminster carpet but stopped in the archway to fasten her cold green eyes on Bonnie.

"I have been here before," Lady Pamela repeated, "and I shall be here again. Long after you are gone, I shall be here."

She walked on out of the saloon, walked unhurriedly down the corridor to the stairs, but Bonnie did not move until she heard the slam of the front door. With that comforting sound reverberating in her ears, she drew herself up and, her knees still alarmingly unsteady, made her own way across the carpet and collapsed on the edge of the sofa. She would have conjectured that she and Lady Pamela had talked for some hours, but when she idly felt the teapot, she discovered it still warm. She poured herself a cup—her hands trembling rather more than her knees—and ventured a cautious sip. But the tea was, in fact, only lukewarm, and Bonnie gulped it down and shakily replaced the cup in the saucer. She then wriggled to the back of the couch, closed her eyes, and began to ponder what she should do.

The apology she had intended to deliver to David was out of the question: her transgressions paled to utter insignificance in comparison to his. No, far from planning to apologize, she was sorely disposed to end their charade at once. It would be fitting punishment for the earl if she packed up the elegant new clothes he had bought her and fled to Aunt Grace—leaving him to explain to Lady Hellier why their "niece" had disappeared as abruptly as she'd arrived. David would be excessively vex of course, but she doubted he would chase her all the way to Nantwich to retrieve a few gowns.

Indeed, now Bonnie thought on it, she doubted his lordship *could* track her to Nantwich. Insofar as she recalled, she had mentioned only that Aunt Grace lived in Cheshire, and David had never inquired the name of the town. So she could probably vanish without a trace, which would overset the earl for a day or two and positively delight Lady Pamela . . .

Lady Pamela. There was the rub: if Bonnie left, it would appear she had yielded to her ladyship's empty threats. And they were empty, Bonnie assured herself, determinedly ignoring the prickle of apprehension at the base of her scalp. What "unfortunate" thing could possibly happen? People were attacked in the streets of London every day; that was true. But not here, in the city's finest neighborhood, mere yards from Grosvenor Square. No, Lady Pamela's threats were so much hollow bombast, and she could not be allowed to suppose they had driven Bonnie away—

"What an astonishing surprise!"

Bonnie had not detected the earl's approach, and she started and opened her eyes. He was standing in the drawing-room entry—one broad shoulder propped against the jamb—and peering at her as though, indeed, he were quite amazed.

"I observed a carriage departing the house, and I assumed you had gone for a drive with one of your many suitors. However . . ." He made a great show of extracting a gold watch from his waistcoat pocket and frowning at the face. "However, I daresay it is a trifle early to repair to the park. Well, do not despair; I expect another of your *partis* will come along at the proper time."

He replaced the watch in his pocket, straightened, turned around, turned back.

"Which of your suitors was it, by the by?" he said casually. "Ravenshaw, I'll warrant; he always did fancy redheads."

"You would be well advised to say no more about my suitors," Bonnie snapped. His jaws twitched, hardened, and he raised his eyebrows. "Inasmuch as it was not one of my suitors who called. It was one of yours, *uncle dear*."

"One of mine?" His jaws and brows simultaneously drooped. "Kate again? Or was it Jane?"

Jane? Bonnie could sit still no longer; she sprang off the sofa and stalked to his side.

"I fervently hope that 'Jane' is Miss Godwin," she said frigidly. "I should hate to discover you're embroiled with *three* barques of frailty. Be that as it may, the caller was neither Kate nor Jane; it was Lady Pamela Everett."

"Hell and the devil!" Evidently David had left his beaver hat in the vestibule, for his head was bare, and he raked his long fingers through his hair. "The woman will give me no peace. I've employed every means I know to rid myself of her attentions—"

"So I collect," Bonnie hissed, "and I'm sure you'll be overjoyed to learn that your latest *means* have succeeded. Lady Pamela is convinced you are sharing your home with a cyprian, and even she is somewhat embarrassed to press her suit in such indelicate circumstances. She came to buy me off. As if I were nothing more than a . . . a . . ." A sudden maddening lump formed in her throat, and she furiously choked it down.

"Good God," David groaned. "Oh, Bonnie, my poor girl."

He seized her hand, and Bonnie felt a familiar tremor in her midsection. Felt the onset of the same odd breathlessness she had experienced when they danced.

"Please believe me when I tell you I never intended it to go so far. I didn't dream Lady Pamela would be so bold as to confront you directly."

"But you did intend her to think I was a bird of paradise, did you not?" His words had rekindled Bonnie's wrath, and she snatched her hand from his. "You correctly calculated that she would cease to pursue you if she fancied you had established a barque of frailty in your very home. And had she *not* been so bold as to confront me, I should never have known what you were at. Admit it, David: was that not your plan?''

"I shouldn't exactly term it a *plan*." He flashed his engaging grin, and Bonnie willed herself not to succumb to his charm. "Though I must own that the situation you describe did . . . ah . . . occur to me."

"Did it also occur to you to consider what would happen when Lady Pamela circulated her delicious *on-dit* the length and breadth of London? Judith and Robert will realize I am not your niece—"

"But Lady Pamela won't circulate such a rumor. That is the beauty of it." David's grin broadened. "As long as she entertains the slightest hope of luring me into the parson's mousetrap, she cannot afford to destroy my reputation. She will consequently be compelled to keep her opinion to herself, and Judith will be persuaded that you're our long-lost niece."

"Judith may be so persuaded if I elect to continue my impersonation." Bonnie essayed a glacial smile of her own. "As it is, I'm inclined to depart for Cheshire on the next stage."

"And what would that achieve?" the earl said soothingly. He reached for her hand again, and Bonnie dodged out of his grasp. "If there was any damage, it has already been done."

"*If* there was any damage?" Bonnie choked. "Lady Pamela believes me a cyprian; is that not damage enough? No, I daresay it isn't." She answered her own rhetorical question. "Not in your view. Which leads me to wonder what other schemes you had in mind when you conceived our project. Am I to expect an even more distressing call tomorrow?"

"To the contrary." David sketched another winsome smile. "Tomorrow we shall *pay* a distressing call on Judith and Robert and Francis. They are scheduled to return to town late this evening, and I propose we visit them early tomorrow afternoon. I shouldn't want Judith to hear the thrilling news of her niece's arrival from anyone but us."

"Very well," Bonnie said stiffly. "But I warn you, David,

that if you do have additional plots afoot, you'd best tell me of them now. Because if I discover you are using me in yet some other devious fashion, I shall leave without a further word.''

"There is nothing." He shook his head with every appearance of sincerity. "Nothing more, I promise you. You've only to deceive Judith and her family, and I am confident—"

"Miss Bonnie?"

She had not heard Kimball's approach either, and she once more started.

"Pray forgive the interruption, miss, but you have another caller.''

Kimball extended his little tray, and Bonnie suspiciously plucked an ivory card from its surface.

"The Earl of Ravenshaw," the butler added as she examined the card. "Shall I advise him you are occupied?''

"Oh, no," Bonnie said sweetly. "No, please show his lordship up without delay. And then, if it would not pose too much trouble, perhaps you could bring us a fresh pot of tea.''

Kimball nodded and bustled back down the hall, and Bonnie was delighted to note that David's smile had tightened round the edges.

"I trust you will excuse me?" he said politely. "I fancy you would prefer to entertain your . . . er . . . friend in private.''

He swept an elaborate bow and retreated into the corridor, and Bonnie was at a loss to say which of them had won the day.

6

The peal of the doorbell reverberated through the house, and Bonnie discovered that her mind had gone quite blank. She could no longer recollect even what bedchambers Judith and Cornelia had occupied during their girlhood—much less the various pets they had owned—and she cast David a stricken glance.

"It will be all right," he whispered. "As I've told you in the past, you might well be able to deceive Cornelia herself. You'll certainly have no difficulty fooling Judith and Robert and Francis."

Did he sound a trifle warmer than he had last night? Bonnie wondered optimistically. He had been infinitely polite at dinner, making no reference whatever to her "suitors." She judged his restraint particularly remarkable in view of the circumstance that Sir Lionel Varden had called just after Lord Ravenshaw's departure, and Viscount Lambeth had appeared later in the afternoon bearing one of his prize puppies for her inspection. But if the earl had been prodigious polite, he had also been excessively cool, and Bonnie had again tossed and turned in her canopied bed. Indeed, she had tossed and turned rather longer than on the preceding night, for—though she could not conceive why—she found David's frigid courtesy more oversetting than his anger. . . .

She became aware that his sapphire eyes had never left her face, and she hastily averted her own eyes and began to fumble with the ribbons of her leghorn hat.

"Perhaps they didn't return on schedule," she suggested hopefully as the echo of the doorbell died away.

"That is possible," the earl conceded. "However, I'm inclined to suspect that Briscoe is sipping brandy in the kitchen. With his faithful tippling companion at his side, no doubt."

On this curious note, he rang the bell again, and Bonnie undertook a nervous examination of the house. It was located very near to David's home—in Orchard Street just north of Oxford—and a stranger to the area might well be excused if he could not distinguish Orchard Street from Grosvenor. The residences in both were more or less alike: tall, narrow structures differentiated only by the presence or absence of pilasters, the style of the windows, the design of the roof.

Except for Sir Robert and Lady Hellier's residence, Bonnie amended grimly. It stood painfully apart from the neighboring homes, and Bonnie collected that—however enthusiastically the Helliers had frittered away David's money—they had not expended a single farthing on the maintenance of their townhouse. The stone facade was grimy with soot, and the paint was peeling off the iron fence. In fact, Bonnie observed upon closer inspection, the fence was beginning to rust. Furthermore, a number of the bricks fronting the arcade were chipped—

"Yes?"

The door creaked open at last, and Bonnie could not repress a gasp of surprise. She had inferred from David's remarks that Briscoe would be as unkempt as the home in which he was employed, but the man across the threshold presented a most impressive figure. He was tall and slender, immaculately clad in black pantaloons and a matching frock coat; and Bonnie calculated that he must have been monstrous handsome in his youth. Indeed, he was still very handsome. He'd kept the whole thick shock of his hair—though it had

turned entirely gray—and possessed eyes so vividly blue that
they almost rivaled the earl's.

"Good afternoon, Briscoe," David said.

"Lord . . . Lord . . ." The butler gnawed his lip, and
Bonnie perceived that he was jug-bitten after all. "Lord
Sedgewick!" he finished, beaming with triumph. "I knew it
was you, sir."

"Excellent," David said dryly. "And now you've ascertained my identity, would you be so kind as to announce me
to my sister? We shall wait in the—"

"Yes, sir!" Briscoe agreed. "Yes, you wait here, and I
shall advise Lady Hellier of your arrival."

He bowed, turned, wove his way across the vestibule and
up the staircase; and the earl shook his head.

"I had thought to tell him we should wait in the saloon,
but I daresay the library will do. With any luck, he will at
least remember that he left us on the ground story."

David closed the front door and beckoned Bonnie toward
the room on the left side of the foyer. The library betrayed
symptoms of deterioration as well, she noted, stepping across
the threshold and stopping to gaze about. She surmised that
the scarlet-and-ecru upholstery of the sofa had once matched
that of the armchair in front of the window, but the latter had
been exposed to the sun so long that its red stripes had faded
to a sickly pinkish hue. The draperies had also faded, but to
orange rather than pink, and the resulting combination of
colors was hideous in the extreme. It was probably fortunate,
Bonnie reflected, that the shield-back chairs were so worn as
to have lost their color altogether: one noticed only the clumps
of stuffing poking through the numerous holes and rents in
the fabric.

Her eyes drifted to the shelves, and for the first time during
the course of her inspection, she was genuinely horrified.
Even from a distance, it was clear the books were cloaked in
dust; and even through the dust, Bonnie could see that many
of the leather bindings were split. Although there weren't

"many" bindings to begin with: the shelves were largely bare—

"I am somewhat comforted to observe that Judith and Robert do not rely entirely on my charity." David's wry voice interrupted her scrutiny. "It appears they have sold the bulk of their library since last I visited."

Bonnie could not but wonder what portion of their library the Helliers had elected to retain, and she traversed the threadbare Brussels carpet to study the remaining volumes on the shelves. When she grew sufficiently close to make out the titles, she was horrified anew because there was not a Shakespeare, a Defoe, or even a Miss Austen among them. In fact, Bonnie was unfamiliar with fully half the works, and those she did recognize were silly novels of the sort she had forbidden the Powell girls to read—

"David?"

Bonnie spun around and sucked in her breath. Though the earl had stated that she looked astonishingly like his sister, the resemblance was so very startling that her jaws sagged with amazement. Lady Hellier was precisely her height, Bonnie judged, and she did not suppose their weights could vary by half a stone. And if they did, her ladyship did not carry a single excess ounce in her face; she had Bonnie's high cheekbones and hollow cheeks, her pointed chin and slightly overlong nose. There was one difference: Lady Hellier's hair was abundantly streaked with gray. But the strands which had not yet turned were the same pale red as Bonnie's hair, and she entertained an unsettling notion that she was seeing herself as she would look a quarter of a century hence.

"To what do I owe such a honor?"

Her ladyship moved from the doorway to David's side, and Bonnie noted that she had, indeed, availed herself of Mrs. Pruitt's services. In sharp contrast to her decaying home, Lady Hellier was clad in a fashionable walking dress which—apart from the circumstance that it was blue rather than yellow—bore a suspicious likeness to Bonnie's own ensemble.

"I am hard pressed to recollect the last time you called,"

her ladyship continued coolly. "Am I to conclude you were eager to assure yourself we had come safely back from France?"

"Of course you may so conclude." His concurrence notwithstanding, the earl's tone was somewhat frostier than his sister's. "However, beyond that—"

"Speaking of France, the most absurd thing occurred when we left our hotel." Lady Hellier sniffed, as if the customs of the country just across the Channel quite defied civilized belief. "Robert discovered himself somewhat short of funds, and the concierge declined to grant him credit. Fortunately, since you had previously patronized the establishment, he agreed to forward the bill to you. The miserable little concierge, I mean. And naturally Robert will reimburse your expense."

"Naturally." David sardonically inclined his head.

"If we are in agreement then, I shall bid you good day."

Lady Hellier turned haughtily toward the door, spied Bonnie for the first time, and froze in her proverbial tracks.

"That was the other reason I called," the earl said pleasantly. "I should like to present—"

"Good God, David," her ladyship hissed, whirling back around. "I have told you time and time again that I will not have your women in my house."

"But Bonnie isn't a woman," he protested. "Well, she is a *woman*," he amended, perhaps perceiving Bonnie's quelling glare, "but not one of my . . . ah . . . But I shall keep you in suspense no longer." He flashed his most engaging smile. "I am sure you will be as thrilled to learn as I was, Judith"—he paused for dramatic emphasis—"that we have a niece. Bonnie is Cornelia's daughter."

"Cornelia's . . . daughter?" Lady Hellier repeated weakly. Her head spun from the earl to Bonnie, back to him, back to her, as though she were watching an especially lively game of tennis.

"I knew you would be thrilled!" The earl clapped his hands with delight. "Come, Bonnie, and give your Aunt Judith a proper greeting."

Bonnie trudged reluctantly back across the ragged carpet, uncomfortably aware that Lady Hellier had ceased to rotate her head and was now observing her every step. Or misstep as the case might be. At length, she grew so nervous that she did, in fact, begin to stumble, and she lowered her own head and concentrated on placing her feet one before the other. She did not look up again until she glimpsed the toes of her ladyship's white kid slippers, and she then perceived a further difference between them. Lady Hellier had her brother's eyes, David's remarkable sapphire eyes. But the earl had told her that, Bonnie recalled, frantically dredging up the endless hours of his instruction. He had told her over and over that—while they keenly favored their mother in every other respect—the Merrill daughters possessed the late Lord Sedgewick's deep blue eyes—

"Your eyes," Lady Hellier muttered. She might have been sharing Bonnie's thoughts. "You look quite like Cornelia except for your eyes. I daresay your father's are brown? I cannot remember."

"Who can puzzle out the mysteries of inheritance?" David said airily.

It was all returning to Bonnie now. All the earl's interminable tutelage was flooding back into her mind, and she recollected that *he* could not remember the color of Thomas Carlisle's eyes either.

"The important thing," David continued, "is that Cornelia has sent her daughter to England. And while her objective was to give Bonnie a London Season, I prefer to regard our niece's visit as an opportunity to heal the distressing rift in our family."

As Bonnie had expected, the earl punctuated this pronouncement by throwing one arm around her shoulders and drawing her fondly against him. However, she had not anticipated that his fingers would dig painfully, pointedly into her flesh; and when they did, she realized she had yet to utter a single word.

"I am pleased to make your acquaintance at last, Aunt Judith," she murmured.

She could not quell an impression that she was once more trapped in a theatrical performance, and she now expected Lady Hellier to seize her niece in a welcoming embrace. But David—though the pressure of his fingers had eased—was still clasping the alleged niece firmly to his side, and her ladyship's expression was far from being one of welcome. To the contrary, she appeared to have recovered her aplomb, for her sapphire eyes were narrowed with disapproval.

"What sort of name is *Bonnie*?" she demanded. "I do not recall any woman in the long history of our family—"

"Her legal name is Elizabeth," the earl interposed soothingly. "In memory of our great-great grandmother on Papa's side of the family."

Having recalled the tedious details of their lessons, Bonnie was quite certain that the great-great grandmother on the Merrill side of the family had been named Joan. But her ladyship nodded—albeit a trifle grudgingly—and David flew on.

"Insofar as the nickname is concerned, Thomas' ancestors were Scottish . . ." His voice trailed off, and, if possible, he pulled Bonnie a bit closer. "But what does it signify? The important thing, if I may repeat myself, is that our dear niece has come to England."

"Umm," Lady Hellier grunted.

"Which does not, of course, in any way tarnish my feelings for Francis," the earl hastened to add. "No more than a father's love for his first child is diminished by the arrival of the second. Indeed"—he sighed—"since I shall never have children of my own, that is a very apt analogy."

He stopped again and bit his lip, as though this tragic analogy had occurred to him only a few seconds before he blurted it out.

"My point being," he went on bravely, "that I have always regarded Francis as a son, and I am overjoyed to discover I have a daughter as well." He clapped Bonnie's shoulder so enthusiastically that she was hard put not to wince. "And like the father I alluded to, I find that my affection is more than sufficient to encompass them both. My affection and"—he provocatively fingered the sleeve of Bonnie's spencer—"and whatever modest wealth I may possess."

Her ladyship flushed to a shade somewhat brighter than the unfaded scarlet stripes on the nearby couch, but before she could respond, there was a commotion in the vestibule.

"Briscoe?" The bellowing male voice was followed by a thud of heavy footfalls. "Where the devil are you?"

The footsteps grew louder, and even as Bonnie glanced curiously toward the entry hall, a man loomed up in the library doorway.

"Judith!" he snapped. "Where the deuce is Briscoe? He took the key to the liquor cabinet . . ." His querulous complaint sputtered off, and he squinted into the room, swaying a bit as he craned his neck over the threshold. "Davey? Is that you?"

"Yes, Robert." The earl's arm, still round Bonnie's shoulders, stiffened with distaste. "Yes, it is I."

Sir Robert staggered forward, and had Bonnie entertained any lingering doubt that he was Briscoe's "faithful tippling companion," it would have been dispelled by the powerful aroma of spirits wafting ahead of him. He was very foxed indeed, and it required no prior intelligence to deduce—from his bulbous red nose and the myriad of broken veins across his cheeks—that this was his normal condition.

"Davey!" Sir Robert repeated.

He had made his perilous way across the rug, and Bonnie observed that, like his wife, he was dressed in the height of fashion. However, the baronet's splendid clothes in no way enhanced his appearance, for years of excessive drinking had rendered him appallingly fat. As a consequence of his great weight, there was a substantial gap between the bottom of his waistcoat and the waistband of his pantaloons—a gap through which an enormous belly protruded—and his swollen jowls sagged well over his high, starched neckcloth. At one time,

Bonnie conjectured, Sir Robert had probably possessed exceedingly fine gray eyes, but now they were nearly lost above the massive mottled pouches of his cheeks. And as if to heap insult upon injury, he had lost the bulk of his hair: a narrow gray fringe, circling from ear to ear, surrounded an otherwise bare scalp.

The baronet extended his hand, swaying again as he did so, and Bonnie suspected he was seeking as much to maintain his tenuous balance as to offer a gesture of welcome. But David reluctantly lowered his arm from her shoulder and proffered his own hand, and Sir Robert energetically pumped it.

"Davey," he said once more. "If I could but locate Briscoe, I should offer you a glass of brandy."

"Forget your brandy, Robert!" Lady Hellier hissed. "Did you fail to notice that David has brought a guest?" She grasped Bonnie's wrist and yanked her into the baronet's full, if dubious, view. "This is Bonnie Carlisle, Cornelia's daughter."

"Cornelia?" Sir Robert released David's hand and shook his head in puzzlement.

"My sister, you goose!" The fingers snaked round Bonnie's wrist were quivering with vexation. "I learned but a few minutes since that my sister has a child. Whom she has sent to us all the way from the Indies. Bonnie is my niece. David's niece. Francis' cousin."

"How delightful!"

The baronet lurched to Bonnie's side, and she was terribly afraid he would clasp her in the warm embrace Lady Hellier had eschewed. But he merely snatched her free hand and began to pump it up and down as he had David's.

"Francis' . . . cousin," her ladyship repeated slowly, emphatically. "Related to David in the same degree as Francis himself. Indeed, David tells me that—just as he's always regarded Francis as a son—he now regards Bonnie as his daughter."

"Davey is so generous." Sir Robert sighed with admiration, then knit his gray brows. "Where is Francis, by the by?"

"He went out in the phaeton," Lady Hellier reminded him icily.

"So he did."

Sir Robert nodded and dropped Bonnie's hand, Lady Hellier simultaneously freed her wrist; and having adjusted her stance to the pressures on either side, Bonnie nearly lost her own balance.

"You must see my new phaeton, Davey," the baronet said as Bonnie regained her equilibrium. "It is magnificent."

"And magnificently expensive, I'll warrant." David's dry tone prompted Bonnie to remember that this was the carriage he had been compelled to pay for. "I trust you purchased it from Hatchett's?"

"Of course." Sir Robert indignantly squared his plump shoulders. "I should patronize no one else. But since it isn't here, perhaps you can return tomorrow. You'll wish to introduce Barbara to Francis at any rate."

Bonnie cleared her throat, but before she could deliver a correction, she heard the creak of the front door and the rapid tap of footsteps in the foyer.

"Uncle David?" A male voice again. "It *is* you." The figure attached to the voice had materialized at the library door. "I thought I recognized your curricle."

The new arrival could only be Francis, Bonnie reasoned as he hurried across the room, and she stifled another gasp of surprise. She had collected from the earl's reference to a "lad" that his nephew was still an adolescent, but the man now wringing David's hand was approximately her own age. Four-and-twenty at the least, she estimated; more likely twenty-five or -six. And while Bonnie didn't personally favor his type, she fancied that by any objective standard, Francis Hellier would be counted quite handsome: he was tall and huskily built, with arresting blue-gray eyes and dark blond hair. Though his hair was already thinning, Bonnie noticed, and she speculated that, like his father, he was doomed to baldness in his middle years.

"You have not yet met our other caller, Francis," Lady Hellier said shrilly. "This is your cousin, Bonnie Carlisle. The daughter of your Aunt Cornelia."

"Cousin?" His eyes briefly widened with shock, but he soon recovered himself and—again displaying a keen likeness to his father—enthusiastically pumped Bonnie's hand. "Cousin!" he repeated happily. "What a bang-up surprise! And such a pretty cousin! It is clear that Aunt Cornelia must be as beautiful as Mama."

If Lady Hellier was comforted by this gallant compliment, she betrayed no hint of it; to the contrary, she emitted a little sniff of exasperation. Francis dropped Bonnie's hand, and she discreetly flexed her fingers, fearing they had been quite crushed by the fervor of his and Sir Robert's greetings.

"What a marvelous surprise!" Francis reiterated, smiling down at Bonnie. "But why did Aunt Cornelia not notify us you were coming?"

"Cornelia realized it would require some months to exchange letters across the Atlantic," the earl said smoothly. "By then, the Season would long have been over, and naturally she wished Bonnie to be introduced into society at the most advantageous time."

Francis bobbed his head in agreement, but Bonnie noted the sudden narrowing of his mother's sapphire eyes.

"Come along now, Davey!" Sir Robert spoke so very loudly that Bonnie started. "Come and see my phaeton before it's unhitched and put away. You, too, Francis; you've mastered its modern features better than I. Come and show your uncle how everything works."

He lumbered toward the door, Francis obediently trailing behind him; and David, with a grimace of annoyance, began to plod in their wake.

"I . . . I should like to see the carriage as well," Bonnie screeched.

In truth, she was not remotely interested in Sir Robert's

phaeton, but she was terrified by the prospect of a private conversation with Lady Hellier. She stumbled forward, intending to race after the men, but her ladyship's fingers once more clamped around her waist.

"Don't go, dear," Lady Hellier said sweetly. "Let us avail ourselves of their absence to become more closely acquainted."

Bonnie could offer no objection—not unless she was prepared literally to wrestle herself from her ladyship's grasp—and she stared miserably at the library doorway until the earl had disappeared. At length, the front door squeaked open, slammed closed; and Lady Hellier released her wrist so abruptly that Bonnie stumbled again.

"Sit down, dear," her ladyship suggested kindly, waving at the sofa.

Bonnie desperately needed to sit, and she walked unsteadily to the striped couch and perched on one end, expecting Lady Hellier to occupy the other. However, her ladyship assumed a position just beside the sofa, a position from which she could peer directly down at her guest, and Bonnie belatedly perceived that she had been outmaneuvered. Mr. Powell—who had never been burdened by a surfeit of modesty—had often described the various techniques he utilized to intimidate his business rivals, and chief among these was his practice of remaining on his feet after cleverly inviting his opponent to sit. But Bonnie's knees were so weak she doubted they could have supported her long at any rate, and she gazed up at Lady Hellier with as much bravado as she could muster.

"He is putting a very good face on it," her ladyship said, now expelling a little sigh.

Bonnie could not but concur; indeed, she had initially been astonished by the obvious sincerity of Francis' welcome. She had then recollected the earl's opinion that his nephew was a trifle "skitter-brained," but since she could scarcely relay this view to Francis' doting mother, she groped for an innocuous response.

"I daresay Cousin Francis realizes he has no reason to be

overset,'' she rejoined at last. ''As Uncle David stated, he continues to regard Francis as a son—''

''I wasn't speaking of Francis,'' Lady Hellier interposed. ''I meant to convey that *David* is putting a very good face on it.''

''I don't understand.'' Bonnie politely shook her head.

''My dear child.'' Her ladyship's warm words were belied by the glitter of her eyes, which shone as hard and cold as the jewels they resembled. ''Surely you were told the circumstances of your parents' marriage.''

Bonnie essayed a cautious nod.

''Then you must comprehend that your presence is prodigious embarrassing. Embarrassing to myself as well as David; I shan't pretend to an entirely unselfish interest in the matter. But since you're residing with your uncle, the brunt of criticism will inevitably fall on him, and he is far too much the gentlemen to turn you out. I consequently judge it my duty to advise you of the proper course.''

''The proper course,'' Bonnie echoed carefully.

''Did it not occur to you to wonder why your mother you to England without warning?'' Lady Hellier's voice was once more growing shrill around the edges. ''David mentioned the short duration of the Season, but if Cornelia wished you to be brought out this spring, she could have written months ago. She deliberately neglected to do so because she knew neither David nor I would consent to receive you.''

''But Uncle David *did* receive me,'' Bonnie protested.

''He received you because he had no choice,'' her ladyship hissed. ''That is precisely my point: when you arrived unannounced, he was forced to take you in. And if you remain in England, the scandal of your parents' elopement will be revived and haunt us all for years to come. Which is why you must return to Jamaica at once.''

''Barbados,'' Bonnie corrected absently.

''Barbados.'' Lady Hellier inclined her head. ''I am delighted you agree.''

Bonnie had agreed to nothing, of course, but she elected

not to issue another correction. "I fear it is too late, Aunt Judith," she said instead. "Too late to keep my visit a secret, that is. Apparently you are unaware that Uncle David escorted me to Lady Lambeth's assembly Tuesday evening."

"That is unfortunate but hardly fatal. At the risk of wounding your feelings"—her ladyship sketched a brittle smile—"I must remind you that the city abounds in handsome young women at this time of year. A few of the people you met may inquire your whereabouts at the next ball, but after that, you will be forgotten. After David explains that you grew homesick and sailed back to Antigua."

"Barbados," Bonnie snapped. "And at the risk of wounding *your* feelings, I must advise you that I've no intention of leaving. My mother wanted me to have a London Season, and I shall abide by her wishes."

Lady Hellier's eyes narrowed to the merest sapphire slits, but before she could speak again, the front door creaked open and there was a tattoo of footfalls in the vestibule.

"Davey was most impressed by the phaeton," Sir Robert reported as the men strode up to the library doorway. "Were you not, Davey?"

"Oh, yes," the earl said dryly. "Yes, I believe it is worth every groat you paid."

"How nice," her ladyship cooed. "And while you were inspecting the carriage, dear Bonnie and I had a *lovely* chat. I pledged to do all I can to ensure she's introduced to the most eligible young men in England. I am certain that was also your objective, David, but a girl's debut really should be supervised by a woman. I shall therefore take Bonnie *personally* under my wing at General Whitfield's assembly tomorrow evening."

This was so far from what Lady Hellier had actually said that Bonnie was compelled to bite her lip lest her mouth drop open with amazement. She detected a flicker of surprise on David's face as well, but Francis and Sir Robert were happily nodding; and the latter declared that if only they could locate Briscoe, they would have a glass of brandy to celebrate the family reunion. However, the earl declined this offer with somewhat indelicate speed, insisting that the Helliers needed to recover from their strenuous journey.

"Indeed," he added, "I should not have called the very day after your return had I not been so eager to share the joyful news of Bonnie's arrival. But now you've met her, we shall leave you to rest and look forward to seeing you at General Whitfield's. Come along, Bonnie."

She rose and—the Helliers chirping more or less in unison how thrilled they had been to make her acquaintance—hurried to David's side. Since there was still no sign of Briscoe, they let themselves out of the house, then descended the front steps and crossed the footpath to the earl's curricle. A groom was just climbing the ladder to the seat of Sir Robert's fabled phaeton, and David silently assisted Bonnie into the seat of his own carriage, took the place beside her, and clucked the matched black geldings to a start.

"How very odd," he mused as they trotted beyond the servant's earshot. "Judith's initial reaction was quite what I'd anticipated, but it now appears she is fairly dying to launch you into society—"

"That isn't what happened at all," Bonnie interjected grimly.

She related the substance of her conversation with Lady Hellier, and she was reminded of the day she had described her life with the Powells; for the earl began to chuckle halfway through her narrative, and by the time she had finished, he was howling with laughter.

"We have won then," he crowed triumphantly when, at length, he was able to control his mirth. "Did you not perceive what she was at? Judith knows very well that the presence of Cornelia's daughter would not embarrass me in the slightest. And insofar as her own reputation is concerned. . . ."

He chuckled again and shook his head. "Robert's antics have so damaged my dear sister's respectability that she has monstrous little reputation left to preserve. No, Judith urged you to return to the Indies because she fears that if you stay in England you will further worm your way into my affections. Robert was too foxed to see the danger, and Francis doesn't possess the first grain of sense, but Judith realized at once that their inheritance is in jeopardy. However, as she thinks on it . . .''

His voice trailed off, and they clattered on in silence a moment. Then David cleared his throat, and when he continued, he spoke with not trace of amusement.

"As she thinks on it," he repeated slowly, "Judith will come to understand that the time of your departure doesn't signify. She will recognize that no matter when you leave, I shall continue to entertain fond memories of my . . . my niece. And could readily decide to bequeath her a substantial portion of my estate. . . .''

He stopped again, coughed again; Bonnie had never before seen him so uncertain.

"Let me not hide my teeth," he resumed at last. "Yesterday you expressed a . . . an inclination to take the next stage to Cheshire. And if that is still your desire . . . Well, now you've deceived Judith, I am prepared to release you from our agreement.''

His words were like a physical blow, a fist unexpectedly slamming into Bonnie's stomach and sucking the air from her lungs.

"Is . . . is that what you want?'' she managed to stammer, struggling to regain her breath. "For me to go on to Cheshire at once?''

"Good God, no!'' The earl sounded peculiarly breathless himself. "I believed it was what *you* wanted. In view of our numerous . . . ah . . . misunderstandings. But I promised you a London Season, and I shall be very . . . very pleased if you consent to stay.''

"Then I do consent to stay,'' Bonnie said shakily.

She was weak—almost faint—with relief, and she surmised she must be dreading her confrontation with Aunt Grace even more than she'd fancied. There was no other explanation for her panic—

"Excellent." David interrupted her speculation, and she thought she detected a tremor of relief in his voice as well. "I trust you will accept my apology for anything untoward I may have said. Or anything I might have done to offend you."

Bonnie glanced at him suspiciously from the corner of her eye, but he looked altogether sincere, and she nodded.

"Yes," she murmured. "And I should like to apologize if my behavior at Lady Lambeth's assembly distressed you. I did not intend to take advantage of your largess."

"Say no more about it," David said kindly. "I am confident we can complete our project in perfect harmony. We need spend only a few more weeks together after all."

A few weeks. Bonnie's relief evaporated, and her stomach once more knotted with panic. In a few weeks, she would return to her own gray world, never to see the infuriating, engaging earl again . . .

It was a magnificent day—warm and bright—but Bonnie felt as though a cloud had suddenly formed above the carriage. A cloud which blotted out the sun and froze her very bones, and she burrowed into the squab and drew her spencer as close as she could.

7

*H*aving been so rudely reminded that the Season would soon be over, Bonnie decided the following morning to advise Aunt Grace of her forthcoming arrival. If she wrote ahead, Bonnie reasoned, she could make it appear that the termination of her employment in the Powell household had been planned. She would explain that Maria and Anne had grown too old for a governess, and Aunt Grace would be unable to utter her dreaded I-told-you-sos.

There was no desk in Bonnie's bedchamber, but she well recollected the handsome Sheraton writing table in the library. The table at which she and David had sat, hour after hour, while he reviewed the design of Sedgewood and jotted the names and events she must remember . . . She swallowed a peculiar lump in her throat, squared her shoulders, and hurried to the ground story.

As Bonnie also remembered, there was a supply of heavy ivory stationery in the center drawer of the desk, and she plucked out the top sheet and snatched the quill pen from the inkstand. The first paragraph of her letter—the one stating that Mr. Powell no longer required her services—was easy to compose, but Bonnie was compelled to hesitate before she began the second. Since the end of the Season was not inscribed in stone, she didn't know exactly when the earl intended her to leave for Cheshire, but she was certain Mr. Powell would have specified the precise date her employment was to cease. The date would fall at the end of a month, she eventually concluded, and surely David wouldn't object if she remained in the city an extra day or two. She dipped the pen in the inkstand again and informed Aunt Grace she would quit London the first of July and reach Nantwich on the second. She signed the letter, but as she reached into the drawer for an envelope, she felt a tremor of doubt.

Had she ever mentioned the ages of the Powell girls to her aunt? Bonnie wondered anxiously. She believed not, but if she had, Aunt Grace would see through her ruse in an instant. Would readily calculate that even the elder daughter was only fourteen . . .

So it would be better, safer, to fabricate some other excuse for her resignation; and Bonnie crumpled the letter, took a second sheet of stationery from the drawer, and frowned down at it. At length, she determined to tell Aunt Grace that Mr. Powell—in view of his far-flung business enterprises— had elected to relocate his family on the Continent. Yes, that was very good. She would say that the Powells were removing to France or Prussia or some such place, and she had no wish to accompany them.

Bonnie penned a few opening words to this effect, but as she paused to debate the particular country to which she should exile her former employer, she perceived another— and far graver—problem: the possibility that Aunt Grace would respond to her letter. Indeed, as she thought on it, Bonnie recognized that her aunt could scarcely fail to acknowledge her communication; she must agree to the proposed schedule, suggest an alternate date for Bonnie's arrival, or decline altogether to receive her niece. And when Aunt Grace's letter was delivered to Portman Square, Mr. Powell would count himself obliged to send it back with a note advising Bonnie's correspondent that his erstwhile governess had mysteriously disappeared.

Which wouldn't do at all, and Bonnie crushed the second

letter, tossed it on the writing table beside the first, and withdrew another sheet of stationery from the drawer. If she was to write to Aunt Grace, she must include her new direction in the message, and she groped for an explanation that would encompass her brief sojourn in Grosvenor Street as well as her imminent journey to Cheshire. As she deliberated, her eyes strayed to the window, and she could not but notice the brilliant sunlight coursing through the panes and splashing across the Brussels carpet. Perhaps, she thought, a brisk walk would clear her mind, and she sprang up, crossed the library, and slipped out the front door.

Bonnie strode east on Grosvenor Street, marveling that it was virtually deserted. If she had learned nothing else about London during five years of residence, she had learned that its weather was notoriously foul, and she could not conceive why David's neighbors were failing to avail themselves of this rare bright day. Not until she reached the intersection with Bond Street, at which point a gust of chill wind whipped the skirt of her walking dress well above her ankles. The sun was radiating a great deal of light but prodigious little warmth, she realized with a shiver, and her lutestring spencer provided scant protection against the cold. She pulled it around her nonetheless and—when the wind once more assailed her— instinctively reached for the brim of her hat.

But she was not wearing a hat, she belatedly recalled, as her fingers found empty air above her forehead. She had left the house without a bonnet, without gloves, and she shivered again when she registered the shocking impropriety of her attire. Or lack of attire, as the case might be. She whirled about, intending to retrace her steps as quickly as she could, but a lone man was now walking toward her on Grosvenor Street. A man who looked familiar, and Bonnie spun back round and ground her fingernails into her bare palms.

Though she had seen the man behind her sufficiently well to ascertain that he was not one of her "suitors," she assumed she had encountered him at Lady Lambeth's assembly. And inasmuch as she had allegedly been the belle of the evening, she feared he would recognize her if he caught her up. Recognize her and—quite possibly—circulate the small but juicy *on-dit* that Miss Carlisle had been disporting herself about the town in a most immodest manner. So there was nothing for it, Bonnie judged, but to proceed into Bond Street and hope he would turn in the opposite direction. Or, barring that optimal outcome, hope he would pass her by without obtaining a clear view of her face.

Bonnie rounded the corner and hurried toward Piccadilly, dismally aware that she was compounding her sin. Should she now be recognized, by the man she had glimpsed or anyone else, it would be said that Miss Carlisle had not only been clad in highly unsuitable fashion but had also been observed walking *unaccompanied* in Bond Street. She turned her face to the shop windows, as though examining the merchandise within, and fervently prayed that none of her acquaintances was peering out from the other side.

Bonnie stopped when she reached the intersection with Bruton, wondering if she dared rotate her head enough to determine whether the man was still behind her or had, in fact, turned north toward Oxford. She gazed into the window of a millinery establishment as she debated the matter and narrowly repressed a gasp of dismay when her unwelcome companion—as she had come to think of him—halted beside her, not six feet away, and began to stare into the same window. Fortunately, he seemed quite enthralled by the display of bonnets arrayed before them, and Bonnie seized the opportunity to study his reflection in the glass.

He was a tall, lean, handsome man, with thick dark hair and—Bonnie believed, though she could not be sure—deep blue eyes. Indeed, he was so very attractive that she knit her brows in puzzlement, for she felt certain she would have taken particular note of such a splendid gentleman had she seen him at Lady Lambeth's. But he was not a gentleman, she suddenly perceived, glancing down at his reflected clothing: his breeches were perhaps a dozen years old, his tailcoat scarcely newer; and even in the window glass, she spied several holes in his neckcloth.

So she had not seen him at the ball, Bonnie concluded with a flood of relief, and she could only surmise that he resembled someone she knew. In fact, if one overlooked his shabby attire, he bore a vague likeness to David, but Bonnie was persuaded he more nearly favored someone else. Someone she had recently met . . .

But she was wasting precious seconds in speculation, she chided herself. The man beside her—whomever he resembled—could not identify her, and it was imperative to return to Grosvenor Street before she enountered anyone who could. She spun away from the window and strode briskly up Bond the way she had come.

Still counting it best to keep her face averted from the street and the footpath ahead, Bonnie once more watched the shop windows as she passed them; and she had traversed approximately half the distance back to Grosvenor Street when she caught a reflected glimpse of her "companion" behind her. Her first reaction was one of idle amazement that a man should amuse himself by window-shopping, for shopping of any sort was an activity both Papa and Mr. Powell had resisted with a desperation bordering on frenzy. However, she shortly realized that her mysterious friend could not have been pausing to admire the wares in the windows—he had matched her pace, and she had not stopped since she left the milliner's establishment—and she entertained an absurd notion that he was following her. A ludicrous notion indeed, but he was rendering her prodigious nervous, and she ground to an abrupt halt at the next window she reached. This chanced to feature the merchandise of a corsetiere, and Bonnie strove to affect fascination with the various undergarments on display while she waited for the now-familiar figure to pass her.

But he did not pass her; he halted as well and inspected the display with every evidence of equal absorption. He *was* following her then, Bonnie thought, her stomach knotting with apprehension. No man, not even David, could be genuinely interested in a back-laced dimity corset. Her handsome, out-at-heels companion was following her, and she wildly wondered why. Probably—she answered her own question—because she appeared to be wealthy. Her seedy friend had not observed that she was wearing neither hat nor gloves; he saw only an unaccompanied woman clad in an expensive dress. Though, surely, he *had* noticed that she wore no jewelry either and was not carrying a reticule . . .

But he had not, Bonnie grimly perceived, or he would not be plotting—as so clearly he was—to rob her. Not here in Bond Street; he wouldn't confront her in full view of dozens of witnesses. No, he intended to trail her back to Grosvenor Street, hoping to find it as deserted as it had been when he followed her out. His efforts would avail him nothing, of course, but she feared that his very frustration might goad him to violence, and she pondered the best means of escape.

Her initial inclination was to remain at the window; sooner or later the robber would tire of waiting and set out in search of a more cooperative victim. But perhaps he wouldn't, she realized, her stomach constricting again. Perhaps, instead, he would precede her into Grosvenor Street and lay an ambush. She briefly toyed with the notion of stepping inside the corsetiere's establishment and pretending to shop, but she soon perceived that this course might well produce the same result. Yes, knowing she must ultimately return to David's house, the robber also knew he could lurk along her route and launch an attack when she appeared. And since Bonnie could not predict the exact time or place of the attack, he would inevitably gain the advantage of surprise. It therefore seemed best to keep her prospective assailant in view, even if she was required to wander aimlessly up and down Bond Street for several hours.

Bonnie glanced about as surreptitiously as she could, deliberating whether to walk back toward Piccadilly, proceed north to Oxford, or cross the street and amble along the opposite side. Whatever way she chose, she comforted herself, she could, indeed, be confident that the robber would not dare an immediate assault. The footpaths were fairly thronged with pedestrians, and there was an unending stream of carriage traffic in the street . . .

A carriage! Good God; why had she not thought of it before? She had only to hail a hackney coach, and she would be safely home within the space of a few minutes. The driver would be puzzled— and excessively vexed, she feared— when she engaged his conveyance for such a short journey, but she would provide an enormous tip in compensation for his trouble.

Having glimpsed an avenue of escape at last, Bonnie was now inclined to move to the edge of the footpath. But it wouldn't do to reveal her plan too early, she decided; the robber, in desperation, might act prematurely as well. She consequently leaned toward the window, as if wishing to study the garments within more closely, and watched the reflection of the traffic.

Inasmuch as everything was backward, Bonnie found it prodigious difficult to get her bearings. At length, however, she adjusted her perspective, began looking left rather than right; and shortly after that, she spotted an approaching hackney coach. She should wait as long as she could to signal the driver, she reminded herself, and when she estimated the coach to be some twenty feet away, she whirled around, dashed across the footpath, and raised her hand.

But her sense of distance had also been distorted, Bonnie belatedly realized: the carriage was nearer thirty feet away than twenty. So far away, at any rate, that the driver had evidently failed to see her because the coach showed no sign of stopping to take her up. Bonnie stepped into the street, frantically waving her hand, and—to her immense relief—the carriage began to slow. Began to slow, but it was still traveling quite briskly, and she instinctively retreated to the footpath.

Well, she *tried* to retreat to the footpath; in the event, she was most rudely jostled by one of her fellow pedestrians. Though perhaps, Bonnie owned, the fault was hers, and she started to turn and murmur an apology. She was halfway round—slightly off-balance, her head tilted at an awkward angle—when she felt a strong hand in the small of her back and another between her shoulder blades. And before she could register what was happening, the hands gave her a mighty shove and sent her stumbling toward the hackney coach.

It was precisely like the day she had crashed into David's curricle, Bonnie thought wildly as she fought to regain her equilibrium. The hackney driver was shouting, as David had then, and desperately attempting to rein in his horse, but the carriage was rolling relentlessly closer. Closer and closer until, at the end, the scenario changed. With inches to spare, seconds to spare, Bonnie's left ankle twisted beneath her, and she fell to the cobblestones not a foot from the horse's hooves.

"Good God, miss!" the driver shrieked. He clambered down from his perch, his face ashen, and stalked to her side. "I seen you well enough," he said furiously, glaring down at her. "You didn't need to run into the street and nearly kill me horse."

"I did not run into the street," Bonnie snapped. "I was pushed by that man on the footpath."

She rotated her upper body and extended an accusing finger, but the robber had disappeared. No, not the robber, she amended grimly; the man she had foolishly supposed to be a robber.

"Well, it's good ye weren't hurt," the driver grudgingly muttered. "Get in the coach, and I'll take you wherever it is ye were in such a rush to go."

He extended his hand, tugged Bonnie up, and she moaned as her ankle once more buckled beneath her.

"I . . . I cannot walk," she gasped, literally breathless with pain. "If you would perhaps assist me . . ."

In point of fact, the driver scarcely *could* assist her: he was several inches shorter than she and, Bonnie estimated, at least a stone lighter. But he eventually managed to drag her to the coach and shove her inside, and Bonnie, for her part, managed to groan out David's direction. As she had anticipated, the driver was not at all pleased to be engaged for such a short journey, but—apparently conceding that the circumstances were somewhat unusual—he contented himself with only a small, dark scowl of annoyance.

As Bonnie had also expected, they reached David's house within a few minutes, at which juncture the driver announced that he really did not judge himself strong enough to wrestle her out of the carriage, across the footpath, and up the front steps to the door.

"No," Bonnie agreed, biting her lip against a new on-slaught of agony. "No, go up to the house and ring the bell. When Kimball answers, explain what has occurred, and he will help you."

The driver nodded and trotted away, and Bonnie gazed in his wake a moment. But her pain had grown so excruciating that her vision was beginning to blur, and she wondered if her ankle was broken. She looked down, gingerly lifted the skirt of her dress, and gasped again when she beheld the mass of blue flesh which had swollen well beyond the collars of her shoe. She could not determine whether her ankle was broken or not, but the mere sight of it set her stomach to churning; and as she glanced quickly back up, David rushed out of the house and bounded to the carriage.

"Good God!" The earl's face was utterly devoid of color, and his sapphire eyes were wide with horror. "What the devil happened? The driver indicated you were involved in an accident."

"It was no accident." Bonnie stifled another moan. "I was pushed in front of his coach—"

"Do not try to talk," David interposed sternly. "Oh, my poor girl . . . Kimball!" he roared. "Kimball! I need you *at once*!"

"At once" extended to above a minute, Bonnie calculated, but at length, the butler raced through the front door and panted to a halt at David's side.

"Kimball!" The earl was panting himself. "Give this man a pound or two." He jerked his head toward the driver, whose own eyes widened with astonished delight at the news

that he was to be rewarded so generously for his ordeal.
"And then fetch Dr. Selwin *immediately*; you are to *run* all
the way to Charles Street. Fetch Dr. Selwin," he reiterated,
"and bring him to Miss Bonnie's bedchamber the *instant* you
return. I shall carry her up while you're gone."

David returned his attention to Bonnie, spread his arms,
and she shook her head.

"I needn't be carried," she protested. "If you will just
support me a bit, I can hop up the stairs—"

"Nonsense," he crooned. "Nonsense, sweetheart; you're
in no fit state to be hopping about. Come now, and I'll have
you comfortably abed in a trice."

She wriggled to the carriage door, and he scooped her
effortlessly out; she would never have guessed him to be so
strong. He bore her toward the house, and—recognizing that
her dangling arms could only impede his progress—Bonnie
twined them round his neck. And felt the strangest, loveliest
sense of security: a warm well-being she had not experienced
since her childhood, when Papa had laughingly carried her up
the rectory stairs to bed. She melted against David's chest,
eagerly inhaling his clean masculine scent, her ankle almost
ceasing to hurt; and sighed with regret when they reached her
room and he deposited her carefully on the bed.

"There," he said soothingly. He perched on the edge of
the mattress, took her hand, began to pat it. "Dr. Selwin will
be here in a moment. And I'm confident he will find that the
injuries you sustained in this accident are no more severe than
those you suffered in the last."

"It was *not* an accident," Bonnie insisted, wincing as her
ankle once more started to throb. "I attempted to tell you in
the street that—"

"Hush." The earl laid one gentle, reproving finger over
her mouth. "I don't wish you to talk until Selwin confirms
that you were not concussed."

Since her head had been altogether unaffected by the "accident," Bonnie was quite certain she had not been concussed.
And if, against all odds, she had, she could not suppose that

speech would in any way exacerbate her condition. But it was clear David would brook no argument even had she been able to utter one, which—inasmuch as his finger was still blocking her lips—she could not. So she stared silently up at him and concluded that she must have been concussed after all, for his eyes looked peculiarly dark. Indeed, they looked more nearly black than blue, and they were regarding her with such intensity that her cheeks began to warm. Such unbearable intensity that she was eventually compelled to shift her gaze to the bedchamber door, and as she did so, a man loomed up on the threshold.

"I am thoroughly tired of your emergencies, Sedgewick," he growled. He snatched off his beaver hat, belatedly realized there was no convenient place to put it, and hung it on the doorknob. "No," he corrected, "I am more than merely tired: I am *appalled* to learn that you've run down another young woman in your curricle."

"I did not run her down," the earl said, leaping to his feet. "But the circumstances of the accident do not signify—"

"However, I cannot honestly profess to be surprised." Dr. Selwin stalked on across the room. "No, as a physician, I can only lament the current passion for excessively fast carriages. A vehicle like yours, even if competently driven, is a fearful instrument of destruction. And when, as in your case, it is *not* competently driven, the destruction can be most frightful indeed."

Much as Bonnie's ankle pained her, she was hard put to repress a giggle, and consequently—or so she feared—she was wearing an exceedingly foolish grin when Dr. Selwin reached the bed and peered critically down at her. He was not at all what she had pictured, she reflected distantly. She well remembered his frosty gray eyes, but she would never have associated them with a round face, a short, stocky body, an unruly shock of sandy hair.

"It is the *same* woman!" the physician screeched in the high-pitched voice Bonnie also remembered. "Good God, Sedgewick, one might almost collect you were deliberately pursuing her. Though this time, I see, you got her ankle."

Dr. Selwin seized said ankle, and Bonnie briefly feared—
nay, *prayed*—that the pain of his inspection would render her
unconscious. But she was not to be so fortunate: she was
forced to lie writhing in agony while he tore off her shoe and
twisted her foot expertly about. It was, perversely, only when
he finished that her head began to swim, and she barely heard
his pronouncement that her ankle was merely sprained. Hardly
felt the pressure as he wrapped it in a bandage. Scarcely
registered his advice to David that she should stay off her feet
for three or four days. Three or four days at the least, the
physician added; longer should her injury continue "unduly"
to trouble her. Bonnie was at a loss to conceive that his
definition of "unduly" might be: perhaps he would bestir
himself to return if she lapsed into a terminal coma. She
watched, her vision once more clouding, as Dr. Selwin strode
across the Aubusson carpet and out of the room; and when he
had vanished, David resumed his place on the edge of the
mattress.

"There," he said again. "Did I not tell you? You suffered
only a little sprain, and as you heard, it will be healed in a
few days."

His words once more reminded Bonnie of the day they had
met, but there was no mistaking the ragged note of relief in
his voice. Indeed, she recalled upon reflection, he had been
fairly frantic with alarm when he rushed up to the hackney
coach, and she essayed a grateful smile. David stroked the
hair at her temple— hair damp from the agony of Dr. Selwin's
ministrations—and at that moment, Bonnie detected a rustle
at the bedchamber door.

"David! Bonnie!"

Even as Bonnie recognized the voice as that of Lady
Hellier, her ladyship galloped into view and ground to a halt
beside the bed.

"Good God!" She stared down at Bonnie, her sapphire
eyes seeming quite as horrified as her brother's had been
earlier. "I drove over to bring David a jar of my cook's
bilberry jelly." She held it aloft in confirmation. "He adores

bilberry jelly. But when Kimball advised me of your terrible accident, I insisted on coming up straightaway. My poor, dear child.''

Lady Hellier sank on the mattress next to David, and their combined weights were so much in excess of Bonnie's that she was compelled to grasp the opposite side of the mattress lest she roll into them.

''My poor, dear child,'' her ladyship repeated, sorrowfully shaking her head. ''Well, it is clear, of course, that you must now return to Bermuda.'' Bonnie wearily elected to allow this latest misidentification of her alleged homeland to pass. ''Yes, when one is gravely ill, there is no substitute for a mother's loving care.''

''That is absurd, Judith,'' the earl snapped. ''To begin with, Bonnie is not 'gravely ill'; she has merely sprained her ankle. And if she *were* seriously injured, the worst possible course would be to subject her to a long, arduous voyage.''

''I daresay you are right.'' Lady Hellier frowned. ''Yes, such a lengthy journey might prove detrimental to Bonnie's delicate health. Consequently''—she brightened—''we shall send her to Robert's and my estate in Shropshire. As most of the staff remains in residence, she will be in excellent hands.''

''That is nearly as ridiculous as your prior suggestion.'' David's tone was one of great disdain, but Bonnie observed a tiny twitch at one corner of his mouth. ''Evidently you failed to register the information that Bonnie has only sprained her ankle. Dr. Selwin predicts she'll be up and about again in three or four days.''

''Doctors!'' Lady Hellier sniffed. ''Physicians are invariably too optimistic in their pronouncements; I fancy they calculate that a cheerful patient will be less inclined to object to their exorbitant fees. No, I am very much afraid that dear Bonnie will be crippled for months, and you are prodigious ill-equipped to care for her.'' She waved her hand about, as though she had just glimpsed a horde of rats scuttling along the bedchamber walls. ''If you do not wish her to go to Shropshire, at least permit me to take her to Orchard Street—''

"No," David interposed firmly, his lips once more twitching. "I am quite prepared—and quite able—to supervise Bonnie's convalescence myself. Even should it require months, which I am confident it will not. I expect Bonnie to resume her social activities within the week, and I daresay that by the end of the Season she will be engaged to a suitable gentleman. A suitable *English* gentleman," he pointedly elaborated, "and then we shall have dear Bonnie near us for many years to come."

If the earl had expected his sister to leap to his fly, he was doomed to disappointment, for her ladyship merely emitted a small, delicate cough.

"The . . . Season," she echoed carefully, as if the subject were almost too painful to discuss. "That is another reason I proposed that Bonnie return to Jamaica or settle herself in Shropshire."

She redirected her attention to her alleged niece, and Bonnie saw that her eyes were now glittering with their customary coldness.

"I am certain, dear, that your mother sent you to London with every hope that you would, in fact, meet and marry a respectable gentleman. Therefore I can only collect—and I am sorry I must be the one to tell you—that Cornelia's long residence in Antigua has altogether distorted her memory of English ways. Her scandalous elopement alone would render it monstrous difficult for you to make a good match, but occasionally, if a girl has a great deal else to offer, a man will forgive her unfortunate background."

Lady Hellier tendered a kind smile, but her eyes did not warm a whit. "However," she went on, "you have *nothing* else to offer, and you can only find the Season a most wretchedly humiliating experience. No man will overlook the background of a poor Jamaican farmer's daughter—"

"Poor!" David gasped. "Good God, Judith, did I fail to mention . . . Well, obviously I did." He sheepishly shook his head. "The truth is that Thomas has been immensely successful in Barbados. His principal plantation is three times the size of Sedgewood . . ."

This was but the first of many embellishments the earl added to the tale he had previously told Lady Lambeth. Bonnie's father, she soon learned, owned no fewer than six plantations, as many sailing vessels, a rum distillery, numerous inns and retail establishments . . . The list went on and on, Lady Hellier's eyes growing wider and wider with every word her brother uttered, until Bonnie was compelled to bite the insides of her cheeks most painfully lest the laughter welling in her chest burst forth.

"I . . . I see," her ladyship stammered when, at last, David had finished his narrative. "Well, that does . . . does cast a different light on Bonnie's future, doesn't it? Let me . . . ah . . . think on the matter." She sprang off the bed so hastily that she nearly tumbled to the carpet. "Meanwhile, pray do enjoy your jelly."

She sped out of the room, and Bonnie clapped one hand over her mouth, fearing her mirth would escape before Lady Hellier had safely departed the house. She stole a glance at David, but his tightly compressed lips, his indrawn cheeks, fueled her amusement, and she quickly looked away. At length, she heard the distant crash of the front door, and she and the earl simultaneously exploded with hilarity.

"Well, I erred in one respect," he sputtered when he eventually regained the power of speech. "Judith has not yet perceived that the time of your departure doesn't signify. Had she done so, she would not be so dreadfully eager to spirit you out of my sight."

"Yes, she was eager, wasn't she?" Bonnie succumbed to a fresh attack of giggles. "When she realized my injuries weren't sufficiently severe to warrant my removal from London, she seized upon my *unfortunate background*—"

"No, you have reversed it," David interrupted. "Judith didn't know of your injuries until she reached the house. When she set out, her intention was to persuade me—as she attempted to persuade you yesterday—that you should sail back to the Indies before you could embarrass the family any further. It was only when Kimball informed her of your mishap that she glimpsed a more convenient reason to send you away.''

"When Lady Hellier set out," Bonnie corrected, "her intention was to bring you a jar of bilberry jelly."

"That was merely an excuse. Since Judith has never called on me before, she had to fabricate some credible motive for her visit, and I do chance to adore bilberry jelly."

"I see," Bonnie murmured, though she was not entirely certain she did. "And then, when circumstance forced her to confront me directly, she conjured up the argument that I should also be humiliated if I stayed in town for the duration of the Season."

"Precisely." David chuckled. "And I wonder what she will do now I've advised her of your fictional wealth. If I know Judith, she will contrive to wed you to a marquis or a duke. . ."

His voice trailed off, and his grin faded. "Yes, if I know Judith, she is already plotting how to capitalize on your imaginery fortune. Just as she sought to turn your accident to her own advantage." He smiled again, but the merriment had left his eyes.

Her accident! So distracted had she been by Lady Hellier's antics that Bonnie had almost forgotten the terrifying incident in Bond Street. The last vestiges of her amusement evaporated as well, and she squirmed upright in the bed.

"It was not an accident, David," she said. "I tried to tell you so before. A man had been following me from the time I left the house, and he shoved me in front of the coach."

"You were attacked in *Bond Street*?" The earl's brows knit with astonishment. "Why did you not scream for assistance?"

"Because he caught me by surprise. I had just signaled the hackney, and I was stepping away from the street when I felt his hands on my back."

"So you did not actually see him push you." Bonnie shook her head. "Then I fancy the attack was a trick of your imagination. The pedestrians in Bond Street can be frightfully discourteous; I myself have been jostled off the footpath more than once."

"I was not *jostled*," Bonnie insisted. "I was *pushed*. And inasmuch as the man had been following me—"

"You are certain?" David interjected. "Could that not also have been a figment of your imagination?"

"I think not," Bonnie snapped. His skepticism was beginning to try her patience. "I first noticed him in Grosvenor Street and next at the intersection of Bruton and Bond. At that point, I turned around, and I shortly realized that he had turned too. I halted in front of a corsetiere's window to let him pass me by, and he stopped as well. Stopped and stood beside me for ten or fifteen minutes, I judge. And why would a man, if he were not following me, study a display of women's undergarments for nearly a quarter of an hour?"

"Some men have rather peculiar tastes," the earl said dryly. "But let us suppose, for the sake of argument, that he *was* following you. Perhaps he thought to rob you."

"That was my notion exactly. Indeed, that is the reason I hailed the hackney—"

"Or perhaps he merely found you handsome." David flew on. "And followed you in hopes of striking up a conversation. In either case, why should you suppose he wanted to do you physical harm."

"I think he was hired to do me physical harm," Bonnie replied. "Hired by Lady Pamela Everett."

"Lady Pamela!" The earl stared at her in consternation, as though collecting that whatever Dr. Selwin's diagnosis, she had been knocked altogether senseless by her mishap.

"Not Lady Pamela herself," Bonnie amended. "She appealed to her father and brother, and they engaged someone to attack me. Precisely as she threatened they would."

"Threatened?" David barked. "When did Lady Pamela threaten you?"

"At the end of her call." Bonnie swiftly related the final portion of their conversation. "I chose not to mention it," she concluded, "because I believed her threats were so much hollow bombast. However, it's now apparent I was wrong."

"No, you were not wrong." David shook his own head. "Haverford and Walsingham are barefaced scoundrels, and I've no doubt they do often employ questionable means to achieve their ends. But they would not stoop to committing violence on a woman."

"Then why was I pushed in front of the coach?" Bonnie demanded.

"You were pushed—if you were pushed—by a particularly rude pedestrian. The man who was following you—if he was following you—had nothing to do with it. And if you were pushed or followed either one, I assure you that Lady Pamela was in no way involved."

"If?" Bonnie echoed irritably. "I *was* followed, and I *was* pushed—"

"Hush now." David once more patted her hand. "Remember that Selwin counseled you to rest."

In point of fact, Bonnie did not remember this, but she was not prepared to dispute the earl's claim, for she suddenly discovered herself very tired. So immensely, achingly tired that she was hard put to keep her head from wobbling on her neck, and she did not object—could not object—when David stood and gently maneuvered her to a prone position on the bed.

"I shall send Nell up to undress you," he whispered, stroking the hair at her temple again.

"Umm," Bonnie muttered, and before the bedchamber door had closed behind him, she tumbled into blackness.

8

By midafternoon of the following day, Bonnie had decided that invalidism was quite a delightful state. Temporary invalidism, she amended; permanent debility would probably grow excessively tiresome for the victim and all of his or her associates. But at present, David and his staff appeared determined to cater for poor Miss Bonnie's every whim.

Her royal treatment had begun early the preceding evening when she wakened—splendidly refreshed—from a deep sleep and discovered that, indeed, Nell had removed her walking ensemble, dressed her in a nightgown and tucked her under the bedclothes. She shortly concluded that the abigail had also been instructed to look in on her every thirty seconds or so, for she had scarcely drawn herself to a sitting position when the bedchamber door flew open and Nell hurtled to her side.

"Miss Bonnie!" the old servant wailed. "Oh, what a terrible thing to happen!"

She smoothed the bedclothes, then felt Bonnie's brow for signs of fever, which seemed a prodigious unlikely complication in view of the nature of her injury. At length—evidently persuaded that her charge was not at the point of imminent death—Nell announced that Mr. David had declared that

Miss Bonnie was to have *anything and everything* she wanted for dinner.

"He does not expect you to go to the dining room, of course," the abigail assured her soothingly. "No, he has directed that your dinner be served in your room, and he will join you here."

And so it came to pass. Some two hours later, Nell marched back into Bonnie's bedchamber, Kimball in tow, both of them bearing trays of roast beef, asparagus, and tender new potatoes. In point of fact, Bonnie was only moderately fond of roast beef, but—recollecting that it was the earl's favorite dish—she had ordered it in deference to his kindness. Bonnie's tray was placed on the nightstand beside the bed, David's on the dressing table where she customarily took her breakfast; and as they began to eat, she murmured her appreciation that he had forgone General Whitfield's assembly to be with her.

"My dear girl!" the earl protested jovially. "I should rightly have been judged the most shameless cad had I gone merrily off to a ball and left my niece to suffer alone. Say no more about it."

As if to ensure that she would not, he launched into an account of the carriage mishap he himself had been involved in on the day of his twelfth birthday. He had "borrowed" his father's gig, he reported, and promptly run down a dairy maid. Fortunately, the only immediate injury suffered by either party was a grave wound to his pride; but before the day was over, the late Lord Sedgewick had vented his wrath on the rear portion of his son's anatomy.

"Do birthdays always bring out the worst in children?" David finished plaintively. "Or was I an especially horrible specimen? Mama claimed I was, and I did perpetrate a more insidious prank every year till I went up to Oxford."

"No, it wasn't just you." Bonnie was laughing so hard that she feared she might ingloriously choke to death on an asparagus tip, and she paused to gulp it down. "On my eighth birthday, I climbed the tree behind our house and fell out and got the most *awful* paddling . . ."

They continued to exchange similar anecdotes until their meal was over, and when the earl bowed out of her bedchamber, it appeared his good humor had been entirely restored. In fact, Bonnie reflected, one might almost collect he preferred her in a helpless state, for she did not believe they had got on so well since the afternoon of their precipitate meeting.

Nor had David's solicitousness diminished by the next morning. When Nell delivered Bonnie's breakfast, she brought with it the news that his lordship feared Miss Bonnie would become most dreadfully bored if she were confined to her room during the remainder of her convalescence.

"So," the abigail concluded, "I am to get you dressed, and then Mr. David will carry you down to the library and help you locate the books you might wish to read."

Bonnie was perfectly amenable to this procedure, but inasmuch as she insisted on bathing before she dressed, the execution of the earl's plan occupied nearly two hours. It was astonishingly difficult, she discovered, to *hop* into a tub and prodigious awkward to bathe with her bandaged ankle dangling over the side. The actual donning of her clothes proved almost as challenging: she had never before realized how often the simple act of dressing required a person to stand first on one foot and then the other.

At length, however, the earl was summoned to take her to the library, whereupon a new obstacle arose. Bonnie belatedly remembered from her own experiences that it was easier to bear a cumbersome burden up a staircase than down, and David—compelled to negotiate *two* flights of stairs—found this to be the case as well. Or so Bonnie surmised, for he stumbled so many times that she began to fear she had survived her encounter with the hackney coach only to be dashed to death on the marble floor of his foyer.

But she was not; at half past eleven by the vestibule clock, the earl staggered through the library door and deposited her rather unceremoniously on the Hepplewhite sofa. He collapsed in a nearby armchair, gasping for breath, and before he could recover sufficiently to make his way to the book-shelves, Kimball and Nell appeared to set the sofa table for lunch. This meal, too, had been prepared according to Bon-nie's specifications, and she happily wolfed down generous servings of beef broth, pigeon pie, and chocolate blancmange.

When the luncheon dishes had been cleared away, David proceeded to the shelves and commenced to announce the titles available for Bonnie's reading enjoyment. She had sup-posed he intended her to make three or four selections, which would be ample to see her through even a week's recovery. However, it soon became clear that his plan was to catalog his entire library, volume by volume, and his consideration was so touching that Bonnie lacked the heart to object. She consequently identified some two dozen books she was fairly dying to read, and the vestibule clock was striking half past two by the time the earl had stacked them on the carpet beside the couch.

"There!" he said cheerfully. "Do you want some tea while you read? Or a cup of chocolate?"

"Thank you, no. I am still quite stuffed from lunch."

"Too stuffed even for a piece of chocolate candy?" he teased.

"You have some?" Bonnie had never been too full for chocolate candy.

"No, but I can readily procure a box. There's a shop in Oxford Street."

"You're not to go all the way to Oxford," Bonnie pro-tested. "Had you chanced to have it at hand . . ."

But she was talking to empty air; David had raced out of the library, and she shortly heard the slam of the front door. Yes, she thought contentedly, invalidism was a most delight-ful condition. She bent down and sorted through the books at her feet, selecting a volume of Mr. Coleridge's newest poems; and as she straightened, she spied her crumpled letters to Aunt Grace on the surface of the writing table.

She must compose some sort of communication soon, she

reminded herself, and as she sat back on the couch, she perceived a credible—nay, a *splendid*—explanation for her confusing circumstances. She could say that Mr. Powell had removed to the Continent at the end of April, and the Earl of Sedgewick had subsequently engaged her to tend his children during the Season. The earl had needed her services, Bonnie would further explain, because the children's regular nanny had abruptly resigned her post. Or taken ill, perhaps, or even died; she could fabricate the details when she actually wrote the letter.

Yes, it would work out exceedingly well, Bonnie reflected, opening the book to the first page. Her formidable aunt would be satisfied, and David would never know he had been saddled with a fictional wife and several mythical children. Though she would have to be very careful when she reached Nantwich and Aunt Grace pressed her to describe the family of her most recent employer. Very careful indeed because the mere notion that the rakeshame earl might wed, much less sire a gaggle of obstreperous offspring, brought a twitch to Bonnie's lips—

"Miss Bonnie?"

Kimball's voice interrupted her reverie, and Bonnie started and glanced up.

"Forgive me, miss. Mr. David said you were not to be disturbed, but Mr. Francis is here, and I thought you'd wish to grant him an exception."

To say the truth, Bonnie did *not* wish to receive her alleged cousin, but she feared it would be monstrous rude to send him away. She nodded reluctantly at Kimball and closed her book, and a few seconds later, Francis Hellier strode into the library.

"Bonnie!" he said sorrowfully. "I should have come earlier, but Mama insisted I give you ample time to rest. And I daresay she was right"—he brightened—"for you look far better than I had anticipated."

"Thank you," Bonnie murmured.

Francis, for his part, looked considerably better than she

recollected from their initial meeting, and she was briefly at a loss to conceive why. Then—somewhat tardily—he removed his beaver hat, and she realized that his appearance was much improved when his thinning hair was out of sight.

"I brought you a box of chocolates," he said, plucking it from beneath his arm and setting it on the sofa table. "I trust you like chocolate?"

"Yes, thank you. Yes, I am very fond of chocolate."

"So am I."

He gazed longingly at the box, and Bonnie perceived that courtesy now compelled her to open it and offer the delicacies within to her guest. She waved Francis to the armchair, tore off the string, raised the lid; and they passed the exposed treasure back and forth for a time, munching in happy silence.

"Well." As there were no napkins in the room, Francis licked the residue of his feast from his fingers. "As I indicated, I am delighted to find you in such high force. Mama was *immensely* concerned for your condition."

Fortunately, Bonnie was just swallowing her last morsel of chocolate, and she was able to create the impression—or so she hoped—that her sudden fit of coughing was due to this rather than to Francis' words.

"Yes," she choked when she found her voice. "Yes, Aunt Judith was excessively . . . ah . . . thoughtful. Indeed, she was kind enough to propose that I recuperate at your estate in Shropshire."

"So she mentioned." Francis nodded. "But I well understand why you declined to be banished to the country during the very height of the Season. A handsome young woman such as yourself . . ."

He stopped and smiled, and Bonnie noted a rather large gap between his upper front teeth.

"However," Francis went on, "I should like to take this opportunity to invite you—*personally* invite you—to visit Hellier Manor when the Season is over. I daresay you will discover it quite different from your own estates in . . . er . . ." He stopped again and cleared his throat.

"Barbados," Bonnie supplied.

"Barbados! Mama was sure it was Barbados, but she wasn't absolutely certain."

Try as she might, Bonnie could not keep her countenance, and she buried her face in her hands and affected another great attack of coughing.

"Are you taking a cold?" Francis asked anxiously. "I fancy our climate is also very different from that of the Indies."

"No," Bonnie wheezed. "No, I fear I ate my chocolates too quickly."

"Good. Well, it isn't *good* that you're strangling on your food," he amended, "but I should hate to think you'd be struck down by illness even as your ankle was healing. Your many friends would be most disappointed to be further deprived of your company."

"Friends?" Bonnie echoed, daring to raise her head.

"Yes, you were sorely missed at General Whitfield's assembly last evening. Viscount Lambeth inquired after you, and Sir Lionel Varden, and . . ." Francis frowned with concentration, then shook his head. "The rest of their names momentarily escape me. At any rate, they were all *horrified* to learn of your accident, and several of them stated an intention to call on you today. Luckily, Mama was there to advise them that you were too weak to entertain guests."

David had predicted his sister's behavior with remarkable accuracy, Bonnie thought dryly: having been advised that her presumed niece was wonderfully rich, Lady Hellier was apparently scheming to wed her to the very pink of the *ton*. And since none of Bonnie's extant suitors was a marquis, much less a duke, her ladyship had cleverly discouraged their attentions. Bonnie was more amused than annoyed, for she had never been attracted to any of them—from the radical Mr. Aldrich to the cultured Earl of Ravenshaw—

"Lord Ravenshaw!" Francis said. Bonnie briefly collected he had read her mind, but she soon surmised that he was

remembering and enumerating still more of her "friends."
"And Lady Pamela Everett—"

"Lady Pamela?" Bonnie repeated sharply. "She inquired
after me as well?"

"Umm." Francis once more knit his brows. "Now I think
on it, she asked why Uncle David was not at the ball.
Whereupon I explained that you had suffered an accident, and
he had remined behind to nurse you."

"And what was her reaction?" Bonnie said casually. "Was
she . . . surprised?"

"Why should she have been surprised? Any gentleman in
Uncle David's position would have acted as he did."

He had obviously misinterpreted her question, and Bonnie
judged it best not to pursue the subject.

"Be that as it may," Francis continued, "I shall make it a
point to speak with your friends at Lord Blanchard's assembly
this evening. I shall assure them you are recovering from
your mishap, and if you like, I shall relay your thanks for
their concern."

"Yes, please do so." Bonnie nodded. "And be certain,"
she added impulsively, "to seek out Lady Pamela. Be certain
to . . . ah . . . assure her that my injury was minor and I'm
already very much improved."

"I certainly shall." Francis inclined his own head. "It
appears that despite the brevity of your acquaintance, you and
Lady Pamela have formed a close relationship."

"Indeed we have," Bonnie said grimly.

"Bonnie?" The sound of David's voice roughly coincided
with the slam of the front door. "I trust you have not
succumbed to starvation in my absence."

The earl loomed up in the library entry, and Francis jumped
to his feet and hurried forward, his right hand extended in
greeting. David was bearing a box so enormous that it required
both his hands to carry it, but he hastily tucked it under one
arm and grasped his nephew's outstretched fingers.

"You catch me unawares," he said. Why this should be a
source of embarrassment, Bonnie could not imagine, but the

earl's cheeks were unmistakably pink. "I did not notice your phaeton outside."

"No, you did not," Francis agreed, "because I walked from Orchard Street. I wanted to stop in Oxford to buy Bonnie some chocolates."

He dropped David's hand and gestured toward the sofa table, and Bonnie observed—to her mingled shock and mortification—that the box was empty.

"But you got her some chocolates too, I see!" Francis went on, apparently spying the earl's parcel for the first time. "From the very same shop! Well, you will be pleased to learn that Bonnie is monstrous fond of chocolate."

"Is she indeed?" David said coolly.

"Oh, yes. However, you must not collect that she ate the entire box. No, she had only six or eight pieces . . ."

Francis chattered on, gallantly confessing that he had devoured more than his share of the missing chocolates; and—though, again, she could not conceive why—Bonnie noticed that David's eyes grew a bit frostier, his mouth a trifle thinner, with every word his nephew uttered.

"But I shall stay no longer," Francis concluded at last. "Mama cautioned me not to tax Bonnie's limited strength, and I'm afraid I have already done so." He retrieved his hat from the sofa table, swept Bonnie a bow, wrung David's hand again, and retreated into the vestibule.

"What the deuce did *he* want?" the earl growled when the front door had clicked shut in Francis' wake.

"Want?" Bonnie echoed. David's vexation was puzzling in the extreme. "Why should you assume Francis wanted something? You told me yourself that he isn't a bad sort. He believes me to be his cousin, and I daresay his call was in the way of a family duty—"

"Then I fervently hope he now judges his family duty to have been fulfilled," David snapped. "Because if he does not, I fear you will shortly die from an excess consumption of chocolate."

He marched across the room, snatched the candy box from

beneath his arm, and slammed it on the sofa table. And before Bonnie could thank him for his trouble—before, in fact, she could generate any response at all—he spun around and stalked out of the library.

By the next morning, Bonnie was able to hobble down the stairs unaided. Which was not to say that she accomplished the journey without difficulty: to the contrary, her *Step*-hop, *Step*-hop required upwards of a quarter of an hour. But at length, she limped through the library doorway, collapsed on the couch, propped her bandaged ankle on the sofa table, and congratulated herself for her perseverance.

Indeed, she thought darkly, were it not for her perseverance, she might well have been left to languish in her bedchamber all day, for David seemed to have grown quite bored with his resident invalid. Well, that was not entirely fair, she conceded: he had helped her back to her room at the end of the afternoon and had once more joined her there for dinner. But his good humor had altogether vanished—he had picked at his food largely in silence—and this morning Nell had made no mention of another visit to the library. Bonnie could only collect that the earl remained annoyed because he had walked to Oxford Street for a box of chocolates and Francis had brought one in his absence. As if it were her fault! Bonnie fumed. She had not *asked* David to fetch her a box of candy, had not invited Francis to call—

The doorbell pealed, and Bonnie listened for the tap of Kimball's footsteps in the vestibule. But the house was still, and she shortly remembered that the servants attended church together on Sunday mornings. She sighed, lowered her injured foot to the floor, struggled up, and hobbled to the door.

"You are walking!" Francis said cheerfully. "That is a marvelous sign indeed, but you mustn't strain yourself. No, permit me to assist you."

He removed his hat, again exposing his unfortunate hair, and more or less dragged Bonnie from the foyer to the library, where she sank back on the Hepplewhite sofa. She was relieved to note that he had not brought another box of candy, for she feared she was, in fact, suffering from an excess consumption of chocolate. She had eaten nearly half of David's box after dinner and had felt distinctly queasy when she wakened—

"You look *splendid*!" Francis said, lowering himself to the armchair. Evidently, Bonnie reflected wryly, her gluttony did not show on her face. "Just as I told your friends last evening. That is why I came," he added. "I was sure you would wish to know what transpired at Lord Blanchard's assembly."

To say the truth, Bonnie had almost forgotten Lord Blanchard's ball. But she fancied it would be impolite to say so, and she essayed a grateful smile.

"Thank you," she murmured. "I should offer you some tea, but all the servants are at church."

"Yes, I am en route to church myself," Francis said piously. "I merely stopped to tell you that I had conveyed your messages. Beginning with your message to Lady Pamela. I sought her out straightaway and assured her you were recovering from your injury."

"And what was her response?" Bonnie was becoming keenly interested in the conversation after all.

"She said you must take care not to suffer another such mishap in future."

A wonderfully ambiguous remark, Bonnie reflected. Her ladyship might have been obliquely admitting that her father and brother had arranged Bonnie's "mishap" and would order another at the earliest opportunity. On the other hand, she could have been implying that—while the Everetts had not commissioned the attack in Bond Street—they were perfectly prepared to engineer a like assault when Bonnie was up and about again.

"After that," Francis said, "I spoke with your other friends. Lambeth and Varden and the rest of them. They were delighted to learn you were faring so well, and several of them inquired whether you were ready to receive callers. Mama advised them that despite your remarkable improvement, you should rest a day or two more.''

"Umm," Bonnie grunted. She was still attempting to decipher Lady Pamela's words.

"They were disappointed, of course," Francis went on. "However, they all agreed you should be left in peace until you are fully recovered from your accident."

"Umm," Bonnie mumbled again.

She had perceived yet a third interpretation of Lady Pamela's statement, and she gazed down at her hands. Perhaps her ladyship had merely glimpsed a chance to endow her empty threats with some degree of credibility. If—as David insisted— Lord Haverford and Lord Walsingham would never do violence to a woman, Lady Pamela had known from the outset that she could not cause Bonnie any physical harm. But she had cleverly created the impression that she *might* have instigated an attack in Bond Street and, more to the point, could arrange a similar one whenever she chose.

Yes, this interpretation made perfect sense. Except for the circumstance that it compelled Bonnie to admit that her mishap had been just that—an evil stroke of fortune—and she had been so sure . . . She peered at Francis through her lashes and impulsively decided to test her theory on him. A somewhat diluted theory, she amended: she would not mention Lady Pamela's possible involvement. But she would tell Francis of the man who had followed her and the deliberate way she had been shoved in front of the coach. And if he agreed with David that she had permitted her imagination to trick her, she would put the incident entirely out of her mind.

"I'm not altogether sure it was an accident," she said, raising her eyes. "My . . . my accident, that is."

She had got off to a very bad start, and Francis, not surprisingly, frowned with confusion.

"What I meant to say," Bonnie continued doggedly, "is that I am inclined to believe my mishap was not an *accident*. A man had been trailing me from the time I left the house. . ."

She related the gist of the story, and when she had finished, Francis shook his head.

"A crusher," he said. "One sees them every day. Men dressed in all their finery and following women about the streets in hopes of making an improper advance. Which is why," he added severely, "you should not have been in Bond Street alone."

Bonnie judged this a point best left ignored. "He was not dressed in finery," she protested instead. "In fact, his clothes were exceedingly shabby—"

"A robber then," Francis interposed. "But neither a crusher nor a robber would deliberately push you into the street. No, it was a passing pedestrian who tripped you up, and I wish I could profess to be astonished by such rudeness. However, I cannot, for I myself was quite *upended* in Piccadilly last autumn. I must own that the street was slick with rain at the time, but I should not have fallen had a most uncivil fellow not sent an elbow into my ribs."

"I daresay you are right," Bonnie murmured. "Uncle David is persuaded that is what happened as well. The most ironic aspect of the situation is that I probably should not have noticed the man at all had he not chanced to look familiar."

"You thought him to be someone you knew?"

"No one I had actually met," Bonnie replied, "but I initially thought I had seen him before. Later I realized that he only resembled someone of my acquaintance. He was tall and lean and had unusually thick hair. Dark hair. And very blue eyes, I believe."

"I . . . I see." Francis abruptly leapt to his feet. "Well, I must depart at once if I'm to reach St. George's prior to the start of the service. Do not trouble yourself to show me out."

He clapped on his hat and bounded into the vestibule, and Bonnie shortly heard the creak of the front door, followed by an indistinguishable rumble of voices. The door clicked closed again, and even as she reached for her book, the earl appeared in the library entry.

"Francis!" he snapped. "I am excessively tired of my nephew's constant skulking about."

Bonnie could hardly term two brief visits "constant," but she bit back a sharp retort. Not that she would have been granted an opportunity to deliver one, for David had already whirled around and begun to stomp up the staircase. His miftiness was really growing most irksome, Bonnie reflected, glaring in his wake. But in the interest of preserving whatever slight harmony remained between them, she hoped Francis would not call again tomorrow.

9

*P*apa had frequently included quotations from the classics in his sermons, and one of his favorites had been Aesop's statement that we would often be sorry if our wishes were gratified. Bonnie had occasion to remember this the next morning when—as she had hoped—Francis did not call, but Lady Hellier appeared in his stead.

"Good day, dear," her ladyship trilled, sailing into the library. "I hesitated to come before noon, but Francis assured me you are an early riser. That is a very commendable quality and one you will discover to be most advantageous when you are mistress of your own household. Why are you lounging about, Kimball?" she snapped. "Pray bring us some tea."

"Yes, ma'am."

The butler scurried away, and Lady Hellier sank into the armchair.

"I am excessively pleased to see that Francis' information was correct." She favored Bonnie with an excessively pleased smile. "It is clear you are making a *remarkable* recovery."

Inasmuch as Bonnie had been seated since her ladyship's arrival, her bandaged ankle hidden from view, she did not see how this could be clear at all. But she nodded and reluctantly laid aside the Fanny Burney novel she had been reading.

"Thank you, Aunt Judith," she murmured. "I deeply appreciate your concern."

"Which is not to suggest that I am surprised," Lady Hellier said. "Our family have always been a hardy lot, quick to rebound from illness and injury alike. That is another quality you will find enormously helpful when you are married and have a family to care for."

Evidently, Bonnie thought wryly, her ladyship was composing a list of her niece's many virtues. An interested duke or marquis would soon be assured that not only was Miss Carlisle reasonably handsome and monstrous rich, but a "hardy," energetic young woman as well.

"Of course," Lady Hellier continued, "a strong constitution means nothing if one lacks the proper spirit. And you, dear, have displayed the most wonderful courage in the face of adversity."

Courage, Bonnie added to the list. Miss Carlisle was also exceedingly brave.

"I firmly believe that a mishap such as yours is often beneficial." Her ladyship did, indeed, sound quite firm on this head. "Hardship gives one the opportunity to build one's character, does it not? And in your case, yet another benefit accrued. Had you not chanced to suffer an accident, you would have been caught up in the festivities of the Season, and I daresay you and Francis would scarcely have exchanged a word. Fortunately, however, your confinement has enabled the two of you to become close friends."

Bonnie would hardly have deemed Francis Hellier a "close friend," but she was compelled to own that he had been admirably attentive to his alleged cousin. So attentive, she recollected, as to vex his uncle beyond all reason. "Yes," she rejoined aloud. "Yes, Francis has been extremely kind."

"How I wish we had had cousins!" Lady Hellier lamented. "David and Cornelia and I, that is. Well, as you no doubt know, there was rumors that Josh the footboy was our cousin. Compliments of our rakeshame Uncle Albert. Josh and several other children in the neighborhood. But we had no *legitimate* cousins, and I was fearfully lonely . . ."

Lady Hellier chattered on in this vein for some fifteen

minutes, her discourse only briefly interrupted by Kimball's
delivery of the tea tray. Cornelia and Lady Amanda Rawlins
had been inseparable companions literally from infancy,
Bonnie learned, and David had befriended every boy for
miles around—from the finest young gentlemen to the sons of
the lowliest servants. But though Lady Hellier had made
friends of her own from time to time, these relationships had
invariably, inexplicably, died an early death; and she had
spent her childhood largely in solitude. Had Bonnie not recalled Nell's advice that Miss Judith was a wicked child, she
would have been driven nearly to tears by her ladyship's
tragic narrative. As it was, she sipped her tea in silence and
tried to incline or shake her head at all the appropriate points
in the story.

"But you will happily be spared such unhappiness," Lady
Hellier concluded with a tremulous smile. "Since you have a
cousin, and since you and Francis have grown so fond of one
another, you can always be confident of having at least *one*
friend in England."

"I was confident of that from the outset," Bonnie said
politely. "But it was very good of you to come and . . . er
. . . reinforce my confidence."

"That is not why I came." Lady Hellier returned her
empty teacup to the tray on the sofa table. "I came to see for
myself that you will soon be entirely recovered from your
injury."

"I do hope I shall," Bonnie said. "My ankle is considerably stronger today than it was yesterday—"

"Because I have conceived the most wonderful idea."
Her ladyship flew on. "I should like to conduct an assembly
in your honor."

Bonnie's first reaction was one of utter astonishment; she
would have been somewhat less surprised by an announcement that the Prince Regent had at last divorced his estranged
wife and offered for Miss Carlisle's hand. But even as she
shakily set her own cup and saucer on the tea tray, she
realized that such a proposal was quite in accordance with

David's prediction: a come-out ball would afford Lady Hellier the opportunity to present her niece to only—and all of—the most desirable *partis* in the realm. The assembly, while relatively small, would therefore have to be prodigious elegant, and Bonnie had no doubt the earl would ultimately be saddled with the bills. Which meant that she must nip her ladyship's "wonderful idea" in the bud at once.

"What . . . what a generous notion," she stammered. "But Mama didn't intend me to have an actual debut. She recognized that I am too old for a come-out—"

"As you are," Lady Hellier interposed, "and I do not intend to give you a debut either. I merely thought to invite a few of our friends—Robert's and Francis' and mine—to meet our lovely colonial relative. An intimate gathering; perhaps fifty people. Or seventy-five. A hundred at most."

Her ladyship's "intimate gathering" was growing more costly by the second, and Bonnie groped for a discreet way to say so.

"I couldn't dream of putting you to such trouble," she protested at last. "To say nothing of the"—she essayed a delicate cough—"the expense."

"It will be no trouble at all!" Lady Hellier said cheerfully. "I *adore* to plan parties. And why should you suppose expense to be a problem? You will learn when you have a home of your own that bills trickle in very slowly and can be just as slowly paid."

Or not paid at all until one's brother could no longer bear the embarrassment, Bonnie thought grimly. She cast frantically about for another objection and, miraculously, found one.

"I daresay an assembly would be most pleasurable," she said. "Except that there is no time to have it." She tried to sound regretful. "Uncle David has mentioned that there is an event scheduled every night for the remainder of the Season."

"There *was*," her ladyship said smugly. "By a great stroke of luck, Mrs. Maitland has been forced to cancel her ball, which was to take place this Friday evening. Her sister unexpectedly took ill and died within four-and-twenty hours."

Only Lady Hellier could regard sudden death as a "stroke of luck," and Bonnie was hard put to quell a laugh. But she kept her countenance carefully straight because her ladyship had unwittingly provided further grounds for opposition. It was impossible to arrange an assembly in four days, and Bonnie parted her lips to point this out.

"Indeed, were it not for Mrs. Maitland's cancellation, I could not arrange an assembly so quickly." Lady Hellier might have been reading Bonnie's mind. "However, in the circumstances, I shall be able to engage her orchestra and her florist and her caterer; they will be eager for substitute employment. And inasmuch as her ball was to be one of the grandest of the Season, I fancy virtually the whole of the *ton* is now free Friday night."

She paused a moment, tapping one long fingernail against her teeth. "So perhaps it would be best to invite them all," she finished with a martyred sigh. "I should hate to wound anyone's feelings."

Good God! Within the space of five minutes, her ladyship's cozy assembly had become the grandest ball of the Season, and—worse—Bonnie's every hope of preventing it had been dashed. Her mouth was still foolishly hanging open, and she glimpsed only one other avenue of escape.

"Permit me to . . . to discuss it with Uncle David," she mumbled. Surely the clever earl could fabricate some inarguable objection to his sister's plan. "Yes, let me be sure Uncle David approves—"

"Be sure I approve of what?"

Bonnie had not heard David's approach, and she started and spun her head toward the library entry. She could not determine whether the earl was leaving the house or returning: his immaculately tailored black pantaloons, his charcoal frock coat and dove-gray waistcoat, the beaver hat in his hand, merely indicated that he had dressed with the intention of going out.

"David!" Lady Hellier said brightly. "We are speaking of an assembly. I wish to conduct a ball in Bonnie's honor, and while she has agreed it is an excellent idea, she wants to secure your consent.''

Agreed? Bonnie's mouth fell open again, but before she could issue a denial, she realized that she might, in fact, have appeared to concur in her ladyship's proposal. Yes, she had carelessly remarked that an assembly would be most pleasurable. At the time, of course, she had spoken with the objective of forestalling the ball, but it was scarcely surprising that Lady Hellier had misinterpreted her words. She looked desperately at the earl, hoping somehow to signal him; but his eyes were on his sister, who was now describing the "lucky" circumstances that would enable her to conduct an assembly Friday night.

"How could I conceivably decline to approve?" he said frigidly when she had finished. "It is clear that you and Bonnie have anticipated and resolved every problem."

"Oh, I was certain you'd consent!" Evidently Lady Hellier had failed to register his tone, for she clapped her hands with delight and leapt to her feet. "I shall begin writing the invitations at once. Naturally, dear"—she turned her attention to Bonnie—"I wish you to participate in the planning, but I shan't tax your limited strength by insisting you come to Orchard Street. No, we shall use Francis to carry messages back and forth between us."

The earl's jaw tightened, and, if possible, his eyes grew a trifle frostier.

"But I can waste no further time." Lady Hellier squared her shoulders with determination. "If the ball is to be a success, I must start work *immediately*."

She raced out of the library, and when the front door had slammed in her wake, David granted Bonnie a sardonic nod.

"I am compelled to give you considerable credit," he said. His voice was fearfully calm; he might have been commenting on the weather. "I did not dream you would be so devious as to prevail on Judith to give you a come-out."

"*Prevail* on her!" Bonnie gasped. "To the contrary, I— "

"A come-out which I shall have to pay for." He went on

as though he hadn't heard her, and Bonnie dismally suspected he had not. "You do realize that, I trust? That the expense will inevitably devolve on me?"

"Yes, I do." Bonnie frantically bobbed her own head. "It is for that very reason that I attempted to dissuade her—"

"But you've been determined from the outset to have a debut, and it is now in Judith's interest to give you one. Especially since it will not cost her and Robert a single farthing."

"Please, David," Bonnie pleaded. "Please listen to me. The assembly was entirely Lady Hellier's idea, and I did not agree to it. I admit that I may have *seemed* to agree . . ."

But it was obvious he did not intend to listen—he was already turning away—and Bonnie snatched at a final straw.

"Believe what you will," she said stiffly. "Fortunately, there is yet another way to prevent the ball. I shall leave for Cheshire at once, and you can tell Lady Hellier I suddenly grew homesick and returned to Barbados after all."

"That is absurd," the earl snapped, whirling back round. "You are in no condition to undertake such a journey. You can hardly walk, much less climb in and out of a coach."

"I can walk very well," Bonnie lied. "In fact, my ankle is so much improved that I had decided to accompany you to Lady Cunningham's assembly tomorrow evening. So there is no reason I cannot travel to Cheshire instead."

David hesitated, and Bonnie clenched her hands. She had spoken impulsively, spoken from sheer desperation, and it appeared she had gone too far . . .

"No," he said at last.

Bonnie's fingers weakened with relief, and she saw that her nails had left little crimson crescents in her palms.

"No," he repeated, "your departure would make me seem a cad indeed. I will not have it said that the Earl of Sedgewick blithely permitted his injured niece to sail off to the Indies. You will stay in London, and you and Judith will have your ball. However, I further trust you will understand and forgive my lack of enthusiasm for the project."

His tone was still perfectly level, but his eyes had narrowed to the merest slivers of glittering blue ice. "I shall pay for the assembly, and I shall attend it, but pray do not expect me to assist in the planning. Should Francis bring a dozen messages a day, I shall not be available for consultation."

He jammed on his hat; apparently he had been going out. "If you will excuse me," he continued, as though in confirmation, "I was at the point of leaving for my club." He bowed, turned away again, turned back. "In fact, as I think on it, I fancy it would be best if I spent my days at Brooks's until arrangements for the ball are complete. I should hate to intrude on you and Francis."

He swept another bow and stalked into the vestibule, and Bonnie winced as the front door crashed to behind him.

Papa had also been wont to preach that liars were invariably trapped in their falsehoods, and by half past nine the following evening, Bonnie was compelled to own him right on this head as well. No, not altogether right, she amended, for after nearly an hour of practice in her bedchamber, she could, in fact, walk quite smoothly. Well, perhaps it would be more accurate to say that she could *appear* to walk smoothly: if she placed all her weight on her right foot, then quickly slid her left in front of it, she fancied her gait would look normal to any but the most critical observer.

But she had failed to consider the possibility that she would be required to stand—endlessly stand—in the corridor outside Lady Cunningham's saloon, and her right ankle soon began to ache almost as much as her left. Had she designed the human body, she thought grouchily, she would have anticipated such circumstances and provided an emergency limb. As it was, she could only rock awkwardly from one leg to the other until, at last, the butler announced them and David escorted her into the drawing room.

"Lord Sedgewick!" Lady Cunningham said brightly. "And Miss Carlisle." Her face fell, and she sorrowfully shook her head. "How unfortunate that you should have been exposed to the very worst of our British ways so soon after your arrival. Perhaps you will be comforted to learn that you are not alone in your travail. No, I myself was nearly pushed off the footpath in Oxford Street last spring. Or was it the spring before? Well, it doesn't signify. The point is that an excessively rude pedestrian somehow got between me and my footman . . ."

Her ladyship rattled on, and Bonnie understood why David had insisted they come to the assembly early. And why—despite this precaution—they had been left to languish in the hall for almost half an hour. If Lady Cunningham devoted such attention to each of her guests, there would soon be a line extending well into the street. Bonnie began shifting from foot to foot again, and just as she reached the point of collapse, her ladyship reached the end of her narrative.

"Be that as it may," she concluded, "I am delighted that you are recovered sufficiently to attend my ball. However, if you will forgive an old woman's advice, I daresay your ankle is not as strong as you fancy. You should sit and rest awhile so that when the orchestra starts to play, you will be ready to dance."

Bonnie doubted she would be ready to dance if she rested her ankle a week, but she nodded and permitted David to guide her to a chair in the corner of the drawing room.

"Would you care for a glass of champagne?" the earl said politely.

"Yes, thank you. It would be very kind of you to bring me one."

He bowed and strode out of the saloon, and Bonnie sighed. Though he had, in fact, been from home Monday afternoon and all day today, he had returned to Grosvenor Street for dinner last evening, and the meal had been grim in the extreme. Indeed, Bonnie soon came to wish that he had elected to dine out as well, for she did not believe he uttered twenty words in the whole hour they sat at table. At one point, she thought to inquire whether his gaming had been successful, but it then occurred to her that he was probably spending his time with Miss Godwin rather than at Brooks's. So she had picked at her food in silence . . .

Bonnie suddenly entertained a notion that she was being watched, and when she glanced around, she spied Lady Pamela Everett gazing in her direction. Following her conversation with Francis, she had sincerely tried to put the incident in Bond Street out of her mind, but she had been unable to do so. No, she was still persuaded—half-persuaded at least—that she had been pushed in front of the hackney coach, and she searched Lady Pamela's face for some hint of confirmation. But her ladyship was situated just inside the drawing-room entry, too far for her expression to be readable, and Bonnie lowered her eyes and discreetly inspected her ankle.

Upon removing the bandage that afternoon, she had been encouraged to note that her ankle had shrunk nearly to normal size and retained only a faint bluish tinge. And, she was pleased to see now, her hours of walking and standing had done no visible damage. It would have required a critical observer indeed to detect the slight remaining swelling, and that last trace of blue might almost appear to be a reflection cast by her periwinkle slipper. Yes, her ankle looked quite acceptable, and she would have been excessively happy if it didn't *hurt* like the very deuce—

"Bonnie!"

She started and peered up just as Francis sank into the chair beside hers.

"I crept past Lady Cunningham," he whispered. "I should not ordinarily be so discourteous, but people are strung all the way to the street, and I had matters of grave importance to discuss with you."

What matters these might be, Bonnie was at a loss to conceive, for Francis had not left Grosvenor Street until half past five that afternoon. And that, if she recollected aright, had been his fourth call of the day. To say nothing of the three visits he had paid on Monday. The messages he had so dutifully borne ranged from the merely trivial ("Should we invite Clement Aldrich? Though he is Sir James Clayton's cousin, his political views have rendered him decidedly unpopular . . .") to the utterly ridiculous ("Should we place a potted palm on the *left* side of the orchestra or the *right*?"). But Francis was only doing his mother's bidding, Bonnie reminded herself, and she essayed a tolerant smile.

"To begin with," Francis said earnestly, "Mama now believes we should put a *fern* in front of the orchestra instead of a palm. On the left side, of course; we agreed to that yesterday."

Bonnie would have sworn they had agreed to place the palm on the orchestra's right, but she bobbed her head. "Yes," she muttered. "A fern would be fine."

"And then there is the question of your attire," Francis went on. "Mama feels—since the roses are to be yellow—that you might wish to wear a yellow dress."

It was fortunate, Bonnie thought dryly, that most of her ball gowns chanced to be yellow. "Yes," she said again. "I shall wear my—"

"Francis," the earl said coolly. He was carrying two glasses of champagne, and he thrust one into Bonnie's hand and sipped at the other himself. "Your conversation with Lady Cunningham must have been one of historic brevity."

"To say the truth, I have not yet spoken with Lady Cunningham," Francis confessed. "'I own it was rude of me to avoid her, but I was eager to talk to Bonnie."

"That is quite understandable, but since you and Bonnie have finished your chat, I am sure she will permit you to pay your belated respects to our hostess." David drained his glass and slammed it on the bow-fronted commode next to Bonnie's chair. "In your absence, I shall stand up with your cousin."

Bonnie had been only distantly aware of the strains of music in the background, but she now realized that the orchestra was playing a waltz and that the dance floor—such as it was—was thronged with guests. David snatched her glass away, crashed it to the commode beside his, extended his hand; and Bonnie shook her head.

"I fear I cannot dance," she murmured. "As Lady Cunningham suggested, my ankle is not so strong as I'd fancied."

"Then we must certainly leave," the earl said kindly. "I shall summon Kimball at once."

"We needn't go on my account," Bonnie protested. "I shall be perfectly comfortable as long as I'm sitting."

"And I shall keep her company," Francis promised.

"How very noble." David shook his own head with admiration. "But such suffering is entirely unnecesssary, I assure you. No, I shall send for Kimball; allow me ten minutes. Then, Francis, you can desire one of Lady Cunningham's servants to assist Bonnie down the stairs."

In the event, it was Francis who assisted her down the stairs, through the vestibule, and across the footpath; and she greeted the dozens of puzzled stares they received with a fixed bright smile. A smile which indicated that it was altogether natural to leave an assembly not long after ten o'clock. To her relief, David's barouche was waiting, and Francis and Kimball between them boosted her into the forward-facing seat. Francis waved a rather dubious farewell, Kimball remounted the box; and a few seconds later—amid the curious frowns of the guests still milling in the street—the carriage clattered to a start.

"We did not have to go so early," Bonnie reiterated as they turned a corner and, blessedly, trotted beyond view of Lady Cunningham's house. "As I stated, I should have been perfectly comfortable—"

"And as *I* stated," the earl interposed, "I could not subject you and Francis to a long, dull evening. No, it is clear you attempted to resume your activities too soon, and Lady Cunningham will understand your premature departure. I shall also send word to Lady Jersey that we cannot attend the assembly at Almack's tomorrow night."

"Not go to Almack's!" Bonnie's eyes widened with disbelief. The servants in the Powell household had often debated how many of her children Mrs. Powell would trade for a voucher to Almack's. The most conservative estimate was two; several on the staff had insisted she would readily give all six.

"It is really very boring," David said. "On the whole, I vastly prefer to play macao at Brooks's, which is what I shall do tomorrow evening. But I can understand why you might wish to go to Almack's once in your life, and I shall take you next week. When your ankle is completely healed."

Once in your life. There it was again: the chilling reminder that her days in London were fearfully numbered. "Yes," she mumbled, "I daresay that would be best. I couldn't possibly appreciate Almack's if my ankle was still troubling me."

Once-in-your-life, once-in-your-life, once-in-your-life. The carriage wheels sang the refrain endlessly to the cobblestones as they rolled on through the darkness.

10

*B*onnie had often pondered the awesome power of Fate: the enormous changes that a day, an hour, even a few minutes could create in one's life. If, for example, Mr. Powell had chosen to visit his Stafford office on some other date or at some other time, he would have had no opportunity to engage her as his governess. And if she had chanced to be wearing her oldest gown rather than her newest when the Powell boys poured ink in her chair, she probably wouldn't have fled the house in Portman Square. No, the ink would scarcely have showed on her ancient black bombazine dress, and Bonnie would not have cared a whit if it had. And then, of course, if she had raced into Oxford Street mere seconds sooner or later than she did, she would not have met the Earl of Sedgewick.

Despite her frequent meditations on the subject, Bonnie had never decided whether the changes thus wrought were generally for good or ill. Nor did she reach any such conclusion the next morning when she realized that—a scant twelve hours after her humiliating retreat from Lady Cunningham's ball—her ankle was perfectly healed.

"You are not limping!" Nell said happily as Bonnie walked into the breakfast parlor. Two days earlier, the abigail had declared that in order to "get the morning stiffness out of your ankle," Miss Bonnie must henceforth take her breakfast downstairs with Mr. David.

"No, I am not," Bonnie agreed.

She glanced around the room, but she couldn't determine whether the earl had eaten or not. The pristine tablecloth in front of his empty chair proved nothing; Kimball would have captured and destroyed every wayward crumb the instant his master departed. And inasmuch as the entire Wedgwood breakfast service was kept on top of the sideboard, it was impossible to judge if one plate was missing.

"I seem to have recovered literally overnight," Bonnie went on. Papa would no doubt have termed her dramatic improvement a "miracle," but Bonnie had always been a trifle skeptical on this head. "Indeed, I was thinking to advise Uncle David that I can go to Almack's after all."

"I fear it is too late." Nell shook her head. "Mr. David has already left for Brooks's, and he stated he would remain there through the evening."

"I see," Bonnie murmured. "Well, I can go to Almack's next week, can I not?"

Invalidism having long since lost its charms, Bonnie had mastered the art of expanding every remotely interesting activity to the maximum, and she dawdled over breakfast for nearly an hour before repairing to the library. Though she had by now discarded her abortive letters to Aunt Grace, she well remembered that she must soon send a communication to Cheshire; and she proceeded directly to the desk, withdrew a sheet of stationery from the drawer, and seized the pen. But her heart wasn't in the project, and when Nell appeared to announce lunch, she was still laboring over the first paragraph.

Lunch occupied another hour, and afterward—abandoning any notion of completing her letter today—Bonnie settled on the sofa with one of William Beckford's gothic novels. But she was unable to concentrate on it either, and at length, she laid the book aside, gazed toward the window, and wondered if she should risk a walk. The weather was marginal, the sun only occasionally peeping out from behind a bank of scudding gray clouds. However, there had been no rain, and if she didn't venture far from the house, she could quickly scurry back if it did start to rain . . .

Unless Lady Pamela's father and brother had stationed a man outside to watch for her. As they so obviously had last Friday. Well, she amended, as they *might* have done last Friday. She clenched her hands in frustration, desperately wishing she knew. Until she was persuaded that her mishap had truly been an accident, she was virtually a prisoner, not daring to step into the street alone—

The doorbell pealed, and Bonnie spun her head eagerly toward the vestibule, so monstrous bored that she was prepared to welcome even one of Francis' calls. Which was fortunate because it was, indeed, Francis who shortly loomed up in the library entry.

"Francis!" she said warmly, leaping to her feet.

"B-Bonnie," he stammered. "I am immensely pleased that you are so pleased to see me."

He did, in fact, blush with pleasure, and Bonnie felt a little stab of guilt for having misled him. Francis really was a "good lad," and she counted it excessively cruel of Fate to have rendered him so very dull.

"Mama and I were most alarmed by your relapse," he continued, "and I came to inquire as to your condition. You . . . you seem somewhat better."

"I am vastly better," Bonnie assured him. "No, not merely *better*: I have altogether recovered from my injury. Indeed, I was thinking to go out, but I . . ." She recollected that he didn't know her suspicions of Lady Pamela, that he—like everyone else—believed she had been jostled off the footpath. "I remembered your advice that I should not leave the house unaccompanied," she finished rather lamely.

"And now you need not!" Francis said. "Mama was in hopes you'd be well enough to come to Orchard Street and discuss the final arrangements for the assembly. She intended me to drive you, of course, and we can detour through Hyde Park."

Bonnie was far from wishing to discuss the ball with Lady

Hellier, but she did long for a dose of fresh air, and she enthusiastically bobbed her head. "Yes," she agreed. "Let me fetch a bonnet and gloves, and I shall be back in a moment."

She hurried up the stairs to her bedchamber, where she found Nell waving a feather duster in the general direction of the dressing table. Bonnie had previously observed that these daily "cleanings" produced scant result: however formidable her talents as an abigail, Nell was a perfectly wretched chambermaid. But Bonnie had not complained and never would, for she had come truly to love the crusty old woman; and as she snatched her leghorn hat out of the wardrobe and put it on, she explained the nature of her and Francis' outing.

"I shall be back in ample time for dinner," she concluded, drawing on her gloves.

"And what will you be wanting to eat?" Nell asked. "Alice has both chicken and veal, and as Mr. David won't be home, the choice is entirely yours."

Bonnie had forgotten that the earl would be dining at Brooks's, and she shook her head. "Do not tease yourself about dinner; I shouldn't want Alice to cook a meal just for me. When I get hungry, I shall go to the kitchen and prepare a sandwich." She hurried out of the room before Nell could protest and sped back down the stairs.

Though Bonnie had seen Sir Robert's high-flyer phaeton—had even noticed the ladder—she had failed to register how prodigious elevated the seat was from the ground, and she stumbled to a halt at the edge of the footpath and stared upward in sheer horror. The longer she looked at the carriage, the more it came to resemble the oak tree behind the rectory, and she had learned a bitter lesson from that ill-conceived adventure. No, she would never climb so high again—

"Come along now," Francis said cheerfully. He had clambered nimbly up the ladder and was extending his hand. "I can raise the top if it rains"—he waved his free hand toward the increasingly threatening clouds—"but that isn't half such fun. Let us try at least to make it through the park with the roof open."

Bonnie gritted her teeth, gripped his hand, began to ascend the ladder, and—via another of Papa's miracles—safely reached the seat. Francis stowed the ladder and clucked the horses to a start, and they trotted up Duke Street and into Oxford.

How far she had come, Bonnie thought wryly as her terror subsided and she began to enjoy the ride. A little more than two weeks ago she had been observing the daily parade of the *ton* to Hyde Park. In fact, she recollected with a shock, she had walked down Orchard Street to Oxford; that ironic circumstance had not occurred to her before. Another twist of Fate.

At any rate, she was now ensconced in the very sort of vehicle she had so admired, and instead of gazing enviously up at the elegant passengers in the carriages, she was peering down at the pedestrians on the footpath. She glimpsed a young woman at the intersection of Oxford and Park—a girl carrying a portmanteau—and wondered if she, too, might be fleeing an unreasonable employer. Bonnie started to give her an encouraging smile, then remembered, with another jolt, that her own future was far from settled. If Aunt Grace refused to take her in, she might be standing at just this corner a few weeks hence. . .

But there was no point in dwelling on such a depressing contingency: Fate would have its inevitable way. So Bonnie smiled at the girl after all, and when she returned her eyes to the road, she saw that they were entering Hyde park. This might also be a once-in-a-lifetime experience, she reflected, and—emulating Francis' example—she bowed to or merely nodded toward the various carriages they passed.

They reached the house in Orchard Street at half past five, which was not a moment too soon, for fat drops of rain began to fall even as Francis shepherded Bonnie into the vestibule. Lady Hellier was seated at the rickety *bonheur-du-jour* desk in the library, pawing through an enormous sheaf of papers on the surface, but she jumped to her feet as they entered the room and rushed forward to greet them. After some ten minutes of happy clucking over her niece's astonishing recovery, she got to the point of her summons: with the assembly now only two days away, they must review *every detail* so as to ensure that the evening would be flawless. Bonnie stifled a sigh, removed her bonnet and gloves, and trailed her ladyship to the desk.

As Lady Hellier had indicated, the ensuing discussion was a review; they had covered every detail before, and many of them more than once. But Bonnie nodded politely as her ladyship leafed through her voluminous papers, and agreed again that the roses would be yellow and she would wear a yellow gown to match and they would serve sweetbreads and saddle of mutton for supper.

At length—at great length—Lady Hellier checked off the last item on the last sheet of paper, whereupon Bonnie learned that she had yet a further duty to perform: she must accompany her ladyship to the saloon and determine the arrangement of the furniture. She managed another nod, albeit a weary one, and trudged in Lady Hellier's wake up the stairs to the drawing room. Inasmuch as the saloon furniture was nearly as dilapidated as that in the library, Bonnie's honest opinion was that it should be hidden in the attic on the night of the ball. But she couldn't say so, of course, and she approved her ladyship's plan to move the Adam couch to the front wall and the mahogany sofa to the back . . .

"I believe that is it," Lady Hellier said brightly when the last piece of furniture had been accounted for. "And we finished just in time. Dinner will be served in five minutes."

"Then I certainly shan't trouble Francis to drive me home," Bonnie said. "If it wouldn't be too inconvenient, perhaps you could desire one of the grooms—"

"Nonsense!" her ladyship interposed. "I intended you to eat with us; your place is already set."

"No, thank you," Bonnie protested. "No, I really couldn't."

"Well, you cannot drive about in that." Lady Hellier gestured toward the window, and Bonnie heard the furious tattoo of rain on the glass. "I'm sure David would concur, but if you fear he will be worried, I shall send a message to Grosvenor Street.''

''No, Uncle David is at Brooks's—''

''It is settled then,'' her ladyship said firmly. ''You will dine here, and with any luck, the rain will end before we're done.''

She was trapped, Bonnie realized, repressing another sigh. It would, indeed, be absurd to set out in a driving rainstorm when nothing but a sandwich—a sandwich of her own making—awaited her at the other end of the journey. She reluctantly inclined her head and followed Lady Hellier back down the staircase and into the dining room.

Evidently Francis had also intended Bonnie to stay for dinner, for he met her just inside the archway and guided her to one of the threadbare chairs. Sir Robert, already seated at the head of the table, watched this proceeding with considerable puzzled interest, as though he was vainly attempting to recollect the identity of their mysterious guest.

''You do remember Bonnie?'' Lady Hellier prompted as she sank into her own chair. ''Cornelia's daughter? From Barbados?''

''Betty. Betty, of course. To your health, my dear.'' The baronet lifted the glass beside his plate, drained it, held it aloft. ''More brandy, Briscoe,'' he commanded.

''Briscoe is indisposed this evening,'' her ladyship snapped. ''You told me so yourself.''

Bonnie surmised that the butler was ''indisposed'' to approximately the same extent as Sir Robert himself, who was so foxed he could barely sit erect. But the attending footman obediently trotted to the table and refilled the baronet's glass, and Lady Hellier went on.

''You no doubt recall, Robert, that Bonnie suffered an accident last week. But she has fortunately recovered, and it is in her honor that we're conducting our ball Friday night.''

''Ball.'' Sir Robert frowned. ''Yes, I believe there was some mention of a ball.''

''Some mention!'' her ladyship screeched. ''I've been talking of nothing else since Monday . . .''

But she apparently decided she must start all over again, and she proceeded to describe the plans for the assembly in excruciating detail. The same plans Bonnie had heard twice or thrice or half a dozen times before, and in normal circumstances, she would have been fairly wild with boredom. As it was, however, she found it quite challenging to pretend to consume her food, which—from the watery broth at the start of the meal to the watery lemon pudding at the end—was uniformly inedible. She wondered if David would be comforted to learn that the Helliers were not expending undue sums for a cook. Perhaps she should warn him to steer well clear of his bilberry jelly.

". . . and I am confident the ball will be a grand success," Lady Hellier concluded as the pudding bowls were cleared away. "No, more than merely confident. I believe Bonnie will be so pleased that she'll permit me to arrange her wedding as well."

"Wedding!" Francis choked. "You are speaking somewhat prematurely, Mama."

Somewhat prematurely indeed, Bonnie thought dryly: she had yet to *meet* an eligible duke or marquis, and her ladyship was already planning the nuptial ceremony. She was more amused than embarrassed, but she appreciated Francis' concern for her feelings, and she flashed him a grateful smile.

"I believe the rain has stopped," Lady Hellier said, tilting one ear toward the dining-room window. "Just as I predicted it would." Her smug expression suggested that, far beyond predicting, she might well have *ordered* this improvement in the weather. "Have the phaeton brought back round, Nixon." She waved peremptorily at the footman, and he galloped out of the room. "And pray bid Bonnie a proper good-night, Robert."

"Umm?" The baronet shook his bald head, and Bonnie suspected he had dozed off long since.

"Bonnie is leaving," her ladyship said frostily.

"Umm, yes. To your health, my dear."

Sir Robert fumbled for his glass, but before his swollen

fingers could find the stem, his head began to droop again. With an apologetic smile of his own, Francis rose, assisted Bonnie out of her chair, and escorted her into the foyer. Lady Hellier retrieved her hat and gloves from the library, and as Bonnie tied her bonnet ribbons, Nixon opened the front door and announced that the carriage was ready.

Once she had conquered her fear, Bonnie had come quite to like the high-flyer, and the drive back to Grosvenor Street was especially pleasant. The clouds had blown over, leaving a full moon behind them, and in its brilliant light, the wet streets and houses fairly sparkled. Indeed, she rather regretted that the journey was so short, and when the carriage stopped in front of David's house, she gave Francis another appreciative smile.

"I thoroughly enjoyed our excursion," she said. She judged it best not to mention dinner. "Thank you for a lovely time."

"You are welcome," he mumbled.

Bonnie waited for him to position the ladder, but he did not. Instead, he continued to sit, staring straight ahead, and had he not been fumbling with his neckcloth, Bonnie might have collected that he had fallen asleep as well. But eventually he cleared his throat and turned in the seat to face her.

"I . . . I pray you will not feel that I am also speaking prematurely," he stammered. "When I tell you that despite the brevity of our acquaintance, I have grown most . . . most fond of you."

"I'm very fond of you too, Francis." She was speaking sincerely: whatever his mother's sins, Francis had been excessively kind.

"Yes, I dared to hope as much when you greeted me so warmly this afternoon. Were it not for that, I should have sought to postpone my . . . er . . ." He gulped. "Well, let me not hide my teeth. What I wish to say is that I . . . I am offering for your hand."

Bonnie was so startled that her head began to spin, and she briefly feared she would topple out of the carriage. She gripped the seat to steady herself and gazed at him in consternation, desperately groping for some sort of response.

"My hand?" she gasped at last. "Good God, Francis, I am your *cousin*."

"That presents no obstacle," he said eagerly. "The Regent himself is wed to his cousin."

"But . . . but I—"

"You needn't answer now." Francis awkwardly patted her shoulder. "Consider it for four-and-twenty hours, and we shall discuss it at Viscount Peyton's assembly tomorrow evening."

Bonnie wanted to tell him that there was nothing to consider, nothing to discuss, that her "fondness" in no way resembled love. Well, in no way resembled the emotion she had always fancied love to be. But even as she attempted to gather her wits, Francis secured the ladder, climbed out of the phaeton, and raised his hand to help her down. They crossed the footpath in silence, and when they reached the door, he smiled down at her. She feared for one awful moment that he intended to kiss her, but he merely doffed his hat, then opened the door; and she fled into the vestibule, slammed the door behind her, and collapsed against it.

Dear God! she inwardly moaned. Dear God, how had she got herself into such a bumblebath? She *had* been happy to see Francis, but she had never dreamed he would so utterly misinterpret her reaction. And now she had created the impression that she was actually considering his proposal . . . She spun around, threw the door back open, and peered into the street, but the carriage had disappeared. So it was too late to undo the damage yet tonight, and she crashed the door to again and dashed up the stairs, her mind churning rather faster than her feet.

Her initial inclination was to dispatch a note to Francis the first thing tomorrow morning; it would be cruel to keep him in suspense all day. But perhaps, she decided as she pounded down the first-floor corridor, it would be equally unkind to write a curt message of refusal and send Kimball to deliver it. Equally unkind and cowardly in the extreme. No, she owed it to Francis to decline his offer personally, and she could only hope that during the ensuing four-and-twenty hours she would find some gentle means of doing so.

Bonnie reached the second-floor landing and sagged against the newel post. Her frantic race up the stairs, added to the shock of Francis' proposal, had quite snatched her breath away, and rivulets of perspiration had begun to trickle down her brow. She tore off her bonnet, fanned her face a moment, then drew herself up.

"Where the deuce have you been?" David hissed.

Bonnie whirled toward the sound of his voice and saw him at the end of the hall, bathed in the lamplight splashing through the open door behind him.

"David!" she wheezed. "Thank God you are home." She flung her hat on the newel post and tottered down the corridor to his side. She had not realized how very weak she was, and she clutched his arm for support. "The most dreadful thing has happened—"

"I asked where you have been," he snapped, jerking his arm away. "I returned at six, and Nell assured me you would be back in ample time for dinner."

"I did plan to be back, but—"

"As it was," he interrupted coldly, "I was compelled to dine alone."

"And was that my fault?"

A rhetorical question. Of course he thought it was her fault: he invariably twisted events in such a way as to put her in the wrong. Bonnie clenched her hands and swallowed a sudden maddening lump in her throat.

"I planned to come back in time for dinner," she reiterated as levelly as she could, "but it seemed foolish to do so. You had told Nell you'd be eating at Brooks's, and I had told her to prepare nothing for me, and it was pouring rain. In the circumstances, I perceived no harm in accepting Lady Hellier's invitation to dine with them."

"And you were quite right." The earl sketched a sardonic smile. "In the circumstances you describe, there would have been no harm. Had I remained at Brooks's, I should never have discovered your latest deception.''

"My latest deception," Bonnie echoed wearily. "I presume you are suggesting that I deliberately plotted to visit Lady Hellier in secret. You no doubt believe she and I are scheming to make the ball as grand and expensive as possible. We did, in fact, discuss the assembly, and you may draw from that whatever conclusions you will. I am tired of arguing the point." She was dangerously near to tears, and she bit her lip and started to step away.

"I wasn't referring to the ball." David's fingers snaked around her wrist, drawing her to a halt. "I was referring to your statement that you were too unwell to go to Almack's this evening."

"I did not make that statement!" The tears had begun to sting her eyelids—tears of impotent rage—and she blinked them furiously away. "*You* pronounced me too unwell to go to Almack's. And had you not left the house at the very crack of dawn this morning, I could have told you I'd recovered."

"I returned early from my club." As so often happened, he had altogether ignored her protest. "Expecting to find you literally bedridden and sorely in need of companionship. I found, instead, that you and Francis were disporting yourselves gaily about the town."

"I shan't argue that point either." Bonnie snatched her wrist from his grasp. "Nor shall I listen to any more of your baseless accusations. If you will excuse me—"

"No, I will not excuse you." His voice was as brittle and chill as ice. "And you will listen to one thing more. A question. I should like to know how Judith's other project is progressing."

Bonnie was briefly at a loss to conceive what other project he meant, but at length, it came to her. "It has not progressed at all," she said. "Lady Hellier has yet to present me to a duke or marquis either one."

"Spare me your innocence, Bonnie." Even in the dim glow of the lamplight, the earl's eyes glittered like great blue jewels. "I did initially suppose that Judith would contrive to wed you to some such exalted person, but I was wrong, was I not? She has no duke or marquis in mind for her wealthy niece. She is plotting to wed you to *Francis*."

Bonnie began to grow dizzy again. Not with shock this time—she recognized at once that he was right—but with astonishment that she had failed to perceive the situation herself. Of course Lady Hellier would attempt to wed her to Francis. It was the perfect solution to her ladyship's dilemma: with one stroke, she could ensure that her son would inherit David's estate and lay her greedy hands on Thomas Carlisle's mythical fortune as well. Indeed, Bonnie now recalled, Francis had hinted as much just before he stammered out his proposal. Yes, he had said that were it not for her fervent greeting, he would have "sought to" postpone his offer—the offer Lady Hellier was obviously urging him to tender.

"And evidently the project has your enthusiastic endorsement," David continued. "Or so I collect from the shameless manner in which you are throwing yourself at Francis' head."

Throwing herself at Francis? The earl's charge was so abrupt, so absurd, that Bonnie was struck quite speechless.

"You went to Lady Cunningham's assembly with the specific objective of chatting cozily with him all evening." David went relentlessly on. "Thinking to claim your ankle was still too weak to permit you to dance with anyone else. But I insisted you leave, and while I was summoning Kimball, you told Francis you would decline to go to Almack's tonight. Leaving you free to dine with him."

He had distorted the facts so grotesquely that Bonnie couldn't decide which of his allegations to counter first. Should she remind him that when he was summoning the carriage, she had assumed he would be home this evening? That he had not announced his intention of playing macao at Brooks's till they were halfway back to Grosvenor Street? Remind him, again, that it was he who had proposed they wait until next week to go to Almack's?

She parted her lips, still not certain what she planned to

say, and in the event, no words came. In the event, the tears which had been lurking in her throat, hiding just behind her eyelids, burst forth, and she dissolved in a fit of weeping. She would not let him watch her cry, she thought fiercely, would not give him that satisfaction, and she spun around and began to run down the corridor.

"Bonnie!"

She shook her head and stumbled on, and he caught her as she reached the staircase, seizing her elbow with such force that she fell against him.

"Good God, I didn't mean to make you cry. Hush now; there's a good girl. Please, Bonnie, I can't bear it."

His arms were around her, her face buried in his chest, and her sobs subsided first to little gasps and then to sniffles, and eventually the sniffles died away. And it was then, when they stood in silence, that she became suddenly, intensely aware of his nearness. She could feel the beat of his heart against her, the stir of his breath in her hair, and she experienced a sensation she had never known before. Not the warm well-being she had felt when he carried her up the stairs—though there was some of that as well—but a peculiar weakness in her knees and a sweet, throbbing ache in her midsection.

His arms tightened, pulled her so close she could scarcely breathe, and she raised her head and found his eyes upon her, eyes that seemed blue-black in the shadows of the corridor. He stared at her for an endless moment, then released her and hurriedly stepped away.

"Go to bed now," he said hoarsely. "We shall discuss the matter tomorrow."

He turned and strode back down the hall, and Bonnie retrieved her hat from the newel post and walked unsteadily in the opposite direction.

11

*B*onnie woke with a vague, indefinable sense of apprehension, but even as she lowered her feet to the carpet, she remembered the cause. *Causes*, she amended grimly: David and Francis by name. Both had declared an intention to "discuss" matters with her today, and the prospect filled her with dread. She glanced at the bellpull beside the bed, then shook her head. She needed an interval to think, and she would be unable to do so with Nell bustling about the room and reporting the latest neighborhood *on-dits*. She rose and trudged to the dressing table, sat down and began idly to brush her hair.

Her discussion with David would be much the more unpleasant of the two, Bonnie judged. Infinitely more unpleasant, for at some juncture, she must advise him of Francis' proposal, and she could scarcely bear to contemplate the earl's reaction. In his present frame of mind, he would surely conclude that she had somehow enticed Francis to offer for her hand. And when—if—she succeeded in persuading him otherwise, how was she to explain her failure to render an immediate answer? He would never believe she had been struck literally dumb with shock; he would assume, as Francis had, that she had wanted to deliberate the matter.

Yes, the conversation would be unpleasant in the extreme,

and Bonnie fancied she would do almost anything to avoid it.
Might well sell her soul if she didn't have to tell him . . .

But she did not have to tell him. The realization came so
suddenly that Bonnie dropped her hairbrush and gazed wide-
eyed at her reflection in the glass. Not this morning at any
rate. The time to inform David of Francis' proposal was after
she'd refused it; he need never know she had waited four-and-
twenty hours to do so. And a postponement of the discussion
would resolve yet another problem: once she declined to wed
Francis, he would cease his attentions. The earl would consequently forget his ludicrous charge that she had thrown herself at his nephew's head, and within a few days—a week
perhaps—he would receive the news of Francis' offer with
perfect equanimity.

Bonnie's mirrored image nodded its approval of this reasoning, and she reluctantly turned her attention to Francis.
Their conversation could not be delayed beyond this evening,
but as she thought on it, her dread began to subside. She was
inclined to believe that Francis was genuinely fond of her; she
doubted even the formidable Lady Hellier could persuade her
son to marry a woman he did not care for at all. But Bonnie
equally doubted that Francis had fallen over head and ears in
love with the alleged cousin he scarcely knew, and she suspected he would be more relieved than disappointed when
she rejected his proposal. She would take care not to wound
his pride, of course . . . Her reflection bobbed its head in
eager agreement to this plan as well, and she jumped up, sped
to the wardrobe, and donned her peach-colored morning dress.

Bonnie had entertained a distant hope that David might
already have left for the day, but he was still seated in the
breakfast parlor when she reached it. Though he had apparently finished eating, she observed: he had pushed his plate
aside and was leafing through a copy of *The Times*. She
paused in the entry to watch him, her cheeks warming with the
memory of their embrace.

Embrace, she chided herself. What an absurd notion.
Papa had held her just that way a hundred times, permitting

her to sob out her childhood agonies against the buttons of his waistcoat. Well, not quite that way, she corrected. She had never been aware of Papa's heartbeat or his breathing, had never felt that strange, delicious ache—

"You may come in," the earl growled, raising his eyes from the paper. "I shan't bite you."

He had caught her unawares again, and Bonnie started and hurried to the sideboard. Since she had eaten virtually no dinner, she fancied she should be ravenous, but the mere sight of the eggs and bacon and simmering kidneys set her stomach to churning. After some deliberation, she took a single muffin and one pat of butter and sank into the chair across from David's.

"Shall I order you a cup of chocolate?" he asked gruffly. "You can hardly survive on that." He frowned at her plate.

"No, thank you. I am not very hungry." She broke the muffin in two and began to apply butter to the smaller half.

"I wasn't hungry either."

David gestured toward his own plate, and Bonnie saw that it was, in fact, still heaped with food. The earl was silent a moment, but at length, he laid his newspaper on the table and cleared his throat.

"I daresay we both remain somewhat overset about the . . . ah . . events which occurred last night."

Bonnie's knife slipped through her muffin and came to rest on her palm. Fortunately, the knife was not sharp, and the only casualty was the muffin, which had disintegrated to a pile of crumbs.

"I now own . . ." David emitted another cough. "I now own that certain of my remarks were unjust. As I reviewed the circumstances, I came to recognize that you did not arrange to dine with Francis before you left Lady Cunningham's ball. I am sorry to have . . . have distressed you by suggesting you had."

Bonnie hadn't dared to dream he would actually apologize, and her bones fairly dissolved with relief. "That is all right," she murmured.

"However," he continued, "I count it only fair to remind you that you did deceive me."

"Deceived you?" she said sharply, her relief evaporating.

"Perhaps 'misled' would be a better word; call it what you will. You created the impression that you were too unwell to leave the house, and I altered my schedule accordingly. Whereupon I learned that you were *not* too unwell to go out with Francis."

"But I explained last night—"

"I don't wish to discuss it any further." The earl waved her to silence. "I simply wish you to know that I shall be prodigious overset indeed if you deceive me again in future. Deceive or mislead me either one. I trust you will not."

He had, as usual, twisted the facts to his own advantage, but Bonnie bit back an angry retort. They were at relative peace, and it would be excessively foolish to rekindle his wrath. "No," she muttered. "No, I shall not."

"Excellent. Now what was the dreadful thing you alluded to last evening?"

Dreadful thing? Bonnie knit her brows in puzzlement, then recollected that she had started to tell him of Francis' offer. Which was now out of the question, of course, and she groped for a credible reply.

"It . . . it was more embarrassing than dreadful," she stammered at last. "Briscoe was so jug-bitten he had taken to his bed, and Sir Robert was scarcely better off. Indeed, he fell asleep at table—Sir Robert, that is—and it was most . . . most disconcerting."

Her words rang false even in her own ears, but David nodded.

"It is hardly the first time," he said sardonically. "But I well understand that it might appear dreadful to one unfamiliar with their conduct." He tossed his napkin next to the newspaper and stood up. "I assume you are sufficiently recovered to attend Viscount Peyton's assembly tonight?"

"Yes," Bonnie mumbled.

"Then pray be ready to depart at half past eight. I should

guess, based on prior experience, that it will be the largest rout of the Season.''

He bowed and strode out of the room, and Bonnie gazed miserably in his wake. She *had* deceived him now, deceived him quite deliberately, and she shuddered to ponder the consequences if he discovered her lie. But how was he to discover it? Francis wouldn't mention his unsuccessful suit to David or anyone else. Whatever the degree of his affection, Francis' male conceit alone would impel him to keep the rejected proposal a secret.

Bonnie buttered the undamaged half of her muffin, but she could not quell a nagging inkling that there was some flaw in her logic. Her stomach began to churn again, and she returned the muffin to her plate and crept back to her bedchamber.

It was not until she was dressing for the ball that Bonnie perceived the elusive error in her reasoning: Lady Hellier. Eager as she was to wed her son to his fictional cousin, her ladyship would naturally have demanded an accounting of his conversation with Bonnie the instant he returned to Orchard Street. She would have collected, as Francis had, that Bonnie was considering the offer; and so long as she was laboring under this misapprehension, she might well remark on the proposal in David's hearing. Therefore, Bonnie concluded, it was imperative for her to speak with Francis at the earliest opportunity, and she rushed to the vestibule at twenty-five past eight and impatiently waited for the earl to appear.

David arrived at half past eight precisely, but he brought with him the grim news that their departure was to be delayed. There was a problem with the barouche, he said, and though he went on to explain the malfunction in exhaustive detail, Bonnie registered only that it had something to do with one of the wheels. Kimball had been working on the carriage all day, but he had completed the repair just ten minutes since, and he now must hitch the horses . . . She gritted her teeth in a fair frenzy of frustration, and at ten minutes before nine, Kimball opened the front door and announced that the vehicle was ready.

The earl had mentioned that Viscount Peyton's home was located in Curzon Street, and Bonnie was initially at a loss to comprehend why the barouche came to a halt at the intersection of South Audley and Mount. She leaned forward, thinking to urge Kimball to hurry, and glimpsed a line of carriages before them extending as far as the eye could see.

"It is as I predicted." David sighed. "An utter rout. I sometimes suspect Peyton of inviting every beggar in the street to his assemblies so he can claim the dubious distinction of conducting the largest gathering of the Season."

"Perhaps we should go round the other way," Bonnie said nervously. "By Berkeley Street and Piccadilly."

"That route will be no less crowded." The earl shook his head. "No, there is nothing for it but to wait our turn. I assure you the festivities will continue into the small hours of the morning."

Bonnie once more surveyed the endless line of carriages and wondered if she should suggest they abandon the barouche altogether and proceed on foot. A walk would require under ten minutes, she calculated, but even as she parted her lips to point this out, she realized that such a suggestion would seem peculiar in the extreme. So she closed her mouth and began to pick imaginary specks of lint from the yellow satin roses around the bottom of her skirt.

Bonnie estimated that some forty-five minutes had elapsed when the barouche rolled to a stop in the general vicinity of Lord Peyton's door. The scene outside the house much resembled her notion of a riot, and she could not but remember the unfortunate occasion, some years earlier, when Carlton House had been opened to the public and four women had been trampled to death in the universal eagerness to be first through the gate. Indeed, it briefly appeared *she* would be trampled to death by the throng on the footpath, but David somehow propelled her safely up the front steps, through the door, and across the foyer to the bottom of the staircase.

Bonnie craned her neck and peered up the stairs, but she did not spy any of the Hellier party ahead. Nor would it have

signified if she did, she realized, for she couldn't possibly
have made her way through the crowd to speak with Francis.
No, she would simply have to search for him the moment she
entered the drawing room. Which could not be long; they had
already ascended three risers . . .

But the assembly was not being held in the saloon, Bonnie
saw as they rounded the first-floor landing. The corridor was
jammed with guests all the way to the end, and she surmised
there was a ballroom on the second story. Up still another
flight of steps. Good God. The press of bodies had rendered
her monstrous warm, and she opened her ivory fan and
waved it about her face.

A long-case clock was situated on the second-floor landing, and it was chiming half past ten when she and David
reached it. Bonnie was genuinely faint by now—her knees
trembling with a toxic blend of hunger and heat and appre-
henson—and she sagged against the earl as they inched their
way toward the ballroom entry. At least, she comforted herself, there would no lengthy receiving line. David had also
mentioned that Viscount Peyton, like the earl himself, was a
bachelor.

But she was wrong in this respect as well, for Lord Peyton
had obviously recruited all his female relatives to hostess his
grand assembly. Well, perhaps not *all* of them, Bonnie
amended: she was not familiar with his lordship's entire
family history. She only knew with certainty that she was
compelled to greet the viscount's widowed mother, three
sisters, two sisters-in-law, and several cousins; and to assure
each of them that theirs was by far the loveliest ball she had
been privileged to attend since her arrival from Barbados.

David was behind her in the line, and as he murmured his
compliments to the last of the cousins, Bonnie gaze despairingly round the ballroom. It was veritable sea of people, and
she could not conceive why Lord Peyton had troubled himself
to engage an orchestra. The musicians were seated on an
elevated platform at one end of the room, bravely sawing
away at their instruments, but their efforts were quite drowned

by the roar of conversation. Not that it mattered, for there
was no space in which to dance. In fact, there was scarcely
space to *move*, and Bonnie began to doubt she would ever
locate Francis. The earl stepped to her side, and at that
moment, she spotted the Helliers perhaps twenty feet away.

"There they are!" she said brightly. "Lady Hellier and Sir
Robert and Francis, I mean. We must bid them good evening."

"We *must* do nothing of the kind," David snapped. "To
the contrary, we can readily claim we failed to see them in the
crowd."

Bonnie had not anticipated this complication, but even as
she groped for an objection, Lady Hellier waved her hand
frantically in their direction. "Well, they have now seen us."
She tried to sound regretful. "So let us greet them at once,
and then we shan't have to speak with them again."

The earl snorted with exasperation, but before he could
voice another protest, Bonnie seized his elbow and tugged
him ahead. She would never have imagined that it could
require nearly ten minutes to traverse a distance of twenty
feet, but in the event, she judged them lucky to complete the
journey at all. Viscount Peyton's guests were packed literally
shoulder to shoulder, cheek by jowl; and when she and David
reached the Helliers at last, Bonnie glanced down at her satin
slippers. As she had feared, they were in ruins—trodden on
so many times that they were nearer black then white. She
sagged against the earl again, panting for breath, and once
more fanned her face.

"What a mob!" Lady Hellier shouted above the ceaseless
din around them. "I should not permit half these people to
darken my door."

"A mob indeed!" Sir Robert bellowed. "I have been
waiting upwards of an hour for my first glass of champagne! I
note that footmen are circulating on the *other* side of the
room. I told you, Judith, that we should go to the left . . ."

The baronet ranted on, and Bonnie drew herself shakily up
and assessed the situation. She was standing immediately beside Francis, but she had recognized long since that they

could not converse in the carnival atmosphere of Lord Peyton's
ballroom. They would have to repair to the corridor or to one
of the lower floors, and she discreetly plucked his sleeve.

"I must talk to you," she whispered.

"Eh?" He bent toward her, cupping his ear. "What was
that?"

"I said . . ."

But the din was not ceaseless after all; as often happened in
large groups, everyone seemed to drop his voice at the same
instant. Even Sir Robert's tirade had sputtered to a close, and
in the relative hush, Bonnie calculated that her next words
would be readily audible.

"I said," she finished lamely, "that it is most uncomfortably crowded."

"That it is." Lady Hellier emitted a sniff of disdain. "And
as I indicated, I should not permit half these people in my
home. You may be assured, dear"—she gave Bonnie one of
her chilly smiles—"that while our assembly will be smaller,
it will be vastly more elegant . . ."

She continued in this vein, and as she did so, the level of
noise in the ballroom once more swelled to a roar. Her
ladyship was compelled to raise her voice higher and higher,
and at length, when she was virtually screaming, Bonnie
judged it safe to tweak Francis' sleeve again.

"I must speak with you," she hissed.

"I cannot hear you!"

Francis shook his head and apologetically spread his hands,
and Bonnie's eyes darted round the room. They were situated
close to a wall, she saw; and perhaps, if she could maneuver
Francis to the nearest corner, it would be sufficiently quiet to
convey at least the gist of her message—

". . . and I fancy we shall have a happy announcement for
our guests!" Lady Hellier shrieked in conclusion.

"Announcement?" David yelled. "What announcement?"

Announcement. Dear God. Bonnie had not considered this
contingency, and as she clenched her hands in horror, she
distantly chided herself for her obtuseness. Her ladyship had

probably planned from the outset to announce their engagement at her assembly. No, there was no "probably" about it: in view of her ultimate objective, she would not have wished to introduce her niece into society. Another of those peculiar hushes descended over the ballroom, and Bonnie clearly heard the snap of her fan splintering to pieces beween her fingers.

"Did Bonnie not tell you?" Lady Hellier said.

The earl frowned in puzzlement, and Bonnie struggled to collect her wits. Fortunately, the background noise had erupted again—had, if possible, reached yet a higher pitch—and she drew David's head down and placed her lips directly against his ear.

"She is referring to the announcement that I am your long-lost colonial relative," she whispered. "She intends it to be very dramatic. Very . . . very happy."

"Umm." He raised his head and nodded.

"So we *are* to have an announcement!" Her ladyship beamed with delight. "There remains but to decide who is to make it. And since you are the head of the family, David—"

The party just behind them burst into raucous laughter, and Lady Hellier stopped and peered irritably over her shoulder. She must remove the earl from the scene at once, Bonnie thought wildly, before the discussion could proceed. She would advise him she had suddenly taken ill, which—inasmuch as her knees were fairly knocking together and her stomach lurching with panic—was far from being a lie. She turned toward him and detected a disturbance at their left; evidently someone was attempting to force his way through the crowd.

"David?"

To force *her* way through the crowd, Bonnie amended; it was a female voice. Miss Elwell or Miss Godwin, no doubt, and she repressed an hysterical inclination to laugh. Maybe it was fitting that she should be rescued by one of his lordship's barques of frailty. The top of the woman's head became visible, and Bonnie observed that she was wearing a leghorn hat. Apparently, she reflected dryly, Mrs. Pruitt had not adequately explained the type of attire appropriate to a *ton* assembly.

The woman forged doggedly ahead, and in the crush, her bonnet slipped from her head and came to rest on her shoulders. Her hair was red, Bonnie saw, the same pale red as her own. Except that it was streaked with gray, like Lady Hellier's . . . Bonnie's heart crashed into her throat, and she desperately assured herself that she was wrong. It could not be—

"Cornelia!" David gasped.

"Cornelia!" Lady Hellier choked.

"David!" She bounded the last few feet to his side and hurled herself against him. "David!" She stood back and fondly studied his face. "It really is my little brother, all grown up!" She glanced past him. "And Judith," she said, her tone unmistakably cooling. "And Robert." It cooled a bit further. "And is this your son?" Her sapphire eyes moved to Francis.

"Yes, ma'am." He reached out and wrung her hand, much as he had Bonnie's on the occasion of their first meeting. "Francis."

"Francis."

Cornelia nodded, then transferred her eyes to Bonnie, and Bonnie braced herself for the inevitable moment of exposure. Perhaps, she thought philosophically, it was for the best. Once she learned the truth, Lady Hellier would abandon any notion of an engagement, and the earl need never know he had been deceived.

"And here is my own dear Bonnie." Cornelia stepped forward and spread her arms. "Come now, child. Haven't you a word of welcome for your mother?"

The outstretched arms closed around her, pulled her close, and Bonnie felt Cornelia's breath in her ear.

"Nell told me what you are at," she whispered rapidly, "and I shall play my part. But I suggest we leave immediately lest we confuse our stories."

"Y-yes," Bonnie whispered back.

Cornelia released her and smiled round the group. "I was so eager to see you that I couldn't bear to wait till the end of the assembly. However, I now discover myself quite exhausted from my journey. So perhaps, David, I could prevail on you and Bonnie to drive me home.''

"So soon?'' Lady Hellier snapped. ''You've scarcely arrived. You have not even had an opportunity to hear of Bonnie's—''

"I shall tell Mama all about the ball!'' Bonnie interposed shrilly. ''Please do let us hurry, Uncle David. Mama is sorely in need of her rest.''

In point of fact, Cornelia seemed possessed of considerably more energy than Bonnie herself, and it was she who took the lead as they struck out across the ballroom. The crowd had thinned a bit, Bonnie observed—it took them only a few minutes to reach the entry—but she soon discovered that the guests had dispersed to other parts of the house. There was a great throng in the saloon, which was serving as a refreshment parlor, and the ground story was crammed with people evidently seeking relief from the crush on the floors above. Indeed, Bonnie saw when they stepped outside, many had carried their search for fresh air beyond the confines of the house; the front steps and the footpath were nearly as crowded as they had been when she and David arrived. Sufficiently crowded, at least, that it was impossible to conduct a private conversation, and they stood in silence while one of Viscount Peyton's servants summoned the barouche.

"Is that Lady Cornelia?'' Kimball gasped, gaping down from the box.

"None other,'' she responded cheerfully. ''But pray drive us out of this bedlam, Kimball. We shall talk at home.''

Bonnie fancied that the ''bedlam'' of Lord Peyton's rout might well be audible for miles around, but as they turned from Curzon Street into South Audley, the roar behind them faded to a mere buzz. Cornelia untied the ribbons of her hat, which was still flapping round her shoulders, removed it, set it in her lap, and burst into laughter.

"Good God, David. I said inside that you were all grown up, but I am compelled to wonder. You are approaching forty years of age, and I find you still perpetrating your pranks.''

"It is hardly a *prank*." He sounded most indignant, but as the carriage rolled beneath a streetlamp, Bonnie detected the flash of his winsome grin. "Did Nell not explain the circumstances of our charade?"

"I granted her no chance," Cornelia confessed. "As soon as she advised me where you were, I set out for the assembly."

"Which was an excessively foolish thing to do," the earl said severely. "Had Judith and Robert started posing questions about your life in Barbados, we should have been in a wretched hobble indeed."

"Perhaps it was foolish, but I truly could not wait another moment to see you. I've missed you, David. I've missed you every day for five-and-twenty years."

"I've missed you as well." His voice was rough, and he elaborately cleared his throat. "And even if your arrival had destroyed our project, I should have been deuced glad to see you."

"Yes, the project." Cornelia cleared her own throat. "As I said, I gave Nell no opportunity to explain. She had time only to warn me that you had engaged a young woman to pose as my daughter." She patted Bonnie's knee. "I should guess it has to do with your estate."

"So it does. Judith and Robert have been spending Francis' inheritance somewhat prematurely . . ." He described several of their more flagrant transgressions, then the fortuitous meeting with Bonnie which had prompted him to invent a niece.

"Dear Judith." Cornelia emitted a wry chuckle. "I collect she hasn't changed a whit. I still judge it a prank, David, but I shall be delighted to abet it. Tell me the details you and Bonnie have concocted."

"I shall do so later. First you must tell me how you've fared through the years. Why the devil didn't you write?"

"Because I did not want Tom to suppose I regretted the life I had left behind. And I didn't, David. Much as I missed you, I did not regret my marriage for an instant."

"You speak in the past tense," he said gently. "Is Tom . . . ?"

"Dead." She nodded. "He died of fever six months since."

"I am sorry," David murmured.

"Do not be sorry. We had almost twenty-five good years together, and I daresay that's twenty-five more than Judith has had with Robert. Good years and prosperous ones; he left me exceedingly well-fixed. That is ironic, is it not? That Tom and I should grow wealthy while Judith and Robert slid to the very brink of poverty? I wish Papa could know."

A note of bitterness had crept into her voice, but before she could say anything further, the carriage stopped in front of David's house. As Kimball leapt down from the box, Nell and Alice flew out the door and down to the footpath; and Bonnie feared that the three servants between them might well suffocate Cornelia with the enthusiasm of their welcome. But at length, simultaneously laughing and weeping, they shepherded her up the steps and into the vestibule.

"Are you too tired to relate your adventures yet tonight?" David asked.

"To the contrary; you could not prevent me. And then I must hear everything that has happened at Sedgewood since my departure."

David inclined his head and beckoned them toward the library, but they all began to chatter in unison before they reached the doorway. "You do recollect Josh . . ." ". . . and Lady Amanda has *three* grandchildren . . ." ". . . and the stable was struck by lightning, but luckily . . ."

She had no place in their reunion, Bonnie thought. Nor could she afford to sit up half the night and risk sleeping till noon again. Cornelia's arrival had snatched her from the jaws of disaster, but she could not continue to trust to Fate. No, she must rise early in the morning and go to Orchard Street and advise Francis that she did not intend to wed him. The happy voices in the library rose, and she crept across the foyer and up the staircase.

12

The long-case clock chimed twice as Bonnie reached the vestibule, and a glance at the face confirmed her surmise that it was only half past seven. Far too early to call on Francis, but she had wakened at first light and been unable to fall back to sleep. She shifted her gaze to the front door, reflecting that a leisurely walk to Orchard Street would be most refreshing, but the indelicate rumble of her stomach reminded her that she had eaten almost nothing during the preceding six-and-thirty hours. She sighed, laid her bonnet and gloves on the pier table, and strode through the dining room to the breakfast parlor. She had expected to find it empty, but Cornelia was seated at the table, reading the newspaper as she ate.

Not *Cornelia*, Bonnie chided herself, pausing at the entry. In her conversations with the earl, she had employed his name for his sister, but it would be excessively rude to address her in such familiar fashion.

"Good morning, Mrs. Carlisle," she said.

"Mrs. Carlisle?" She looked up and emitted a disdainful snort. "Nonsense! If I cannot be your mother, I can surely be your friend. You are to call me by my Christian name; I shall answer to nothing else. Now serve yourself and sit down, and let us chat."

Bonnie nodded and proceeded to the sideboard, but as had

happened the morning before, the sight of the food quite destroyed her appetite. However, she fancied she must try to eat something, and she took a spoonful of scrambled eggs, one rasher of bacon, and a scone. Cornelia eyed this meager meal with considerable interest, and Bonnie anticipated some sort of reproof. But—though she could not conceive why—she thought she detected the twitch of a smile at the corners of Cornelia's mouth.

"I did not suppose you would be up so early," Bonnie said, spreading her napkin in her lap. "I assumed you would sit up half the night with David and the servants."

"So I did." Cornelia nodded. "But I've risen before dawn every morning for nearly twenty-five years, and one does not break such a habit in the space of a few weeks. The wealth I alluded to last evening did not come as a gift from heaven. Tom and I worked our fingers to the bone for every groat."

She was folding the paper as she spoke, and Bonnie observed that, indeed, her hands were red and rough and her fingernails broken to the merest stubs. Not at all like Lady Hellier's smooth hands and long, perfectly manicured nails. Nor was that the only difference between the sisters, Bonnie saw, surreptitiously studying Cornelia through her lashes. She had registered last night, when Cornelia embraced her, that they were almost precisely the same height, but she now estimated that Cornelia outweighed her and Lady Hellier alike by some two stone. Which was not to say that she was plump; she could better be described as . . . Bonnie groped for the proper adjective and eventually selected *strong*; Cornelia had the sturdy body of a farmer's wife. And the skin: her face and neck had been burned brown by decades of exposure to the sun, and there was a rash of freckles across her nose.

"In point of fact," Cornelia said, "I was up till almost four. The servants retired at half past one, but after they left, I continued to talk with David. It was a most instructive conversation." Her lips twitched again. "I collect that you and he have had your . . . ah . . . differences."

"Differences?" Bonnie echoed. Was that how the earl had described their numerous bitter arguments? She risked a tiny bite of egg, but the actual taste of food unsettled her stomach even further. She choked the bite down and began chopping the rest of the egg into little pieces.

"Differences stemming from your inexcusable conduct." Cornelia once more inclined her head. "As I understand the situation, you have taken the most shameless advantage of David to launch a search for a husband. Upon the occasion of your first public appearance, you flirted outrageously with any number of eligible young men, and shortly thereafter, you prevailed on Judith to give you a debut. However, you have subsequently fallen in with her scheme to wed you to Francis."

"You . . . you believe that?" Bonnie stammered.

"Of course I do not believe it!" Cornelia issued another sniff. "David is obviously . . . ."

She stopped, and Bonnie surmised that she, too, was seeking just the right word. But when she went on, it was in an entirely different vein.

"At any rate, I reiterated my assurance that I should lend your project my full cooperation. Naturally, since you created the impression that your father is still alive, we cannot tell Judith and Robert of Tom's death."

Bonnie had not considered this complication, and she shook her head in protest. "No, that would be most unfair. I can't ask you to behave as though nothing were amiss."

"You are speaking of outward behavior, dear, which is altogether unimportant. I have mourned Tom in my heart every day since he died, and I daresay I shall continue to do so for as long as I live. But he would not have wanted me in black gloves."

Bonnie glanced from Cornelia's face to her attire and noted that her old-fashioned morning dress was a brilliant azure blue.

"No," Cornelia said, "it will not overset me in the least to pretend that Tom is still alive. I did not come back to England to find a second husband. Someday, after I return to Barbados, I shall write to Judith and advise her very sorrowfully that Tom has expired."

"Return?" Bonnie repeated sharply. "I had presumed you intended to remain here."

"Good God, no! I was wild to see David, and I hope we can exchange visits in future. But my life is in the Indies."

"Do you have children?" Bonnie asked. "I neglected to inquire last night."

"No, that was the one great sorrow of our marriage. But I've a host of friends in Barbados, and their children and grandchildren are nearly like my own. So I shall stay a few months—through the summer, I think—and then sail happily back to my sunshine and my palm trees."

"A few months!" Bonnie's fork slid through her fingers and clattered onto her plate. "Then perhaps . . ." She swallowed her burgeoning excitement. "David must have explained that we planned for me to return to Barbados at the end of the Season. To disappear, that is. So maybe, now you're here, we could . . . could coordinate our departures."

"You would be willing to extend your impersonation till the end of the summer?" Cornelia raised her brows. "I should have assumed you'd be eager to escape David's clutches."

"Not exactly eager," Bonnie mumbled. She snatched her knife from the tablecloth and began dissecting her scone.

"No? How very peculiar. One might almost infer that despite your many differences, you've grown rather fond of my brother."

Fond. Bonnie sifted the word through her mind. She had judged herself to be fond of Francis, but she was not troubled by the prospect that they would soon part and never meet again. There was none of the deep, raw pain she felt when she contemplated her permanent separation from the earl. But perhaps, she decided, language was simply inadequate to distinguish among the various degrees of "fondness."

"I suppose I have," she rejoined aloud. "Though I cannot

imagine why. He is the most difficult person I have ever
met—the very soul of kindness one instant and an irrational
tyrant the next. I am sure he does not treat his male friends so
cavalierly, or he would *have* no male friends. But he seeems
to hold women in utter contempt. It is excessively puzzling.''

"It is not at all puzzling in view of his background,"
Cornelia said. "Recollect that I was nine when David was
born, and Mama was nearing forty. She and Papa had de-
spaired of ever having a son, and they regarded David's
arrival as a miracle. They coddled and pampered him from
the day of his birth—they, the servants, even Judith and I. It
is scarcely surprising he developed the notion that he was
vastly superior to his sisters. His sisters and, by extension,
every other female in the world."

"But *all* men have that notion," Bonnie said dryly. "That
they are superior to women, I mean. It does not prevent them
from wedding."

"True." Cornelia nodded. "Keep in mind, however, that
David was fearfully spoiled. Raised to believe that his needs
and desires transcended those of anyone else. In short, to put
it candidly, he was simply too selfish to marry." She hesitated for a long moment. "Until now," she added at last.

"Until now?" Bonnie frowned. "You think he has
changed?"

"I think he has been forced to change. Or shortly will be."

Cornelia looked expectantly across the table, but Bonnie
could make no sense of her statement. Her frown deepened,
and Cornelia burst into laughter.

"My dear child! Can you possibly be so obtuse? Have you
not perceived that David is hopelessly in love with you?"

"In . . . in . . ." Bonnie's knife crashed to her plate
beside her fork.

"Did it not occur to you to wonder why he is so distressed
by the prospect that you might wed someone else?" Cornelia's voice seemed to come from very far away. "So prodigious overset that he bitterly resents any man who pays you

the slightest attention? I started to say earlier that he is obviously suffering an advanced case of jealousy.''

She peered once more across the table, as if to elicit Bonnie's concurrence, but Bonnie was literally frozen with shock.

"I did not say it earlier,'' Cornelia went on, "because I wished first to ascertain *your* position. I shouldn't have wanted to . . . to embarrass David if you did not care for him in turn. But it is clear that you love him as well.''

How could it not have been clear to her? Bonnie marveled distantly. Of course she loved him. She had loved him from the very beginning, from the instant she'd gazed into his face and thought him to be an angel. Her lips thawed, and she parted them, but no words came. She could only gape at Cornelia—her jaw sagging and her eyes wide with astonishment.

"You must not suppose me a Gypsy soothsayer.'' Cornelia had evidently misinterpreted her expression. "I daresay I should soon have divined the truth for myself, but in the event, I had a good deal of assistance from Nell.''

"Nell,'' Bonnie croaked. She had finally found her tongue.

"Yes. I dissembled a bit about the conversation we conducted before I left for the assembly. After she warned me that a young woman was posing as my daughter, she pronounced her opinion that 'Mr. David' and 'Miss Bonnie' had fallen over head and ears in love. An opinion based on her observation that neither of you was eating as much as you should.''

She glanced at Bonnie's plate and chuckled. "Dear Nell. Appetite had always been her sole measure of the human condition.'' She stopped chuckling and regarded Bonnie with concern. "Are you all right?''

"Yes,'' Bonnie whispered. "Yes, I am all right. But what am I to do now?''

"You need *do* nothing,'' Cornelia replied. "You need only be patient and wait for David to own to his feelings. He will not permit you to leave London; I promise you that. And I suspect he will come to his senses long before the time for your departure. He is fairly ill with jealousy of Francis—''

"Francis!" Bonnie had quite forgotten him, and her mouth fell open again. "David doesn't know . . ." She poured out the story of Francis' offer, her failure to decline it, the announcement Lady Hellier planned to make at the ball.

"I was on my way to Orchard Street to speak with him," she concluded, "but I judged it too early to call."

"Well, it is not too early now," Cornelia said, "and I urge you to go without delay. It wouldn't do at all for David to learn that you deceived him."

"No, it would not," Bonnie grimly agreed.

She leapt up, flung her napkin on the table, and raced toward the vestibule, another of Cornelia's chuckles floating in her wake.

The doorbell pealed, began to echo, and Bonnie shifted nervously from foot to foot, envisioning all manner of terrible scenarios. What if the Helliers were still abed, and Briscoe was once more "indisposed," and no one answered the door? That would not be so terrible after all, she decided: she could remain on the porch, continuing to ring the bell, till someone within the house responded. But what if—against all odds—Francis had risen, dressed, finished his breakfast, and already set out in Sir Robert's infamous phaeton? Well, that presented no great problem either; she could simply wait until he returned.

But what if he did not intend to return for many hours? What if he planned to come back just prior to the assembly, just in time to don his smallclothes and silk stockings and the rest of his evening attire? Bonnie would be compelled to deliver her rejection of his offer to Lady Hellier, and that would be terrible in the extreme. Or what if Francis was home, but his mother insisted on participating in their discussion? Bonnie would have to announce her refusal to them both, which would be more dreadful yet—

The door swung inward, and Bonnie was so startled that she nearly tumbled across the threshold.

"Good morning, Miss Carlisle," Briscoe said pleasantly.

She blinked up at him and started again, for he looked tantalizingly familiar. Well, he *was* familiar, she reminded herself: she had met him on the occasion of her first visit to Orchard Street. But she could not quell an odd notion that she had encountered him somewhere else as well, and—odder still—the notion triggered a little shiver of apprehension.

"I regret to advise you that Lady Hellier is from home," the butler went on.

This was cheering news indeed, but Bonnie's relief was tempered by her obsessive fascination with his appearance. Briscoe did not have a common sort of face; she had previously remarked his unusual handsomeness—

"In fact," he added, "I daresay you passed her en route. She departed on foot only a few minutes since."

Bonnie inferred from this commentary that her ladyship had gone to Oxford Street to purchase some final accessory for her ball gown. An errand which could not take long, and every second she stared at Briscoe was a precious second wasted.

"I did not come to see Lady Hellier," she said, tearing her eyes from his. "I was in hopes of speaking with Francis. Mr. Hellier, that is. Is he awake?"

"Awake but not quite dressed. However, I shall hurry up and tell him you are here. May I suggest you await him in the library? The staff are rearranging the furniture in the saloon. For the assembly this evening."

As if she might have forgotten the assembly, Bonnie thought wryly. Briscoe gestured her into the foyer, closed the front door, escorted her to the library entry, bowed, and sped toward the staircase. He wasn't foxed today, she reflected, gazing after him. Which was no great tribute to his character, for it was only a few minutes after nine. But perhaps his sobriety enhanced his vague resemblance to David. Yes, that must be why she fancied she had seen him in some other place and some other role.

Bonnie stepped on into the library and across the ragged carpet to the sofa, but she was too restless to sit. So very restless that she wondered how she was ever to maintain the patience Cornelia had counseled. How could she pretend, for weeks to come, that she regarded David as nothing more than her fictional uncle? Weeks or months, she amended, her stomach fluttering with dismay. If the earl was not ready to confess his feelings—and apparently he was not—he would probably seize upon Cornelia's visit to continue their charade till the end of the summer. In fact, there was nothing to prevent him from extending the project even beyond Cornelia's departure. He could manufacture one excuse upon another and keep his "niece" alive for *years* . . .

But she was wasting time again, Bonnie chided herself. Pondering the distant future instead of rehearsing her imminent conversation with Francis. She stopped her fitful pacing— she had not realized she was pacing—and furrowed her brow in concentration. She had just composed a brilliant opening ("Francis, there is something I must tell you") when she heard the tap of footfalls on the stairs.

"Bonnie!"

Francis strode through the doorway and hurried across the room, but he did not seem to know exactly what to do when he reached her side. It initially appeared, from the ungainly forward thrust of his neck, that he intended to kiss her on the cheek, but he soon drew back and began to grope for her hand. Before he could find and wring it, however, he changed his mind again and clumsily patted the satin puff at one shoulder of her spencer.

"Bonnie." He sorrowfully shook his head. "I expected you to call this morning."

"You . . . you did?"

"Indeed I did, and I can well surmise what you plan to say."

"You . . . you can?"

"Of course I can, and I quite comprehend your distress. I can only beg you to believe that Mama's remarks shocked me as much as you. I had explained very clearly that you were still considering my offer, and I didn't dream she would publicly mention an announcement of our engagement. I pray her . . her optimism did not cause you undue embarrassment."

His miscalculation of her motives had rendered Bonnie's task infinitely more difficult, and she abandoned the opening she'd devised and cast about for a subtler way to introduce the true purpose of her call. But there was no subtle way, she decided; she could only forge ahead as gently as possible.

"I did come to speak with you about the announcement of our engagement." Her voice was so clogged as to be almost incomprehensible, and she cleared her throat. "And I should like to begin by saying that I am . . . am extremely fond of you. Had we not chanced to be cousins, I feel sure we should nevertheless have become friends. However . . ."

But she could not tell him what she had so recently learned— the vast difference between fondness and love. "However, my affection is insufficient to permit me to wed you," she blundered on. "You must not interpret my refusal as a personal affront—"

"Refusal?" he interposed. "You are declining my offer?"

"I am sorry, Francis. My very last desire was to wound you— "

"Wound me?" He threw back his head and roared with laughter. "To the contrary, I daresay you've made me the happiest man in England."

Bonnie had suspected—indeed, *hoped*—he would be relieved by her rejection of his proposal. But his actual emotion seemed to border on ecstasy, and she instinctively bristled.

"Forgive me." He sobered and awkwardly patted her other shoulder. "I didn't wish to wound you either. I'm prodigious fond of you too, Bonnie: you're handsome and clever and a thoroughly delightful companion. But I should never have contemplated marriage after such a brief acquaintance. Not without . . ." He stopped and peered down at his hessians.

"Not without Aunt Judith's encouragement," Bonnie supplied dryly. "She perceived a union between us as a splendid financial arrangement, did she not? One designed to secure your inheritance and the Carlisle fortune as well."

"Precisely." He raised his eyes and sketched a sheepish grin. "I told Mama you would puzzle it out."

Bonnie saw no reason to advise him that David had been the one to puzzle it out. "What I do not understand," she said instead, "is why you consented to her scheme. Aunt Judith is very"—she searched for a relatively innocuous word—"very forceful. But I can scarcely conceive that you would allow her to propel you into a match you so obviously had no desire to make."

He gnawed his lip a moment, then went to the door, closed it, and came back across the room. "I feared for your safety if I did not consent to wed you." His voice was so low she could barely hear him. "When I discovered that Mama had engineered your accident."

"Aunt Judith!" Bonnie gasped "Of course! She came to Grosvenor Street immediately after I was injured—"

"Shh!" He glanced nervously at the door. "I own, in retrospect, that I should have questioned her visit; she had never called on Uncle David before. But I did not, and she returned with the news of your great wealth and suggested I begin to court you. And I judged it best to pretend to agree. I daresay you think me an abysmal coward"—he flashed another sheepish smile—"but Mama can be monstrous difficult when she is crossed."

"So it appears," Bonnie said grimly.

"My plan was to call on you once a day," Francis went on, "and I honestly perceived no harm in such a course. You would assume I was merely performing my cousinly duty, I calculated, while Mama would collect that I was, in fact, conducting a courtship. On the second day, however—Sunday morning—you told me of your suspicion that you'd been pushed in front of the coach."

"But you didn't believe me," Bonnie reminded him.

"Not until you described the man you fancied had attacked you. I realized at once that it must have been Briscoe's younger brother."

"Briscoe's . . . brother." She wondered how the resemblance could have eluded her. They were the same height and the same build, had the same handsome features and deep blue eyes and thick hair. Perhaps she'd been deceived by the circumstance that the butler's hair was gray while his brother's was still dark.

"A thoroughgoing scoundrel." Francis pursed his lips with distaste. "Mrs. Radway, the cook, insists he was once in Newgate, and if he was not, I daresay he should have been. He has no steady employment, and he invariably comes the day Briscoe receives his wages to beg a few shillings. At any rate, I confronted Mama with my surmise, and she confessed that she had, indeed, engaged Briscoe's brother to arrange a mishap. Her notion was that if you were injured and could not participate in the festivities of the Season, you would sail back to the Indies."

"But that was before she devised her plan to wed us," Bonnie said. "Before Uncle David told her of my fortune. She would not have harmed me again so long as she believed you were courting me. You could have continued your pretense—"

"No, I could not. Mama learned at church that Mrs. Maitland's assembly had been canceled, and she was determined to hold a ball in its stead. A ball for the specific purpose of announcing our engagement. She made it clear that if I didn't offer for you, she would present the offer herself. Consequently, as I indicated, I felt I had no recourse but to pursue my courtship in earnest."

"And now?" Bonnie snapped. "You also indicated that my refusal has rendered you the happiest man in England. Do you no longer care about my safety?"

"Your safety was ensured by Aunt Cornelia's arrival. You would not return to Barbados when your mother is here. So I fancy everything has worked out for the best."

Worked out, Bonnie thought. She wondered if Francis would ever find the courage to defy his mother. Probably not. Sooner or later, Lady Hellier would select another suitable bride, and he would be driven into a loveless marriage. But that was not Bonnie's concern, and she was eager to be gone before her ladyship came back from Oxford Street.

"I fancy so," she muttered aloud. "I trust you will inform Aunt Judith of the situation at the earliest opportunity?" He nodded. "Then I shall bid you good day."

The vestibule was empty, and Bonnie sped through it, let herself out the front door, and hurried along the footpath. She had just crossed Oxford when she spied Lady Hellier walking toward her from the direction of Grosvenor Square. Fortunately, her ladyship was on the opposite side of the street, and Bonnie stopped, averted her face, and watched from the corner of her eye until she had safely passed. Where had she been? Bonnie idly wondered, resuming her forward journey. There were no shops in the immediate vicinity, and Lady Hellier had not had time to walk all the way to Piccadilly and back.

But it didn't signify, Bonnie reflected, heaving a great sigh of relief. Her ordeal was over, and she need not tease herself about "Aunt Judith" again.

13

*T*he vestibule clock was striking ten as Bonnie twisted the knob of the front door, and she paused a moment, marveling that so much could have happened in such a brief expanse of time. For once, she reflected, Fate had behaved in a wholly beneficent manner: Cornelia had appeared at precisely the right instant, and within a few hours of her arrival, all Bonnie's problems had been resolved. As a consequence of her great good luck, she found herself anticipating Lady Hellier's assembly with a remarkable degree of enthusiasm. She would wear her favorite gown, she decided—the gold crepe with the embroidered apron—and perhaps she would look so very handsome that David would be inspired to confess his feelings at once. With this delightful prospect in mind, she pushed the door open and stepped into the entry hall.

"Bonnie!" Cornelia flew out of the dining room and seized her elbow in a viselike grip. "I must warn you," she hissed. "A dreadful thing occurred in your absence—"

"Bonnie?"

David's voice issued from the other direction, the direction of the library, and as Bonnie turned toward it, Cornelia emitted a little whimper and released her elbow. The earl was standing in the library doorway, one broad shoulder casually propped against the jamb.

"It *is* you," he said pleasantly. "How unfortunate that you did not return five or ten minutes since. Had you done so, you would have had an opportunity to chat with your future mother-in-law."

"My . . . my . . ." Bonnie tried to moisten her lips, but her mouth had gone altogether dry. This had been Lady Hellier's mysterious errand, she realized distantly—a call in Grosvenor Street. And the reason for her visit was horribly clear.

"Yes, Judith came to discuss our happy announcement." David might have been reading her thoughts. "She reminded me of our decision last evening that I should be the one to proclaim the news. I initially collected she was referring to the news of our *long-lost colonial relative*; I had somehow conceived the impression that that was the subject of the announcement. Imagine my surprise when I learned we were to announce your engagement to Francis."

"I trust you will excuse me?" Cornelia murmured. She began to creep toward the staircase.

"No, there is no need for you to leave." David's tone remained infinitely, terrifyingly pleasant. "I've nothing to say to Bonnie that you cannot hear. I am merely a trifle curious to know when Francis offered for her hand."

He raised his brows, and Bonnie licked her lips again.

"I am sorry, David." Her voice was the merest croak. "I own that I—"

"I do not believe it could have been last night." He essayed an elaborate frown. "Inasmuch as Judith mentioned the announcement just a few minutes after we joined them."

"David, please listen to me. There is to be no—"

"Nor was it yesterday afternoon. I chanced to inquire of Kimball whether Francis had called, and Kimball said he had not."

"He did not, but I can explain—"

"So it must have been prior to yesterday. Wednesday

evening, I should guess, after you dined in Orchard Street. Or did he propose during Lady Cunningham's ball?''

"It was Wednesday evening. I started to tell you—''

"But you elected not to. You did not tell me then, you did not tell me yesterday morning, and when Judith introduced the matter, you deliberately lied to me about the nature of the announcement. I can only infer that you feared I should advise Judith of your true circumstances. I doubt she would wish to wed her son to an impoverished governess.''

"That wasn't it at all. I—''

"Permit me to assure you that your fears are quite groundless. I shall not inform Judith what you are at. To the contrary, I judge your betrothal by far my finest prank. Little did I dream when we embarked on our charade that I could trick Judith into contracting a ridiculously unsuitable match.''

"David, I beg you to hear me out—''

"But the trick is on you as well, Bonnie.''

He drew himself abruptly up, and his amiability vanished like a cloak slipping from his shoulders. His face was white with rage, and his eyes had narrowed to brilliant sapphire slits.

"I suspect you set your cap at Francis long before you met him.'' His voice had sunk to a savage whisper. "As soon as I explained that he was my heir, you must have begun envisioning yourself as a wealthy countess. Pray be assured that that will not happen either. You will be a countess, yes; I cannot deny Francis my title. But he will receive only the entailed portion of my estate, and—as I fancy I also explained— that comprises only a small fraction of the total. I shall bequeath the rest to various charities. Indeed, I should throw it in the Thames before I left a single groat to you and Francis.''

"David, please—''

"I am sure I need not add that you will have none of my money in my lifetime either. You and your husband and your in-laws can run up the most shocking bills, and I shall not provide a farthing in payment. So unless I have the grace to expire prematurely, you are facing several decades of abject hardship. Perhaps you should consider that before you allow your engagement to be announced.''

''There is nothing to consider.'' Her own voice was shrill with desperation. ''I—''

''You are sincerely in love with Francis? Then I trust you will accept my apology for the injustice of my remarks. Now, if you will pardon me, I should like to return to my breakfast.''

He strode across the foyer, passing so close that Bonnie could readily have stopped him. Could easily have snatched his sleeve or gripped his wrist or simply stepped in front of him to bar his path. But she did not because she perceived that any further protest would be futile. He reached the dining-room archway and spun around, snapping his fingers in sudden—or pretended— recollection.

''It occurs to me that I neglected to report the specific purpose of Judith's call. She feels that Cornelia's unexpected arrival has altered the situation. That your . . . ah . . . mother should be granted the privilege of announcing your engagement. However, Cornelia and I expressed our mutual view that the choice should be left to you.''

He had given her a final chance, and Bonnie clenched her hands. ''If you would listen to me, you would understand—''

''You needn't render a decision immediately.'' He had donned his cloak again; his tone, his expression, were wonderfully kind. ''Judith also requested us to be in Orchard Street at eight o'clock—a full hour before the guests. We shall have ample opportunity to discuss the particulars of the announcement then. Let us plan to depart at a quarter to eight; I shouldn't want to be late for such a thrilling evening.''

He swept a bow, turned away, and stalked on into the dining room. Bonnie watched his retreating figure, entertaining an absurd hope that he would miraculously glimpse the truth and come racing back. But he did not, of course, and when he had disappeared, she gazed despairingly at Cornelia.

''What a bumblebath.'' Cornelia expelled a great sigh. ''I should hate to think I failed you, dear, but by the time I was summoned to the conference, Judith had already let the cat out of the bag. And I did not judge it my place to advise them that you didn't intend to marry Francis. Perhaps I was mistaken.''

"No, you weren't mistaken. My father would have said I was justly punished for my lies.'' Bonnie could not repress a wry grin, and—overset as she was—the mere act of smiling bolstered her courage. "And maybe it isn't such a bumblebath. When we go to the ball and David learns there is to be no engagement, he will listen to my account of what actually occurred.''

"I am afraid he will not.'' Cornelia shook her head. "David is in such prodigious poor humor that he will undoubtedly conclude you terminated the engagement *after* your conversation with him. After he warned you that you would be penniless if you married Francis.''

Yes, Bonnie realized grimly, that was precisely the conclusion the earl would draw. "Then what am I to do?'' she asked, casting Cornelia another stricken look.

"I believe you must swallow your pride and admit your feelings to David. Tell him frankly that you love him.''

"Now?'' Bonnie's stomach knotted, and she glanced fearfully toward the breakfast parlor.

"No, not now. David is excessively angry, deeply wounded, and he should be given some time to regain his equilibrium.'' Cornelia paused a moment, her brow furrowed in thought. "Were I you, I should wait until this evening.''

"Tell him at the assembly, you mean?''

"My suggestion is that you forgo the assembly. Go to David's room just prior to your scheduled departure and speak with him then. I shall alert the servants that you are not to be disturbed. And I myself shall leave for the ball at half past seven so as to afford you total privacy.''

"Lady Hellier will be *furious* when her guest of honor fails to appear.'' Bonnie shuddered, but she could not entirely quell another grin.

"I suspect Judith is quite furious with you already,'' Cornelia said dryly. "And she will have a guest of honor, will she not? I am also her *long-lost colonial relative*."

She flashed a wicked grin of her own, and for the first time in days, Bonnie laughed aloud.

Bonnie withdrew her gold crepe gown from the wardrobe, smoothed an imaginary wrinkle from the apron, then frowned. It was her favorite dress and the one she judged most flattering, but it was scarcely appropriate for an evening at home. She peered once more into the wardrobe, and when her eyes fell on Mama's old black bombazine, she was struck by a sudden impulse. David had accused her of envisioning herself a wealthy countess, and in his present dark mood, he might well suspect her profession of love to be prompted by mercenary motives. Perhaps she would create a favorable atmosphere if she eschewed the finery he had bought her and appeared as exactly what she was: "an impoverished governess." She returned the gold crepe to the wardrobe, removed the black bombazine, and put it on.

She did, indeed, look like a penniless governess, she thought wryly, examining her image in the mirror. It occurred to her that she had grown exceedingly spoiled during the preceding weeks, had come to take her splendid bedchamber and elegant new clothes quite for granted. But had David chanced to be poor, she would cheerfully have consented to live in a garret. To wear Mama's ancient gown every day for the rest of her life. She would love him if he were a simple clergyman like Papa or a tenant farmer like Tom Carlisle or even . . . even a music instructor.

Bonnie combed her hair and applied a bit of rouge to either cheek, and as she studied her finished reflection, there was a light tap on the door. David? she wondered, her heart crashing against her ribs. She hurried across the room, cracked the door, and heaved a sigh of relief when she found Cornelia in the corridor.

"I came to tell you good-by, dear." Cornelia stepped just over the threshold and closed the door behind her.

"Good-by?" Bonnie echoed. Her heart fluttered again. "Is . . . is it that late?"

"Twenty-five past seven, and I desired Kimball to be ready at half past. He will await me at Judith's, of course, and I advised Alice and Nell to remain in their quarters the rest of the night. So you and David will be able to converse without interruption."

Cornelia stood back, inspected Bonnie from head to toe, and nodded her approval. "You look very handsome, dear. That is a lovely dress."

Bonnie initially assumed she was jesting, but when she glanced at Cornelia's gown, she saw that it was rather older than her own. Well, not older, she amended; it showed hardly any wear. But whatever its chronological age, Cornelia's dress was hopelessly outmoded—from the high, square neck to the tier of transparent muslin around the bottom of the skirt.

"Thank you," she said solemnly, biting back a smile.

"You look very handsome," Cornelia repeated, "and I am confident you and David will speedily resolve your differences." She patted Bonnie's shoulder, hesitated, cleared her throat. "I should like to say that had I been blessed with a daughter, I should have wanted her to be exactly like you. Good luck, child."

She opened the door and slipped back into the hall, and Bonnie gazed after her, swallowing a lump in her own throat. She and David would definitely exchange visits with Cornelia, she vowed. Would take their children to Barbados at frequent intervals . . .

But it was a trifle premature to be considering children, she chided herself; she must first survive the evening. She peered nervously at the mantel, then remembered that there was no clock in her bedchamber. It must be half past seven by now, she calculated, and she paced the border of the Aubusson carpet, counting the seconds under her breath and the minutes on her fingers. When the latter count reached ten, she squared her shoulders, gritted her teeth, and marched down the corridor to David's room. She paused at his door, sorting through the several hundred introductory remarks she had composed, but before she could raise her hand to knock, the door swung inward.

"What the deuce . . . ?" The earl started and blinked down at her. "Am I late?" He turned his head, evidently to consult a clock inside the room. "No, it is only twenty to eight." He returned his eyes to her and sketched a chilly smile. "But I can well imagine how eagerly you are anticipating the forthcoming festivities."

He had seized the initiative, put her on the defensive as he always did, and Bonnie could not recollect a single one of the clever comments she'd devised. She could only stare at him, marveling anew that she had not recognized her emotions long since. He was the man she had dreamed of all her life, and she felt such a rush of love that she was hard put to stand erect.

"So let us be off," David said briskly. His eyes swept over her much as Cornelia's had, but—unlike Cornelia—he concluded his inspection with a gasp of dismay. "Good God! You intend to go to the ball in *that*?"

"No," Bonnie mumbled. She discovered that she couldn't look into his face and talk at the same time, and she focused on his left ear. "No, I do not intend to go to the assembly."

"Not go to the assembly?" he barked. "You will not be present for the announcement of your own engagement?"

"There is to be no announcement. I tried to tell you so this morning, but . . ." She stopped; an accusation was hardly the proper opening. "At any rate, Cornelia has already left for the ball, and she will convey our regrets to Lady Hellier. My regrets, that is; you may wish to attend without me."

He was silent for such a long time that she began to fancy he hadn't heard her. "No, I believe not," he said at last. "Would you . . . er . . . care to come in?"

He stepped to one side of the doorway, and Bonnie walked past him and halted in the center of the Axminster rug. Nell's fine touch was visible here as well, she observed: the washstand and bedside cupboard, the chest of drawers and the dressing table were liberally adorned with dust. But it was a handsome room nonetheless—the dark mahogany furniture offering a pleasing contrast to the bright green and gold of the draperies and the counterpane.

Bonnie heard the soft click of the latch, and she ceased her idle scrutiny and turned around. David was leaning against the door, his arms crossed behind his back, his fingers still fastened on the knob.

"You stated," he said gruffly, "that you have terminated your engagement."

"No, I stated that there was to be no announcement." He was sufficiently far away that she was able to meet his eyes. "There never was an engagement, David. I never consented to marry Francis."

"Then why the devil did Judith suppose you had?"

"Because I didn't refuse his offer either. Not immediately, that is. That was the dreadful thing that happened, the thing I started to tell you Wednesday evening. When Francis asked me to marry him, I was so startled that I quite lost my wits. He naturally conceived the impression that I was considering his proposal and so advised Lady Hellier."

David's eyes narrowed with suspicion, but he left the door and ventured a few feet into the room. "Go on," he said tersely.

"I attempted to tell you what had occurred," she reiterated, "but you—"

"I granted you no chance," he interposed. "Upon reviewing our . . . ah . . . discussion, I was compelled to own to that. But the following morning, I specifically inquired what dreadful thing you'd alluded to, and you claimed it was Briscoe and Robert's lamentable behavior."

"Yes, I deliberately misled you; I admit to that. You had charged me with throwing myself at Francis' head, and I was certain you wouldn't believe I had been too shocked by his offer to decline it. So I judged it best to wait and inform you of the proposal after I *had* declined it. Which I intended to do at Viscount Peyton's assembly.''

"You intended to, but you did not.''

"I *could* not,'' she protested. "Surely you recall what a"—she borrowed Cornelia's word—"what a bedlam it was. Before I could gain Francis' attention, Lady Hellier introduced the subject of the announcement.''

"Whereupon you deceived me again. With your statement that she was referring to an announcement of our family reunion.''

"What else was I to do?'' she pleaded. "The noise in the ballroom was such that I couldn't possibly have explained the true situation. Not to you or Francis either one. I could only hope to end the conversation and resolve the matter later.''

"Later meaning this morning, I collect.''

He walked on across the room and halted just beside her, so close that their sleeves were nearly touching. Bonnie's knees weakened, and she willed herself not to look away.

"Yes, while Lady Hellier was here, I was in Orchard Street. Advising Francis that there was to be no engagement.''

"And what was his reaction?''

"He was overjoyed,'' Bonnie said dryly. "He readily confessed that Lady Hellier had forced him to offer for my hand.''

"Forced.'' David snorted with derision. "Francis is far too weak. I daresay Judith will ultimately *force* him to wed someone else.''

"I daresay she will,'' Bonnie agreed, "but in this instance, there was an mitigating factor. It was not Lady Pamela who arranged my accident, David. It was Lady Hellier.''

"Judith arranged for you to be attacked?'' His eyes widened with horror.

"Yes, and after Francis puzzled it out, he feared for my safety. Lady Hellier engaged Briscoe's brother . . .''

She repeated the story Francis had related, the earl's face growing increasingly pale with every word she uttered, and when she had finished, he pulled her into his arms.

"Good God," he murmured. "My poor girl. You insisted you were pushed in front of the coach; how could I have failed to believe you?"

He was holding her only loosely, holding her as an uncle would, but her heart began to pound nonetheless, began to race so madly she was certain he must hear it.

"I failed to believe you, and as a consequence, you might well have been attacked again." He tilted his head back and gazed contritely down at her. "And I should never have forgiven myself if you had come to harm."

"It . . ."

She had started to say it was all right, but her voice froze in her throat. His eyes had darkened, she saw, darkened to the blue-black she remembered from the night he had held her in the corridor. His arms tightened round her, and his breathing quickened, and she realized that this was the moment to speak. Now, now; but even as she parted her lips, he lowered his head and covered them with his own.

Bonnie had imagined being kissed, had imagined the touch of a man's mouth on hers, but she had not anticipated the sensations that followed. Had not dreamed the sweet, throbbing ache that spread all through her, turning her to liquid, fairly dissolving her bones. She twined her fingers in David's hair, parted her lips still further, moaned when she felt his tongue.

"Dear God," he whispered. "I've wanted you so desperately. Surely you saw it. Saw from the start that I could scarcely keep my hands off you."

He took her mouth again, his mouth hungry now, his hands moving urgently over her body; and Bonnie's yearning swelled to meet his. He had unleashed a strange, wild excitement—something else she had never dreamed was there. He moved his lips to her neck, and she writhed against him, weak with longing.

"You won't be sorry," she said raggedly. "I promise you

that. I love you, and I shall make you happy. You'll never be sorry you wed me.''

"Wed!'' he choked. "Love!'' He thrust her away so abruptly that Bonnie nearly lost her balance. "Good God, what have I done?''

He stumbled backward, tugging at his neckcloth, which had come half untied. "I . . . I can only apologize most abjectly for my odious conduct. And express my deep regret if I . . . I misled you. I did not intend to suggest that I thought to marry . . .''

He crashed into the door and nearly lost his own balance. "You cannot stay, of course,'' he muttered. "Not in the circumstances. I shall hire a chaise to drive you to Cheshire tomorrow. For the present, I must beg to be excused.''

He spun around, flung the door open, raced into the hall, and Bonnie shortly heard the frantic tattoo of his footfalls on the staircase. How could Cornelia have so drastically misjudged his feelings? she wondered distantly. Have mistaken mere physical desire for love? The slam of the front door echoed back up the stairs, and she walked unsteadily out of David's bedchamber and down the corridor to hers.

He was right in one respect, she reflected grimly: in the circumstances, she could not stay. Indeed, she could not stay even until tomorrow; after making such a horrid cake of herself, she could never face him again. She pulled her portmanteau from beneath the bed and laid it on the counterpane, opened it and went to the wardrobe.

She had once thought to pack up all her new clothes and flee to Aunt Grace, she recalled, eyeing the ball gowns and walking dresses and morning dresses in the wardrobe. But that had been long ago, on the day of Lady Pamela's call, and now she wanted only to forget the Earl of Sedgewick. She withdrew the white muslin dress she had brought from Portman Square, then proceeded to the chest of drawers and removed her lingerie. After she had placed her clothes in the portmanteau, she crossed to the dressing table, snatched up her brush and comb and cosmetics, returned to the bed, and tossed them in the bag.

The portmanteau seemed rather emptier than it had when she left the Powells', but as she frowned around the room, she recollected that one of her gowns had been ruined when she collided with David's curricle. That memory triggered yet another, and she could not repress a bitter laugh. She recalled very well her opinion—when the earl had proposed their charade—that Fate could not be so unkind as to propel her into a second post as disastrous as the first. But Fate had once more outwitted her; Fate, like David himself, had perpetrated its finest prank. She had not even seen Almack's . . .

Bonnie closed and fastened the portmanteau and carried it to the wardrobe. She donned her threadbare pelisse and ancient French bonnet, hung her reticule over one arm, picked up her bag, and crept into the corridor. She briefly feared she might encounter Nell, but she soon recollected that Cornelia had instructed the servants to remain in their quarters. She strode boldly along the hall and down the stairs, across the vestibule and through the front door. She stopped only when she reached the footpath, stopped and turned around and gazed back at the house.

Memories; so many memories. She swallowed the lump in her throat, blinked the tears from her eyes, and hurried on toward Oxford Street to hail a hackney coach.

14

"*A*re you in service in London, dear?"

Bonnie stifled a sigh. She had suspected from the outset that the elderly woman in the seat across was the talkative sort—the kind of person who would shortly attempt to initiate a conversation. Particularly inasmuch as they were the only passengers in the stage. Well, not the only passengers, she amended: the woman was accompanied by a man of similar age whom Bonnie assumed to be her husband. But it had soon become clear that he was prodigious hard of hearing, and he had already burrowed into the squab and fallen asleep. They had left the yard of the Swan with Two Necks but a few minutes since, and Bonnie prayed the woman would leave the coach at one of the early stops.

"I *was* in service in the city," she muttered aloud. "In a manner of speaking."

"I see." The woman nodded. "But you have now left your post to return to your family?"

"In a manner of speaking," Bonnie said again.

She had never written to Aunt Grace, she recollected, and she still wasn't certain her aunt would agree to take her in. But if Aunt Grace sent her away, surely she could find another position. Perhaps she should hire on with a theater troupe, she thought bitterly. Having proved herself so very adept at the art of impersonation.

"And where might they be?" the woman asked. "Your family, I mean."

"Cheshire," Bonnie replied. "Though I was raised in Stafford."

"Clyde and I are from Staffordshire ourselves! We've been visiting our married daughter in town, but we're headed back to our home in Lichfield."

Lichfield. Bonnie clenched her hands with dismay. Lichfield was many hours along the road—

"I am Mrs. Pennington," the woman announced, "and this is my husband." She inclined her head toward the man beside her, whose own head was drooping toward her shoulder.

"I am Miss Gordon," Bonnie mumbled.

It was the first time she had stated or heard her real name in almost a month, and the unfamiliar sound of it prompted her to wonder how David planned to explain her sudden disappearance. As Francis had pointed out, Cornelia's arrival rendered it most unlikely that Bonnie would return to Barbados. Maybe the earl would simply own that his "niece" had been an invention.

David. Bonnie felt a stab of pain so intense that she was compelled to close her eyes. Perhaps she should have taken her clothes after all, she reflected, for it would require more than the absence of her finery to allow her to forget the Earl of Sedgewick. To forget his engaging grin and his sapphire eyes and the touch of his mouth on hers—

"If you will pardon me for saying so, dear"—Mrs. Pennington cleared her throat—"you look excessively unhappy. Which leads me to believe you quit London due to some trouble with a man."

Bonnie wearily opened her eyes. They had reached the dark fringes of the city, but the light of the moon was sufficient to see that Mrs. Pennington was regarding her with avid curiosity. And maybe it would be wisest to satisfy that curiosity at once, Bonnie decided. If she admitted to "some trouble with a man," perhaps Mrs. Pennington would leave her in peace for the remainder of their long journey.

"Yes, I did have a . . . an unfortunate experience," she murmured. "I had conceived the impression that a man intended to wed me, and I recently discovered that such was not the case."

"Men!" Mrs. Pennington emitted a sniff of disgust. "Take Clyde here."

His head had come to rest upon her, and she irritably shook her shoulder. Mr. Pennington moaned and swayed toward the opposite side of the coach, until his head thudded against the window.

"You wouldn't know it to look at him now," Mrs. Pennington continued, "but Clyde was a shameless rake in his youth. Well, he was a rake far into his middle years, I should have said. Disporting himself with every lightskirt for miles around . . ." She sniffed again. "I can tell you that were it not for our lovely children—we have two sons in addition to the daughter—I should wish I hadn't wed at all."

"Umm," Bonnie grunted.

"Sometimes I even doubt that children are adequate compensation. They soon grow up and leave home, and one still has the man to contend with for many years to come. Yes, spinsterhood has distinct advantages, Miss Gordon. I urge you to keep that in mind."

Bonnie was beginning to fear that, far from securing peace, she had inspired an interminable lecture on the deficiencies of men and marriage; and she cast about for another tack.

"I certainly shall keep that in mind," she said politely. "For the present, however—as I am sure you understand—I am exceedingly overset. And most dreadfully tired. So if you will forgive me, I fancy I should try to rest."

"Of course I understand, dear. Lie down, and I shan't say another word."

In point of fact, it was impossible to "lie down" on the narrow seat of the coach, but Bonnie judged it best to comply insofar as she could. She squirmed to the center of the seat, turned sidewise, lowered her right cheek and shoulder to the upholstery, drew her knees halfway to her chin, and once more closed her eyes.

She was, in truth, most dreadfully tired, but her brain didn't seem to comprehend the aching exhaustion of her body. Her mind was whirling with memories and images and regrets, none of them in any logical sequence. She was sorry she had had no chance to bid Cornelia and Nell good-by; she must write them when she arrived in Cheshire. Or wherever her final destination might prove to be. No, she wouldn't write them; to do so would only fuel her memories of David, and she had quite enough of them as it was. David—the angel—peering down at her, David taking her in his arms, David waltzing her around the floor at Lady Lambeth's assembly, David discussing her wardrobe with Mrs. Pruitt, David conducting their endless lessons—

"I am sorry to disturb you, Miss Gordon." Mrs. Pennington cleared her throat again. "But I feel you should know we are being pursued."

"Pursued." Bonnie opened her eyes and quelled another sigh; apparently the woman would stop at nothing to revive their conversation. "And just who do you think is pursuing us, Mrs. Pennington? A highwayman?"

"That is exactly what I think." She was speaking in a whisper, as though the imaginary highwayman were already clawing at the door. "I heard a shout, and just after that, the coach speeded up."

"I do not believe highwaymen *pursue* their prey," Bonnie said with as much patience as she could muster. "I believe they normally wait along the route—"

"Stop!"

The word was distinct even above the clatter of the wheels, and Bonnie bolted upright.

"There is no reason to be afraid." The quaver in Mrs. Pennington's voice belied her sooothing words. "He will take whatever valuables we have and be on his way. Highwaymen are gentlemen; they do not harm their victims . . ."

Bonnie closed her ears to Mrs. Pennington's nervous chatter and pressed her nose to the window. She was situated in the rear-facing seat, and within a few seconds, she spied a lone horseman approaching the back of the coach.

"Stop!" he yelled again.

The driver's response was a defiant one: the stage once more gathered speed. But a heavy vehicle couldn't possibly outdistance a man on horseback, and the highwayman galloped past the rear wheel, drew abreast of Bonnie, passed her, and raced beyond her limited circle of vision. Shortly after that, the coach came to a shuddering halt, and Bonnie sank back against the squab. She was momentarily inclined to remove her money from her reticule and stuff it down the bodice of her dress, but she soon abandoned this notion. Though highway robbers were, indeed, reputed to behave in a gentlemanly fashion, this one might be the exception. If he did not find what he was seeking in the obvious place, he might undertake a search. Surely it was preferable to surrender the last of her wordly goods to Fate without protest and emerge with at least some semblance of dignity intact.

"He is walking back," Mrs. Pennington hissed. The forward-facing seat now afforded a better view of the robber's movements.

"Do not be alarmed, Mrs. Pennington. As you yourself pointed out, we've nothing to fear." Bonnie fancied she would sound considerably more convincing had her teeth not been chattering with terror. "We shall simply give him what he wants—"

"Is Bonnie Gordon in the coach?" a male voice demanded. "I wish to speak with Bonnie Gordon."

"Good God!" Bonnie gasped. "It is . . ."

She squirmed to the edge of the seat and peered out the window again, but her eyes could only confirm what her ears had told her. He was standing in a pool of moonlight, still dressed in his evening clothes, gazing up at the coach.

"It is David!"

"David?" Mrs. Pennington echoed. "Is he the man who caused you such grief?"

"Y-yes," Bonnie stammered. She was seemingly powerless to move, and her breath began to fog the glass.

"Well, he will not trouble you again," Mrs. Pennington said grimly. "Permit me to handle this, Miss Gordon." She lowered her window and leaned out. "Be off with you, young man," she ordered. "Go back to town and allow us to proceed."

"Is Bonnie Gordon in the coach?" he repeated.

"Yes, Miss Gordon is in the coach, but she wishes nothing further to do with you. Go along now and leave her alone."

"Please, Bonnie," he pleaded. "Please come out and talk to me."

"He had ample opportunity to talk to me in his bedchamber," Bonnie muttered.

"Bedchamber!" Mrs. Pennington stared at her with horror. "He actually *seduced* you?" She thrust her head back out the window. "You beast!" she shrieked. "You have already ruined the poor girl; what more do you want?"

"I want to talk to her!" David's voice rose to meet hers.

"Well, she does not want to talk to you," Mrs. Pennnington said frostily. "So you might as well advise the driver that we can continue."

"Hell and the devil!" the earl roared. "Tell her I love her and I'll marry her tonight if she'll get out of the damned coach!"

"Love!" Bonnie's heart bounded into her throat, and she scrambled up and groped for the door handle. "Marry—"

"Place no faith in what he says," Mrs. Pennington interposed sternly. "Men are all alike. They will invariably attempt to trick you . . ."

She rattled on, but Bonnie had found the handle, and she pushed the door open and peered into the moonlight. David rushed forward, and she was afraid to look away from him, afraid that if she averted her eyes for an instant, he would disappear. Her foot blindly sought the step, missed it, and she tumbled out of the coach and fell into his arms.

"Thank God," he whispered, crushing her to his chest. "Oh, thank God."

"Will you be wanting her bag as well, sir?" an unfamiliar voice inquired dryly.

David loosened his arms, though not by much, and Bonnie turned and saw the driver standing beside the box. He was shaking his head with amazement, but there was a great wad of bills in his right hand, and she surmised that he had been handsomely paid for his cooperation.

"No, thank you," David said. "Leave it at the first stop, and we shall retrieve it later."

"Very good, sir. The first change is at the Crown in Watford. The lady's case will be waiting there."

He remounted the box, clucked to the horses, and the coach lurched to a start, nearly bouncing Mrs. Pennington through the window. The old woman sadly shook her head, then settled back in her seat, and the stage clattered round a bend in the road and out of sight.

"Where were we when we were so rudely interrupted?" The earl flashed his winsome grin. "Ah, yes, I believe I remember."

He pulled her close again, laid his mouth hungrily on hers, and Bonnie succumbed to that wild, delicious ache. How could she have thought to forget him? she wondered distantly, parting her lips and straining against him. How could she possibly have thought to live without him?

"Thank God," he repeated, burying his face in her hair. "Thank God I caught you up."

"You gave us an awful fright." Bonnie giggled. "We were persuaded . . ."

She stopped and stiffened in his arms. Perhaps she had absorbed some of Mrs. Pennington's skepticism, she reflected. Whatever the reason, she suddenly realized that a great number of questions remained unanswered, and she drew away and frowned up at him.

"Why would you try to catch me up?" she asked. "You could have traveled to Cheshire at your leisure—"

"To Cheshire, yes," he interjected, "but what was I to do when I got there? I didn't know in which town your aunt resided. I did not even know her *name*. I should have been compelled to scour the entire county for you, which—be assured—I should have done. But it seemed more sensible to chase you down en route. And infinitely more dramatic."

He sketched another grin, then sobered. "I remembered your statement, the day we met, that you intended to take a public coach from the Swan with Two Necks, so I saddled my horse and proceeded there. I learned that a northbound stage had departed not long since, and I could but pray that you were on it."

'But why did you wish to find me at all?" Bonnie pressed. "You were prepared to hire a chaise to drive me to Cheshire tomorow. How did you come to change your mind so quickly?"

"I didn't *change* my mind, Bonnie; I *saw* my mind. After I left you, I went to Brooks's and lost five hundred pounds in the space of an hour. I could scarcely read the cards, much less concentrate on the play. I couldn't think of anything but you. And I finally admitted what I'd attempted to deny for weeks. That I . . . I love you."

He extended one forefinger and tentatively stroked her cheek, and even that gentle touch weakened her knees.

"As I indicated, I'd been attempting to deny it for weeks. I suspect I fell in love with you at the very start, but I did not recognize that something was amiss until I escorted you to Lady Lambeth's assembly."

"*Amiss!*" Bonnie echoed indignantly.

"Hush." He moved his finger to her mouth. "I meant to say that Lady Lambeth's ball forced me to perceive that my feelings were most peculiar. I was . . . was . . ."

"Jealous?" Bonnie supplied, mumbling round his finger.

"More than merely jealous." He raised his finger and ran it lightly down her nose. "Ravenshaw and Varden and the rest of them are some years younger than I, and I conceived a notion that you visualized me as a middle-aged man. An uncle in sentiment if not in fact. I could not remove the gray from my hair, but I went to Weston and Meyer the next morning and ordered several new ensembles.''

"Good God, David. Six-and-thirty is hardly middle-aged.''

"So I shortly discovered,'' he said wryly. "I soon began acting like a sheep-eyed schoolboy, did I not? Tearing off to Oxford Street to buy you chocolates . . . I was *mortified* when I returned to the house and found Francis in the library, and I couldn't puzzle out why. Could not own to my emotions because . . .''

His voice trailed off, and he toyed with the ribbons of her battered hat. It no longer signified, Bonnie realized; she was confident now of his love. It did not signify to her, but she sensed that he must say the words, and she laced her fingers through his.

"Because what?'' she prompted softly.

"Because, in the first place, I was confused. I believed love to be a myth; I told you so the day we met. And then, when I began suffering the . . . the *distressing symptoms* I had always ridiculed, my confusion started to turn to fright. Perhaps you recollect that immediately after I presented you to Judith, I offered to release you from our agreement.''

"I do recollect that.'' Bonnie nodded. "You said you thought it was what I wanted.''

"I did think it was what you wanted, but I also glimpsed a chance to recover from my mysterious malady. I calculated that if you left, I should quickly forget you, and my life would resume its normal course. But as soon as I had spoken, I was terrified you *would* leave. You cannot imagine my relief when you elected to stay on.''

He disengaged his hand from hers and caressed the curls at her temple.

"The next time the subject of your departure arose was the day Judith proposed her assembly,'' he continued. "And by then, I was hopelessly lost. Angry as I was, I couldn't bear to let you go, and I seized upon your injury to keep you in London.''

"Only to order me out of the house tonight," Bonnie said dryly.

"Tonight." He sighed. "You took me unawares, Bonnie, and I simply wasn't ready to confess my feelings. Not until I fled to Brooks's and endured the most miserable hour of my existence. I raced home, and when I found you gone, I nearly lost my wits. Which does not excuse my earlier remarks, of course."

He paused and once more touched her cheek. "I know I must have wounded you dreadfully, and I can but beg you to forgive me. Though I've discovered love late in my life, I daresay I love you as much as a man can love a woman. And if you'll consent to wed me . . . Well, if I may quote you, you will never be sorry."

"No," she whispered round the lump in her throat. "No, I am sure I shall never be sorry."

He took her in his arms again and kissed her, very gently this time, then lifted his head.

"I am engaged," he laughed unsteadily. "Dear God, what have I come to?"

He released her, took her hand, and led her toward his horse, which was placidly grazing a few yards away. It occurred to Bonnie that one question remained unresolved, and she drew him to a halt.

"What of Miss Godwin?" she said. "Make no mistake on that head, David: I shan't allow you to stray."

"How interesting you should mention Jane." He chuckled. "Now I think on it, I believe that was my first indication that something had gone awry. You no doubt recall that I had a . . . an appointment with Jane the day I escorted you to Mrs. Pruitt's. You had given me a great deal of trouble, and I was eagerly anticipating a tranquil interlude with my . . . ah . . . friend. But after five minutes in her company, I perceived that she was prodigious boring. Realized I should rather quarrel with you than—"

"Never mind," Bonnie interrupted hastily.

"At any rate, I haven't seen her again from that day to this."

"But you went out every afternoon—"

"I went to Brooks's. Hoping to regain my sanity. Which, fortunately, I did not." He smiled and tugged her ahead, boosted her into the saddle and gazed up at her. "I am quite prepared to marry you tonight, just as I promised that awful woman in the coach. But I fancy Cornelia would prefer us to wait a week or two and have a proper wedding."

She had waited for him all her life, Bonnie reflected; she could wait a few weeks more. "Yes, we shall have a proper wedding," she agreed.

"However, we needn't return to town tonight. Your case is just up the road in Watford, and we could—"

"David!" she chided.

"Well, I thought we should begin producing heirs without delay." He flashed his engaging grin, his teeth gleaming in the moonlight. "That is how this whole thing started, is it not? With my invention of a niece to inherit my estate?"

"We shall have ample time to produce heirs after we are married." Bonnie had intended to sound extremely severe, but she could not repress a giggle.

"Umm."

David shook his head with mock despair, mounted the horse, and reached his arms around her to take the reins. Bonnie nestled against him, reveling in the strong, steady beat of his heart upon her back, and she was quite certain Fate was smiling.

About the Author

Though her college majors were history and French, Diana Campbell worked in the computer industry for a number of years and has written extensively about various aspects of data processing. She had published eighteen short stories and two mystery novels before undertaking her first Regency romance.